*Happy Reading*

# Billionaire's Forgiveness

PIERCE BROTHERS SERIES  *Book Two*

## Brenda Pearson
WWW.BPEARSONBOOKS.COM

 FriesenPress

Suite 300 - 990 Fort St
Victoria, BC, V8V 3K2
Canada

www.friesenpress.com

**Copyright © 2018 by Brenda Pearson**
First Edition — 2018

All rights reserved.

No part of this publication may be reproduced in any form, or by any means, electronic or mechanical, including photocopying, recording, or any information browsing, storage, or retrieval system, without permission in writing from FriesenPress.

www.bpearsonbooks.com

ISBN
978-1-5255-1861-4 (Hardcover)
978-1-5255-1862-1 (Paperback)
978-1-5255-1863-8 (eBook)

1. FICTION, EROTICA

Distributed to the trade by The Ingram Book Company

## Chapter One

(PRESENT)

Megan looked at his face and sighed. She couldn't cry, not yet! She had to believe that everything would be okay. She wasn't sure if her prayers would be answered, and could only hope he would pull through. *It's funny how life changed in a blink of eye,* Megan thought. Six months ago, she fell in love with the man that haunted her dreams for three long years.

The beeping of the monitors echoed in the distance as air was forced into him. You sacrifice every day to protect the people you love. You never know what life will throw your way. It's hard to know that the most precious person you love is fighting for his life. She had to remember the good times and focus on that.

The moment that she saw him on that beach, a shirtless stranger running towards her, she knew that her life would change forever. From that first look, that first touch, that first smile, she had fallen in love with him. Love hits you when you least expect it—sometimes not once but twice in a lifetime. What are the odds that it would be the same man? She considered herself the luckiest person on earth. Six months ago she fought him, but knew deep down her heart would win. Her mom always said life and love are risky, but also an adventure when you are with the right man.

Everyone has secrets; it's how the world turns. They also fight demons—well, maybe not everyone, but Megan did. Those demons are buried deep down in the bit of your soul hidden and locked away. It's the only way you can keep moving. But when they finally surface and you set those secrets free, you no longer see the darkness that surrounds you. You are finally set free when the truth is unveiled. You cannot hide it anymore because the one person you are keeping it from sees right through you. You take your mother's advice, take a chance, and let it go. By letting the pain that was holding you back free, only then you can truly be happy. Then, the future doesn't look so scary. Megan took that chance and finally understood what her mother meant by having the right man in her life.

Megan reached out and touched his face, his dark whiskers, his sensual lips, his high cheek bones, to his silky black hair. Yes, she took the chance. He made trusting him easy this time. He fought for her when she couldn't fight for herself. He protected her. Megan rested her head on the side of the bed, holding his un-injured hand, hoping and praying that her happiness would wake up. She would rather die a thousand deaths to have him look at her again; to touch her and kiss her. He was her world now but days had passed and still no movement. They said the surgery went well, but you never know if a patient will ever wake up.

Megan held his hand and raised it to her cheeks, feeling his warmth on her face. She closed her eyes and held her breath, saying a silent prayer. She kissed the inside of his palm and lingered, her warm lips on his hand, breathing in his scent. Four long, excruciating days since that tragic cold winter day at

$$$

the cabin. Megan couldn't remember when she had slept last, knowing if she tried the nightmare would come again. Feeling his hand on her face and holding it in place, she held back tears. If she let them fall, she feared the man she loved would never wake up. She needed to believe he would pull through, would come back to her, because Max Pierce cannot die. She found it funny how six months ago, she was the one fighting for her life. He never gave up on her.

XOXO

## Chapter Two

(SIX MONTHS PRIOR)

Max's patience was running thin; waiting had never been his strong suit. Security gave him two options: they could escort him out, or he could stay with the others in the hospital waiting room. He knew arguing with the head ER nurse would not get him what he wanted. He wanted to stay by Megan's side, but they had refused to let him pass—family members only. He had never lost his control with another person because most people didn't argue with him, they just did what he asked. When the nurse told him that he couldn't follow, he lost it and punched the wall, which didn't earn him any favors. The next thing Max knew, he was being restrained and pulled aside by two security guards. These things did not happen to Max Pierce. Hell, he was usually the one who did this to other people when things got out of hand.

His fists were at his sides and he felt the pain in his knuckles, but it was nothing compared to what he was feeling in his heart. This feeling of being out of control for a woman was overpowering. The sight of Megan lying motionless in her blood kept flashing in his mind. *Why is it taking so long for her family to get here?* he thought.

Max couldn't stand still; he needed to move, but even that didn't calm him. He leaned against the wall in the hospital waiting room, feeling the world around him closing in. He closed his eyes, hoping that the pain in his chest would ease. Tonight was not what he had envisioned when he spotted Megan's car at the construction site. Harrison Construction was building a complex for Pierce Enterprises, and every night for the last month her car was there as he drove by late at night. He hated the thought that she was working those long hours, but that was the stipulation in the contract. The building had to be done by a certain time to avoid a fine. Tonight he had planned to put an end to her long hours when he stopped.

He knew he shouldn't have waited three years. He should have gone after her before this. Three years ago, he knew she was different. Something inside changed him and he didn't see anyone, only her. Her smile, her scent, her laughter, her love of life, and the people that she cared about humble him. He wanted to be a better man just being with her. Megan never took anything for granted and she loved with her heart. She saw the good in people, not like him. He questioned everyone's motives, but not once did he question hers; he knew how genuine she was.

The moment she smiled at him, Max knew his life would change for the better, and that had scared him. Megan made him feel emotions he had not encountered before. His heart beat faster just being in her presence. Women knew how he was. He didn't get involved; he loved sex and that was his main purpose back then. That night was magic. She fit him like a glove and they made love for hours. He took her virginity, but if she had said no, he would have stopped. When she wrapped her arms around

$$$

him, he wanted to die in her embrace. Her skin, her hooded eyes, made him want to please her even more. When they had finally fallen asleep, it felt right, but the moment he woke up in a cold sweat with his heart pounding, he knew he could see the future with Megan. Then he bailed. He ran like a coward instead of embracing those new feelings.

As months went by, he couldn't get her out of his mind, so he decided to track her down. He wanted to explain to her why he ran, or at least try, but the moment he saw her in another man's arms, he knew he was too late. That angered him because she was his, but he had to let her go.

Now seeing her again, he wanted her. He wanted to put that smile on her face again. He wanted to remove the sadness, the hurt, and loneliness that reflected back at him. She hid it well but he knew better. He put those emotions there and she had kept them buried. He would let her have her say. Megan didn't care who he was or how rich he was; she only cared about the man he was with her. The moment he saw her at that fundraiser, he knew there would never be anyone else. The flame was still there, and he was going after her full force. The instant that they touched, he knew she felt it too. *That electricity jolting our bodies*, he thought. *We were made to be together!* He was going to make sure that Megan stood by him as an equal and his life partner.

Max thought back to earlier that day when she walked into his office. She was angry and he could see it immediately. She was upset and he knew he was going to get her anger thrown at him. He knew that in anger there is passion, in passion there was desire, and eventually they combine into amazing sex. He knew she was fighting him all the way and she was not afraid to speak her mind. Maybe the gifts were a little too much and this had

XOXO

finally got to her, but damn the chemistry they had would burn up his office building.

Max thought back about that passionate kiss that left them both breathless that morning, her lying on his desk with her blouse open and her breasts just waiting to be devoured, her legs wrapped around his waist. If the phone had not rung, he would have been inside of her, claiming her. Just thinking about it made him want to fight everyone in this damn hospital just to be at her side, but here he was, waiting until someone from her family arrived.

He was pissed off when he showed up and her car was still there. He was going into that building and he could have envisioned himself hauling her over his shoulder as she squirmed in place, her sweet little ass in his face. He could feel himself lean in and bite her if she didn't control herself. That kiss had changed everything. It meant she still cared. It made her body respond to his touch, his lips. She opened like a wildflower as she arched into him, wanting more. Megan's body had heated up like an inferno, and he felt her nipples harden as he touched them through her silky bra. That changed everything, and he knew she would be screaming out his name in the end.

He looked around the waiting room as more people filled in, but thinking of her had calmed him a little. Soon the tension eased, and he could feel the air in his lungs again. Not knowing if Megan was okay created an aching feeling in his chest. He hoped he had gotten to her in time; her pulse was weak and they had almost lost her in the ambulance. He needed to know for himself that she was going to pull through. Hospital protocol meant that only family members would get information for a patient, but he did make a few calls to make sure she was getting

$$$

the best care possible and to have a room ready for her if she needed to stay overnight.

Max stood at the far end of the waiting room, he took a deep breath and sighed. The sound around him of people murmuring and crying wasn't helping, but they had each other. The hospital was not where he would like to be right now. It left something to be desired—the plastic chair, the smell of industrial cleaners, the sound of the janitor cleaning the floors, the sound of sirens in the distance, and medics screaming stats as they brought in another patient on a gurney. Max moved his shoulder in a circle motion to release the tightness. Never had he felt this buildup of stress before, especially for a woman. He sat down and rested is elbows on his knees as he rubbed his face with both hands. He took another deep breath and combed his fingers through his hair. He moved his head from side to side, trying to crack his neck. He hated not knowing what was happening. Leaving was out of the question, but from this day forward he was going to take Megan into his own hands. She would have security with her; he would do anything in his power to make sure of that. Whoever did this to her would pay.

He reached into his jacket and pulled out an envelope, that someone slip into his pocket. There was no name and nothing written on the outside. He looked it over, opened it, and pulled out the contents.

YOU WILL PAY FOR WHAT YOU DID. WE WILL BE WATCHING. NOW WE KNOW YOUR WEAKNESS.

Max had never bothered with threats before. Business was business. It was always about what you knew and what you could have. He had seen it before during hostile takeovers when CEO didn't agree with new management. This was different, personal, and he knew it. He wouldn't sit around for people to hurt him. He took out his cell phone, took a picture of the contents, and forwarded it to his team of security. They had better find something fast or they would be replaced with someone that can do the job. If they were coming after him, his only weakness that he knew was Megan, and he wouldn't let anyone get close to her. He put the evidence back in his pocket so he could give it to his security team in the morning.

Max held his head low. He took another deep breath and looked at his injured hand. He rubbed the top of his knuckles with his other hand to feel the cuts. *Just minor*, he thought. He pressed his other hand on top, feeling it, making sure nothing was broken. As he extended and flexed it, the soreness was there, but he knew it would only be bruised. Punching the wall when the nurse said no was not the smartest move, but he was angry and had lost his temper.

He looked up at the nurses' station and it was finally quiet. He tempted faith again and hoped he would get some answers without causing a scenes and getting kicked out for good. As he walked toward the nurses' station, he noticed the guards looking at him. He nodded and smiled back, meaning 'I got this and it's okay'. He leaned into the window and couldn't help but watched the young nurse blushed as he smiled back at her. *Yeah, I have this!* he thought. His smile grew bigger and he thought he might just get some answers after all. He relaxed and showed off his dazzling smile with full wattage, the one that said, *hey baby, look at me*. The one that made women melt the moment they saw it. "Evening. I was wondering if there is any update on the condition of Megan Harrison."

Max watched her, not giving away that he was holding his breath, keeping the smile on his face as he watched her turn beat red. Yes, he had that effect and he knew it. He looked at her

$$$

flipping through charts as she tried to push her hair behind her ear. Then she looked up at him and her face changed. He knew he wasn't going to get the information he wanted.

"I'm sorry, sir. I cannot give you that information unless you are family." She looked up at him and smiled.

"That's bullshit and you know it," Max said through clenched teeth, trying to keep his cool. "Do you have any idea who I am? I need to talk to the supervisor in charge and now! I've been waiting here for hours and I need to know the status of Megan Harrison." Max held on to the counter, hoping that he wasn't going to lose his patience with her. He was just about to say that she was his wife when a hand touched his forearm. He turned and looked into a pair of gray eyes full of concern. "Maggie," he whispered and pulled her into a hug.

xoxo

## Chapter Three

Maggie Harrison was Megan's older sister, but not the eldest of the Harrison family. It was midnight when she was just about to pull the covers over herself and shut off the light for a good night's sleep. When the phone rang, she looked at it and sighed. She didn't want to answer it but at the last minute, she did. "Joe, this better be good, I'm just about to go to bed." She was a little irate. She listened to him as he barked out orders, telling her to get to the hospital. "I'm on my way." She jumped out of bed and grabbed the first pair of sweatpants she found and a sweater. Her heart raced. *This can't be happening again*, she thought as she rushed through the condo. "Where are my damn keys?"

Maggie ran down the stairs two at a time, hoping that she wouldn't fall in the process. She rushed out the door and came to a stop when she saw her brother Ethan pulling up in front of her. She was relieved that she didn't have to drive. She ran to the truck and slid in the passenger seat.

"Jesus Ethan, why does this keep happening to our family? What happened?" She leaned her head back on the headrest and couldn't help the old feelings coming back. The pain of losing a family member haunted her. She couldn't lose her sister; she had to believe she would be okay.

XOXO

Ethan looked at her from the corner of his eye. "Not sure. All Joe said was that she was attacked and Max found her unconscious. She lost a lot of blood, Mags. That is all I know. Joe said to wait at the hospital until he got there." Ethan took Maggie's hand and squeezed it in comfort. "Our sister will be okay. We need to believe it." Ethan drove as fast as he could. Thank god traffic was minimal at this time of night.

She hoped Megan was alright. Maggie heard Ethan say that everything would be okay, but would it? After losing her parents in a car accident nine months ago, her brothers and sister were all she had.

Ethan didn't have time to stop and Maggie jumped out of the truck, almost falling as she ran inside the emergency department. She stopped the moment she entered as she watched Max Pierce demanding to see her sister. She looked at him from the door. She knew that Megan had a soft spot when it came to Max, but what she didn't know was his intension for her sister. She saw the attraction a few months ago. Every time Max was near, Megan would stiffen and hold herself back, but she didn't know how far this attraction went. She walked towards him and he hadn't notice her yet as she put her hand on his forearm. At first she thought it would be a bad idea because his body was tense, but when he realized it was her, he pulled her into a hug. This powerful man had a weakness and she realized that it was her sister. He was a man that was always in control, but he looked defeated and tired now.

"Max, where is she?" Maggie was anxious to find her sister and to find out what had happened.

Max looked at her, knowing that finally he would find out if Megan was okay. "Thank God you're here, Maggie. They will not tell me anything. I need to know if Megan is okay. Please!"

$$$

Maggie held on to his arm as she leaned into the window. "Hi, my name is Maggie Harrison. My sister Megan Harrison was admitted tonight. May I see her, please?" Maggie felt Max squeeze her arm. She was worried also and didn't have much information about what happened.

The nurse didn't hesitate as Maggie showed her identification. "This way, Miss Harrison."

"Max, let me go check on her. I promise I will be right back. Ethan should be here shortly." Maggie touched his hand, reassuring him. Seeing the bruises and cuts on his hand, she winced. She had two brothers and knew how hot headed boys can be when they do not get what they want. Max was no different. "You should get that checked," she said. Maggie released his hand and he nodded. "Wait here. Tell Ethan that I've gone to check on her. Please stay out of trouble, Max."

"Maggie," Max whispered as she looked over her shoulder. "Please hurry. I want to know she is all right. We almost lost her tonight." She nodded and walked away.

The smell was like no other, and she didn't like the feeling she was having. She was holding her breath. People lined up in hallway. It was over crowded with old and young, mothers and fathers caring for their loved ones. The smell of alcohol filled the air, and the pungent smell of dry blood lingered in waste baskets that the hadn't been cleaned from the last patient that came in. At some point, there was a strong smell of urine as she walked down the corridor. Maggie hated it here; it just reminded her the last time she saw her parents. They finally stopped and the nurse pulled back the curtain. Maggie saw Megan lying there motionless, her head wrapped in a bandage. She was wearing what we all love, the hospital blue gown. Her clothes were at her bedside in a bag full of blood. She was alive and breathing

XOXO

oxygen through the nose, and she was hooked up with an IV tube in her right hand. "How is she?" Maggie asked the nurse.

"Stable. She should wake up soon. Her pressure is normal and she should be fine, except for a headache." The nurse read her chart again and checked her vitals. "We should have her room soon. Mr. Pierce is a very persistent man but rules are rules. Once she wakes up, we will be able to transfer her."

"Thank you." She watched the nurse leave and approached Megan. Her heart raced in her chest. Maggie sighed, knowing she was still alive. She was grateful. She looked fragile and weak, her face lacking color. She was pale and her dark circles didn't help. *Damn, Joe worked her too hard. She was going to have a word with him,* she thought. She couldn't understand who would hurt her like this. "I'm sorry this happened to you, Baby Girl. What were you doing? Who did this to you?" Maggie held her hand. She felt Megan's hand squeeze her. A sign of relief escaped as she looked up and noticed that her sister's eyes were slowly opening. "That's it, Megan. Open your eyes."

$$$

## Chapter Four

Max knew that eventually his feelings for Megan would surface, but he didn't know it would happen tonight in front of all her family and friends. Having her around made him feel things he had never felt before: passion, desire, love… especially love. To see her smile, to make her his everything—he wanted her to be happy most of all. He just wanted to have a chance to prove to her that she could trust him again. When Joe Harrison arrived at the hospital, Max knew he took his role as big brother seriously after their parents' death. Max watched his friend from afar but knew that was going to be different, because Joe had notice how he reacted to Megan being injured, his weakness. He was not the self-assured businessman that he showed the world. He still didn't know how Megan would respond to him being there. Leaving was out of the question until he could see with his own eyes that she was all right.

 Max watched as Joe asked one of the nurses a question, and in that moment, Maggie finally came out. She looked relieved and went to hug her brother. Max watched as Joe finally turned and seeing only him. He could hear Lizzie in the distance as she talked to Ethan and Josh, but he just stood there waiting for the anchor to fall. Good or bad, he was not going to back down. He

XOXO

knew that it was just a matter of time until he had to explain himself to Joe and by his expression, he wasn't happy. This was personal now, and he couldn't hide the feelings he had for Megan. He watched Joe and Maggie walk into the waiting room

"Megan is okay," Maggie said. "She just woke up and the doctor is with her now. She has a nasty gash on her head and a few stitches. She woke up a little lost about what happened, but the doctor said that's normal." Maggie sighed as she held onto Joe and felt the comfort of her brother's arm around her. With all the anxiety she was holding back, finally she took a deep breath.

"Max, can I speak with you?" Joe Harrison wasn't wasting time. He needed answers. He had known Max for a long time, including how he treated women, but this was different. Joe saw the reaction he had towards his sister. This was more than just friendship. He had never seen Max react like this before and he could sense something more going on. Megan was going to be okay, but there were answers he needed to have. The first was what was going on between Max and his sister. He didn't care how he addressed Max. Yes, his tone was a little louder than usual, and everyone turned when he barked. *Friend or not, this is ending now*, he thought. What he saw tonight was more than friendship. "Let's step outside." Joe gave Maggie a look that meant *don't butt in*. He turned and walked out of the waiting room.

Joe took in the evening air, knowing Max was behind him. He had to treat this like a business meeting, but his family was personal, and Max had overstepped the line between business and friendship. His friends and associates knew that his sisters were off limits. The rules were in place for a reason, or so he thought. "Max, what the hell is going on between you and Meg? How do you know her? By your reaction tonight, I can see that there's more than just a working relationship going on here. I don't like

$$$

it! She's my baby sister, for crying out loud! I know how you are with women, Max. I don't want her to be another mark on your bedpost!" Joe's voice was rising the longer he talked. He could see from over Max's shoulder that his family was watching.

Max looked at Joe. He was angry at him and for good reason, but he didn't want to have this conversation in the middle of a parking lot at the hospital. It was late and everyone was on edge, especially him, but seeing his friend from university getting hot under the collar, he knew that he wasn't winning any favors by keeping quiet. Joe could be intimidating at times, but Max had dealt with a lot of people worse than him, and intimidation didn't scare him. He was known to be an arrogant son-of-bitch on most days. Joe did not scare him, and if he had to take a hit, then he would go head to head with Joe. He didn't know if Megan would ever forgive him, but he had to hope deep down she would. He had had a long day and even longer night and right now he just didn't have it in him to fight.

"Well, Max? I'm waiting. What the hell is going on with you and my sister?" Joe fisted his hands to the side, knowing that he should calm himself, but he couldn't. He was angry at what happened to his sister. Some asshole hurt her and he wasn't there to protect her.

"Nothing, Joe! I swear!" Max kept his cool and looked him in the eye. He could see Joe didn't believe him. He knew that if he said anything, their business partnership would be over, and so would their friendship. His feelings for Megan were real and every time she was near, the attraction got stronger. He pondered, knowing he had to try to control the situation. Joe was no push over, and he would come at him with everything he had because he knew friends didn't date their friend's sister without consequences.

XOXO

"You're saying that nothing is happening between you and Megan." Joe came a little closer and he stood eye to eye with Max. "I…don't…believe…you. I've known you for a long time, and I have never seen you act like you did tonight. I will ask you one more time, what is going on with you and my sister? Don't give me any bullshit!" Joe pointed his finger into his chest, making sure Max was hearing him loud and clear.

Max pushed back. He stood taller than Joe by a few inches and leaned into him. "Joe, don't push me. If it's a fight you're looking for, you'll get one. What happens between Megan and me is between us? Do I make myself clear? You are not going to stand there and be all protective of her. I know you're her brother but she's a grown woman and she can see who she wants. Even if we met briefly a few years ago, that is none of your business." He looked at Joe and knew that he overstepped, but he loved her and like hell he was going to let her brother intimidate him.

"What do you mean briefly? You… son of a bitch! If you hurt her in any way, I swear I'm going to…" Joe watched Max. If he said one wrong word, he was going to deck him. Joe saw more people gathering around, even this late at night, but he didn't care.

"Three years ago, we hooked up in the Hamptons, but I didn't know she was your sister. When the vacation was over, we parted ways. When I realized I made a mistake and wanted her back, she wasn't available and had someone else.

"So let me get this straight. You slept with her and discarded her like another one of the floozies that you date." Joe thought back and everything was falling into place. He remembered how depressed Megan was three years ago. It took months for her to even smile. He turned away from Max and remembered how she was depressed, crying all the time. Whenever he asked his

$$$

mom what was wrong, all she said she was going through some personal pain. "So, it was you. Fuck, Max! She was my sister. Do you know how much you hurt her? How could you?" But rationalizing everything was over rated. Joe leaned back and came up with a right punch, hitting Max in the jaw. He watched him lose his balance and fall.

Max wiped away some blood from his lip and looked at Joe. "Okay, I deserved that." He held his jaw in place. Max knew Joe had a good right punch, but he never wanted to be on the receiving end of it.

"Fuck, Max! She's my sister! How could you?" Joe was leaning over him, ready to punch him again, breathing heavily.

"I swear I didn't know she was your sister until much later. If I had known, I would have never approached her, I swear."

Joe was about to throw another punch when Lizzie pushed him away so Max could stand. She remained between the two men. "Guys! Stop!" she yelled. "Wrong time, wrong place." Lizzie held up both her hands as she held them back from one another before they went at it again. "If Megan could see both of you right now, she would be furious. Joe, I hate to tell you this, but Megan has been fighting her feelings for Max for several months now. Yes, she cares about him. Hell, Megan may still be in love with him, but that is her battle to fight, not yours. As for you, Max, if I didn't love Megan so much, I would not defend you right now. You two need to do some serious talking. Deep down inside, I know that girl still loves you, but she's not ready to tell you this. She needs time, and fighting right now will not solve anything. You came back into her life when she least expected, so she needs time to process this. For now, please let's just kiss and make up or do whatever it is that you guys do—buck chest, or high five, or slap each other's ass. I don't care, work it out for

Megan's sake." Lizzie was breathing hard as she tried to get her point across.

Maggie stood beside Lizzie and couldn't help but clap. "Bravo, Lizzie. Bravo!" Maggie couldn't be more proud of her. Lizzie was a little sister and a good friend for Megan. She looked at her brother. "Joe, Lizzie's right. We all care about Megan, and right now, we should all be there for her. What Megan feels for Max is her business, not yours. I know you think that you need to protect us, big brother, but the last time I checked, Megan and I were both grown up, and we can fight our own battles in love. If Megan needs you, I'm sure she will ask for your help." Maggie looked at Joe, knowing that she was getting through his thick skull. He was looking back at her like she had lost her mind.

"But Maggie, he slept with her and ditched her!" He was still pissed and he still wanted to hit the man. He watched Max bow his head in defeat, knowing that he was done fighting. He knew Max could fight, and not fighting back meant something. Maybe he did love her. Joe took a deep breath and realized that if it weren't for Max finding her tonight, they might have lost her. Max's quick reaction saved her damn life. The more he looked at the man in front of him, he could see a change. He wasn't feeling the anger that he felt just moments ago. Maggie was right. He needed to focus on his sister and make sure she gets better.

"Joe, Max cares about her. You of all people must know how hard it is for a man to ask someone for forgiveness. It's not easy. I believe in my heart that what Max feels for Megan is real. Let them hash it out and if it doesn't work, then I will not stop you. I will let you ruin that pretty face of his. I'm sure that Megan is giving Max one hell of a fight." Maggie leaned up and kissed her brother on the cheek. "Come on, big brother, let's go see our sister."

$$$

Joe didn't like it, but knowing Max cared for his sister, he extended his hand. "Sorry, man! I was just protecting her, you know. I hate what happened to her tonight."

Max took his hand as he gave him a man hug. "No hard feelings. I would have done the same had it been my sister. You still have one good right punch." He held his left side of his face and grinned.

## Chapter Five

*Run, just run, Megan. Dammit,* she kept chanting to herself. *This can't be happening!* Her heart was pounding and her lungs were burning as she gasped for air. *Damn, why didn't I see this coming?* She ran down a dark corridor and the only light was the flashing exit sign in the distance. Her muscles hurt, she felt the tightness in her legs, and the pounding of her feet on the cement made every step feel like a sharp shot through her body. She hated running and didn't believe that it constituted physical exercise, though some people would swear by it. She just wanted to keel over and hack up all the contents of her stomach, but when you have someone chasing you, you run like hell and hope they don't catch you. Megan thought for sure she was going to die or that it was just a bad dream that she couldn't wake up from. She feared that if she stopped running, the people who were after her would catch up. But who were these people? They were monsters, faceless men with crowbars, growling at her and knowing she couldn't scream. She was alone and no one would hear her. Megan could hear their footsteps closing in and pushed herself to run faster. Just a little bit more. If she could just get to the door, that would be her safety. She would be safe there. She could lock herself in the office and call for help. All she had to do was reach out and take hold of the doorknob, but she needed to run faster. She reached out just as she was going to turn the knob but she let out of scream and fell backward. Her breath whooshed out of her and she felt the pain hit the back of her head. Then darkness overtook her. She thought her life was over. She was going to die.

Through the darkness, she sensed that small touch, the whisper of the sweetest, most erotic voice she has ever heard, pulling her toward it, telling her to stay to fight. Then the warmth of the softest lips touched her, coaxing her. "Don't leave me. Fight, baby, fight."

Megan knew that voice. *This has to be a dream*. She tried to move, but couldn't. She felt like someone was calling her name, but why couldn't she feel anything? There was nothing—no voices, no running, no screaming, just total silence.

Every muscle in her body was in pain. She felt like she had done ten rounds of boxing. The only sound she could hear was beeping and moaning, like someone was in pain in the far distance. But why? That noise, where was it coming from? It was an annoying beeping sound. Megan tried to open her eyes but couldn't. They felt so heavy and it was taking everything out of her.

She tried to move as she heard voices asking her to wake up. Why couldn't she move? Why couldn't she open her eyes? The beeping increased and she could hear it more clearly now. Her heart raced and she realized the beeping was coming from her. Then she felt it, just the smallest touch holding her hand, squeezing. Megan knew that voice; it was her sister coaxing her to wake up. "Come on, baby girl, open your eyes." She held on to her hand. As she opened her hounded eyelids and light flashed

$$$

into them, she closed them and tried again. She groaned slightly but then looked into her sister's eyes.

"What happened?" Megan asked in a weak voice. She looked around and noticed that she was surrounded by curtains and people crying in pain. Her head was pounding and she wished that her headache would go away. She gave her sister a weak smile.

"You were attacked tonight. This is why you are here. You're safe now, Megan. Just rest." Maggie looked at her sister and sensed the panic rising in her. "The doctor just wants to check you over. You gave us a scare, but you are okay now. No harm will come to you. Everyone is here and they want to see you, but first let this nice doctor ask you a few questions, okay?" Maggie bent over and kissed the top of her bandaged head, giving her the affection that she needed from her family. Maggie told her she would be back and that she just wanted to let everyone know that she was awake. She waited until she knew Megan could calm down, then looked at the doctor and nodded.

"Miss Harrison, you lost a lot a blood and you will have a headache for a few days, but nothing but rest will help you recover. We still want to keep you for another twenty-four hours, but you should recover." The doctor checked her out. "In the meantime, now that you are awake, a room as been set up for you and we will transfer you shortly. I will let your family know the room and floor number."

"Thank you." Megan's voice was weak and dry as she spoke, but she still didn't understand what happened, it was still not all clear to her. She wanted to go home. She didn't care for hospitals, but at least they were taking her to her room.

*At peace finally,* Megan thought as she closed her eyes. She loved her family and friends but they were too much sometimes. Her head was spinning and she felt dizzy with all the questions

XOXO

being thrown her way. She wished she would remember but the doctor said it would take time and her memory would come back. The nurse had turned the beeping sound off and she could feel the pain medication kicking in. Her head was just a small annoying thump. She felt like she was drifting off to sleep when she heard the door open. "Go away! Let me sleep, please." A shiver ran through her body, and then a hand touched her, gently like a feather. Megan opened her eyes and stared into the most incredible eyes she had ever seen. He smiled down at her. She could see the relief of a man that had lost his best friend or someone he had loved, but just like that it was gone. Just when she was about to say something, Joe walked in and broke the connection. She watched him move aside but his look never left her.

"Baby girl, don't you ever scare me like that ever again." Joe leaned in and kissed her head. "What were you doing there that late? You said you were heading home earlier. There was vandalism happening. It was not safe alone there and you knew it. If Max hadn't stopped there tonight, you might have died." Joe looked down at her with so much worry. He couldn't bear losing another family member.

Tears ran down Megan's cheeks as she watched her brother's concerned and worried face. If only she knew or could remember what had happened. One minute she was with David Smith, the head contractor for Harrison Construction, and the next things she knew she was waking up here. "Joe, I'm sorry." Tears kept flowing down her face. She knew she had scared her family. She didn't want to fight with her brother. Tired and weak, she just wanted to sleep, and having Max in the same room was playing with her head. She didn't want to be this emotional. Joe was always her over-protective brother growing up. She hiccupped as she tried to control her sobs. "I wish I could remember what

$$$

happened, but I don't. All I remember is talking with David, and then dreaming about running, being scared, and waking up here."

"I'm sorry if I'm upsetting you, but I'm happy you are alright. You have been through a lot tonight and you need your rest. We'll talk in the morning, so rest your pretty little head of yours. Maybe something will come back to you." Joe leaned in and kissed Megan's head. "You're safe now, Megan. Nobody will hurt you again."

Megan gave Joe a weak smile as she wiped away the last of her tears. Max was still there watching her. She sensed his concern for her. *He saved me, but why don't I remember?* she thought. She watched him leaning against the wall, waiting to say something. She had never seen him look so lost. He was a man that always had a purpose and controlled everything he touched. She still couldn't figure out why she was so attracted to him. His hair was tousled and his dark whiskers made him looked rogue, like a bad ass, but still beautiful. Max was always so in control and it showed in his stance, but not tonight. He looked tired and defeated. She tried to make sense of it all. She noticed that he had a cut on his left lip with blood. His shirt also had a stain of blood. She worried as she looked at him, then at Joe, then back to Max. "What happened to you?" she whispered. Then she looked at Joe and noticed his right hand. "Joe, what did you do? Why is Max bleeding?" She watched the two men exchange a look, then they both smiled back at her.

"What? This? Just a difference of opinion!" he answered. He looked at Joe and smiled back at her.

"How old are you, Joe? Two? You know punching does not solve anything," Megan told him in the stern voice their mom used to use.

XOXO

"You're right. I lost my temper and Max and I had a misunderstanding. It's all worked out now, baby girl. All I want now if for you to rest. I will see you tomorrow. You were hit pretty hard on the head. Tomorrow, they will run more tests to make sure everything is fine, then we'll take you home." Joe gave her a big hug. "Goodnight, baby girl. I'll see you in the morning. Don't worry about anything." Joe looked at Max and put a hand on his shoulder. "Thank you for being there when I wasn't." He shook his head and looked over his shoulder to Megan, then back at Max. "Take good care of her." He smiled and left.

Megan watched the male bonding between two old friends. Respect went a long way with Joe and she knew that. The moment she met Max, she saw the guy on the beach, the guy who truly showed people the kinder side of him, not the business man who was always in control and didn't show emotions. She knew that these two men had a bond that would never die. Megan was going to find out what had happened; part of tonight was still fuzzy but she knew eventually she would remember. She was too exhausted even to think right now, but when Joe left the room, she felt the charge instantly. Being in the same room as Max Pierce made her heart race, and the damn machine wasn't helping. She tried to think of something else, but all she saw was Max. What he did to her inside made her want him even more. Instead of letting her thoughts go wild, she needed to know what happened. "Please tell me what that was about." She watched as Max approached her from across the room.

$$$

## Chapter Six

When Joe left, Max finally had a reason to be alone with Megan. The anxiety of not knowing, and now seeing her awake and alert, meant he was finally at peace with himself. He walked towards her, knowing that he was affecting her. He leaned in and kissed her on the forehead. Max closed his eyes and felt the warmth as he inhaled her scent. "You scared me, Angel. What were you thinking being there that late again?" Max caressed her cheek with the back of his hand and looked at her sleepy hazel eyes. He wasn't going to fight with her; he needed to be there for her and he wanted her to lean on him for strength for support. For tonight, he was giving her his full attention. The ordeal was over, that was the most important thing right now. Looking at her, he knew she was still under the drugs that they gave her for the pain. You could see it in her eyes and in how white her face was. She was still weak.

"What do you mean again?" Megan looked at him like he was out of his mind. Was he following her? Was he watching her like a stalker. She couldn't think any more, it was just too much.

"Megan, you have been staying late every night for the last three weeks. When I spotted your car tonight, I lost it. I was coming in to haul you out of there, even if I had to throw you over my shoulders. You work too hard! If this project is too much, get Joe to hire an assistant for you." Max was keeping his voice calm. He nearly lost her when he was so close to getting her back.

"Max, I don't want to argue, please. I'm just too tired, and my head hurts." She closed her eyes as she leaned back, hoping to calm herself. This man, this beautiful, god-forsaken Greek god was just too close. Her insides were on full alert, craving this man that haunted her dreams.

"Megan, when I saw you laying on the floor, I thought I lost you, and it scared the hell out of me. I don't want to lose you again, baby."

Just then, the nurse walked in. "Miss Harrison, I will put some medication in your IV to help you sleep, and it should help with your headache. Mr. Pierce, you may use the other bed. The room will not have anyone else tonight." Megan wasn't sure she wanted him to stay with her, but she didn't want to be alone, especially in a hospital where there was so much pain for her.

"You should get some sleep." Max held his warm lips to her forehead. He felt her relax in the tender moment. It let her know he was there if she needed him.

Megan's eyes fluttered. Whatever the nurse injected into her IV made her feel drowsy. "You are right! I'm tired." She just wanted to close herself off and cry. This was too much. She couldn't talk any longer from being tired and emotionally drained, and she couldn't fight him anymore. She couldn't fight the feelings she was having for him. Megan needed to come clean and tell him everything. "Oh Max, there is so much I need to say to you." She mumbled her words, fighting the medication.

$$$

Max squeezed her hand and looked into those beautiful hazel eyes. "Shhhhh. Sleep. We'll talk tomorrow." He held her gaze. His voice was soothing and calm as he touched her face.

"There's so much I need to tell you, Max. I just don't know where to start." Her voice was getting weaker.

He raised her hand to his lips and kissed the inside of her palm. "Tonight, you rest. We can talk tomorrow after you're released. No harm will come to you tonight. Not on my watch."

"Max?" She looked at him and saw the man she fell in love with so long ago, the man that was caring, tender, and passionate—and so damn sexy. Megan knew, even if he did not say it, that deep down, she still felt the love he had for her. She couldn't help but admire his rogue beauty. There was just something about the man. No matter how he looked, he was sexy and attractive. The best part was that he wanted her. She yearned for this man, this one who had stolen her heart. Those feeling were still there. She was too tired to make sense of what was going on, even though she couldn't pull away from his intense eyes that looked at her with so much concern and worry. She leaned into his hand, feeling the warmth, the heat, but behind that look, she felt his pain. He felt hers too, but behind all that affection, there was still desire and passion. Megan couldn't help but remember how it felt to be loved because she felt it all the way to her core. She couldn't explain the feeling that this one man could give her. Would it be so bad to let her guard down just for one night? She just wanted to be held.

"Megan, what's wrong?" Max brushed back a tear that ran down her cheek. She hadn't noticed she was crying. He looked at those sad eyes and knew he would give her anything she wanted. "Move over. Let me hold you for a while until you fall asleep."

xoxo

Megan watched as he removed his jacket. He was still dressed in his work clothes, his black Armani suite and a light green shirt that brought out his beautiful emerald eyes. They could take her to places and make her feel things just with one look. He rolled up his sleeves as he lay down beside her and pulled her tight against him. His masculine scent was intoxicating and she breathed it in. The racing of his heart made hers beat even faster. She had the same effect on him as he had on her. She looked up and he smiled at her with so much longing and protectiveness. She took a few deep breaths, hoping to calm herself. She lay with him and felt his arm around her, holding her as he caressed her back. This felt right and safe, and she knew that during this weakness of letting her guard down that this is what she wanted. She felt at peace with herself and drifted into a sound sleep.

Max rested his head as he listened to the rhythm of her heartbeat. He was thinking about his beautiful little tiger. He knew he had this effect on her. She made him feel alive just being near her. He would do anything for her, even buy her the moon if she'd let him. Just thinking about her made his heart ache. Why anyone would hurt her, he didn't know, but he was going to find out. That letter had something to do with it. He felt damn lucky he found her when he did. Every feeling that he had for her three years ago came rushing back. He wasn't running anymore; he loved her. She belonged in his arms. The words almost come out while he was having a discussion with Joe, but he did say them to her. Did she hear them in the ambulance? He wanted her to fight, to stay alive so that he could give her the world.

Max knew his determination was starting to get to her. Megan was finally letting him in. He could see himself with her now down the road so clearly, by his side and with child. This didn't scare him one bit. He was ready to make a future with this

$$$

beautiful woman. He knew she was asleep so he slowly moved himself of the bed, careful not to wake her. He walked slowly to the door, took his phone out, and dialed the number. "Six am meeting my office." That is all he said and hung up, not giving his security time to respond. As he walked back into the room, not making a noise to wake Megan, he looked down at her sleeping face. "She's alive. You're safe now, Megan," he whispered. "No one will ever hurt you again." She mumbled at his small touch and he knew it was going to be a long night.

xoxo

## Chapter Seven

Megan watched the black SUV pull up to the front entrance of the hospital, knowing that it was Max. Not far behind, a second SUV was on his tail. Two bodyguards emerged, and one she had not noticed at her side approached them. She knew then how powerful this man was, but she didn't understand why he needed all the security. Before she was released, Megan knew something was wrong when she walked in on Max and Joe in a heated discussion, but they stopped when she came in the room. They thought that she hadn't noticed but she had. Even though what happened that night was still vague, the doctor said that her memory should return. She was doing fine, and he asked her not to think about what happened. It should come back to her soon.

She sat in the wheelchair. It was mandatory that she needed to be wheeled out—hospital rules, they said. She looked up, and Max walked towards her with the most amazing smile on his face. Damn, did he look amazing? She couldn't help but want to jump him right now. She had fallen asleep in his arms last night, but when she woke that morning, Max was gone. He told her not to move, and she hadn't when he wheeled her out, but as he bent down and looked into her eyes, she knew that she would never be the same again. She could see the twinkle in his eyes, the passion reflecting into her, but when he smiled, that just made her all gooey inside. "What's with the goons? Is there something wrong or something I need to know, Max? Is your life in danger?" She looked him straight in the eyes as he looked over his shoulder and watched his security men. He looked back at her and shook his head.

Max, knew he was doing the right thing. She had to have someone with her. He thought of the letter he had received and another one that morning that was left on his SUV window saying, WE ARE COMING FOR YOU. He couldn't risk something happening to her. He told Joe what was going on and about the threat. When she put up a fight this morning stating that she wanted to be at her condo and arguing with her brother, he knew she couldn't be alone. Not now, not ever. He could sense she was stressing about it this morning, so when he said he would take care of her, she didn't like it. Was he an asshole to impose himself? Yes, but being with Megan and making sure she was safe came first. Forty-eight hours, that was all he needed to have her back in his life. "Those men are my security guys. Where I go, they go, unless I foresee they are not needed." He leaned down and kissed her nose.

"Oh!" She could feel his closeness, his hot breath just inches away from her lips. If he touched her right now, she would go up and flames. "You know I can take care of myself, right? You do not need to stay with me." Having Max Pierce in the same home was a disaster waiting to happen. She wouldn't get any rest; all she would think about would be him naked in her bed.

Max took her bag and handed it to his bodyguard. He extended his arm to her. "Your chariot awaits!" He helped her up, knowing she would be unstable on her feet. He could also

$$$

see the stubbornness in her. She was no pushover. He loved that she was a fighter and she was not the typical girl that just wanted to please him. He had to work for her trust, and she had no issues saying what was needed. She wasn't the same woman he met three years ago. That woman was still in her, but something in her changed. She protected her heart, and he wanted to bring down those barriers. He hoped that one day soon she would trust him again. "I have a surprise for you waiting in the SUV. Are you willing to see what it is?" Max looked down at her as she took his arm and stood, hoping her legs would hold her.

Megan dislike being care for, but she hadn't walked for two days other than going from her bed to the bathroom. When Max held her up, her legs were weak, but his strength kept her in place. The moment she opened the door, the rich aroma of her favorite drink hit her, and she couldn't help but drool to have that first sip. She turned in surprise. *How did you know?* "You bought me a caramel macchiato. How did you know that was... well, it's my favorite?" Megan watched him lean in and kiss her cheek, and damn if those lips on her skin did not make her libido heat up.

Max helped her into the SUV and entrusted his bodyguards to follow until they reached the condo. He needed to stop to pick up a few things for lunch and once there, they were free to go. He climbed into the driver's seat and heard her moan in pleasure. It made him slightly uncomfortable. "Good?" he asked as they drove away.

"Thank you for this. How did you know it's my favorite?"

"I remember everything about you, Megan—your dislikes, what you enjoy. We spent two weeks together, and you made me stop at Starbucks every morning in the Hamptons to get this for you, so yeah, I remember you like them." Max reached out and took her hand while she drank her sugar rush. He preferred his coffee black with nothing in it, but he knew that Megan liked to have her first coffee with the works.

A few hours later, after running around getting things for lunch, Megan sat back and rested her head on the headrest. Her eyes were getting heavier, and she closed them for just a second. Her head was still a little numb and had that pressure that was constantly there, but it was bearable. She might have drifted off to sleep when she felt a hand on hers.

Max looked at her, and she had fallen asleep. He reached out and put his hand on hers. She jumped. "Sorry, I didn't mean to startle you. Are you feeling okay?"

She looked at his strong dark hand on hers. Her skin was pale compared to his, but she once heard that you can tell a lot from a man's hand and how he took care of himself. Max was a virile man. He kept in shape, ran daily, and was constantly watching what he ate. On the other hand, she would just put anything in her mouth—the sweeter, the better. "Yes, I am fine. I'm just a little tired, that's all. Nothing that a little nap won't cure." Megan knew he was trying so hard to make her relax. Why couldn't she take this for what it was worth, a friend helping a friend? She knew it was more. Could she trust him enough now, put the past where it belonged? No, she had to come clean. She needed to tell him everything if she wanted to have a future with him.

"We're almost there. I'll tuck you in." *Or maybe I'll take a nap with you*, he thought.

"Max, please, I'm a big girl. I don't need another father figure." She was irate that he was giving all his attention to her, but she had survived this far in life without people hounding her.

"Baby, it's nothing to do with a father figure. I want to take care of you and also be inside you, loving you, kissing you,

$$$

making you come over and over again until we both have it out of our systems." He kept holding her hand and caressing the top with his thumb.

Megan gasped at what he was saying. Her brain shut down and her heart sped up. She had to keep her thighs together, knowing that he was affecting her. Three damn years, that was the last time she had sex. Maybe if she had followed Lizzie's advice, she wouldn't be so darn turned on right now. Lizzie always told her that she needed to loosen up and take a chance. Life is full of uncertainties; it's what you learn from them that makes you a better person. She looked at him from the side. He controlled everything in his world. Would he try to control her too? She didn't believe that. Josh would talk about Max, but he never said that he had girlfriends, or even when he did have a date, it was all for show. Megan's heart and brain were in a constant battle with each other. Seeing him now, he was all she ever wanted. He was attentive and loving. The way he looked at her, touched her, even smiled at her. Not once did he think about himself. She needed to let go of the past and move on, but first, she needed to tell him the truth, she hoped he wouldn't leave her again. "Max, please, I'm tired, and my head hurts. I just want to lie down." *Coward*, she thought.

They made it to her condo. Megan opened the door, and they both walked in. It was an open concept living room, dining room, and kitchen off to the side, the big bay window that overlooked the river that flowed below. The only things missing were curtains. The walls were greyish, and the décor suited her. It was homey and reflected her style. Her smell surrounded him as he walked in and that alone would make his cock hard. He couldn't help it; being near her affected him in ways that he had forgotten. She was the only person that made him fell; he could

XOXO

fight any battle and win, she did that. "Nice place! Are you an exhibitionist, Miss Harrison?" He looked at her with a raised eyebrow and watched her blush.

"What? No, I love the view here!" She watched him look around. This place sold her because of the sunset coming through the window, overlooking the river flowing below through the trees. Peaceful it was, it was a good way to get away from the world around her. "This is my favorite place!" She showed him the balcony and sighed as she felt the sun beaming through the window. "Help yourself to anything you need. I'm going to my room to lie down." She turned but felt a strong arms snake around her waist. She looked over her shoulder and watched him. He turned her around in his arms.

Max took her face with both hands, leaned in, and kissed her on the lips so gently. He felt her sway into him. She opened for him as their tongues danced with each other. It wasn't demanding, but gentle and affectionate. Her taste was what he had missed. He then kissed her cheek as he trailed kisses down her neck to her ear and took her earlobe into his mouth. "Sweet dreams, Angel," he whispered. He held her a little longer than released her. Max took her chin with his forefinger and raised her head. He looked into her hounded eyes. "Don't worry; everything will be alright. I will take good care of you." He leaned in and kissed her gently on the lips again. "Now go rest up."

Megan felt a little dizzy just from that one small kiss, but her brain was shutting down. She couldn't speak. She just nodded and walked away before she collapsed on her bed.

$$$

# Chapter Eight

Two days, twelve hours, and thirty-six minutes, that is how long Max was with her, but who was counting. It was tough in the beginning. They argued about him being in her personal space. Megan hated to admit it, but she was going to miss him. Tonight he was going back home. With Max always around, her feelings for him were becoming stronger and stronger every day. Megan knew she would have to talk to him soon. He'd been a perfect gentleman these last two days. He was handling business from her home while she rested.

Megan decided that tonight was going to be the night. What needed to be said would be said. *No more secrets*, she thought. She had to tell him. Once the truth was out, he could leave her again. Or would he stay? Sooner or later, she would have to put this to rest and move on with her life. Maybe by saying this out loud, she would finally have closure. No more pain, no more nightmares; she would finally be free of the secret she had been keeping for years. One thing she knew now is that she still loved Max. Three years didn't change anything. There would never be anyone else who touched her that deeply. Her heart belonged to him and always would. She tried to hate him, but the passion was stronger than the hate.

xoxo

Megan looked at her phone for the millionth time, knowing that Max was on his way. He had some emergency and needed to address it, but he said that it wouldn't take long. She went to bed at night feeling frustrated and needy, aching for him. He was so close but yet far. Every morning he would have her breakfast ready, coffee waiting. Sometimes he was shirtless and barefoot with nothing on but his jeans. This look would drive her crazy; she knew he was commando. His jeans loosely on his hips, his tight ass showing but the moment he turns the evidence proving his manhood busting at the seam. She thought he was doing it on purpose. The bastard knew how this affected her. But she didn't give in. She would take her coffee and sit outside until she gets her libido back in check. Tonight was going to be the end—or the new beginning.

When seven o'clock came around, she heard the buzzer and knew that there was no turning back. A few minutes later, there was a small knock on the door. She looked herself over in the mirror. "You can do this," she said aloud. She said a silent prayer and hoped for the best. Her heart sped up a little just by one look. This man could undress you with his eyes, and he made all her female parts hyper-sensitive. He stood there so casually with a bouquet of flowers in hand, and a gorgeous smile that made her weak at the knees. She watched as he leaned in and kissed her lips gently. The warmth of his lips on hers made her heart thump a little faster, made her tingle inside. She had a weakness, and his name was Max Pierce. She knew when it came to her, he only showed his best—that smile and those dimples on that perfect face, his high cheekbones, his sensual lips, a smile that would brighten up a room. Max didn't keep his hair long, but it wasn't short either, his natural black curls were soft to the touch, but what stood out the most about this man was his eyes.

$$$

They were green, like emerald, and you could easily lose yourself in them.

Max had confidence, charm, and was loyal to his family and closest friends. Those people always saw the best part of him. He was also a man that showed power just being in the same room. People wanted to be him, or just be in his presence. They never saw the other side of him, the businessman. At work, he was an arrogant son-of-bitch that you didn't want to cross. He never doubted himself, and when he wanted something, there was no stopping him. As a lover he had dominance. He knew how to please his partner exceptionally well, but that was a secret she kept to herself. She wouldn't want to give in to his big male ego.

"Please come in; dinner's almost ready. Thank you for the flowers, they are beautiful." She leaned in and smelled them. She always liked lilies and daisy and roses. It was a perfect combination, but if she had her choice, she'd take lilies and white roses. "I just have to go back to the kitchen to finish up. Help yourself to some wine, the bottle is already open and on the table. You mind turning on the music?"

"Anything I can do to help?" Max asked, knowing she had everything under control. He watched her walk away with the flowers in hand.

With the bottle and glasses in hand, Max stopped for a moment, enjoying the view. The trees were full and he could hear the water below flowing down as the waves crashed on the rocks. It was quiet and peaceful.

Megan came out with the plates and took a deep breath. *You can do this*, she thought. She sat down and gave herself a silent prayer, giving her courage to say what was on her mind. If they had any chance for a future, she needed to come clean. "Max, thank you for taking care of me these last two days. I know I haven't been easy on you."

Max opened the screen door for her. When she comes out with the plates, he felt something was wrong. He could see it in her eyes; she was hiding something. He could read her like a book, and something was eating at her. "It was my pleasure. I wanted to be here with you, to prove to you that I changed." Max leaned in and kissed her on the cheek. "This smells good!" He dug in and the flavor of the salmon and the sauce combined and melted on his tongue.

"Thanks! I appreciate what you did for me. Besides, it's the least I could do for you, for being so hard on you." She looked at him as he started to eat. She held her glass of wine to her lips. She needed the liquid courage to calm herself.

"Damn, woman! This salmon is to die for. Maybe I should just marry you."

Max said as he kept eating, enjoying the dinner. He heard her fork drop at those words and smiled. "Megan, I wish you would tell me what is bothering you. I can sense it." He didn't want to waste any time. He wanted to know what was going on. "Where did you learn to cook like this?"

"Mom was an excellent cook, and yes, there are things we need to talk about." She said another silent prayer to herself.

Max reached out and held her hand. "I'm sorry for your loss, Megan. I cannot imagine ever losing my parents."

She took a sip of wine. She couldn't help but wonder as she gazed into the darkness, but she knew that Max was sincere. The loss of her parents last year was devastating on her, and her family. She never thought that she would lose them so young.

$$$

"What's wrong? Are you feeling okay? Do you want to talk about it?" Max looked at her and noticed that she hadn't even touched her meal.

"I just miss her. She was my rock whenever something bad happened. I knew she was there for me no matter what."

"I wish I could have been there for you when you lost your parents. You needed someone to lean on. I can only imagine how everyone must have felt."

"It's okay. I know that Mom is with me every day."

"Megan, at the house, I was serious when I told you that I care about you. I only…"

"Max, stop! I heard what you said, but now there are things that I need to say to you." Megan closed her eyes, trying to find her inner strength.

"Okay, I'm listening, Angel." Max put down his fork and leaned back. He watched her as she bit down on her lip, then drank more wine. "Megan, what is it? Tell me what's wrong. I can see it in your eyes that something is wrong."

She took a sip of wine and looked at him. *Megan, you can do this,* she thought and took a deep breath. "Max, when I first met you three years ago, you came into my life when I least expected, but every day we spent together, the more I care about you. I even thought that once we returned home, we would keep seeing each other. Being with you felt natural. It felt like I had known you all my life. What were the odds of us finding each other, or the fact that we both lived in the same city?"

"Megan, I…"

"Don't! Max, let me finish. Let me say what I have to say before I lose my nerve. This is important to me." She took another deep breath. She needed to do this. She needed to come clean. Reliving that day was horrible for her. She lost so much that day.

"Okay!" He reached out and took her hand in his, caressing the top with his thumb, hopefully giving her the strength that she needed. He was such an ass back then. What an idiot he had been. But it didn't change what he did to her. He cared about her and when he left, well leaving was the wrong thing to do.

"When we made love that night, I knew I was ready, knowing that you stole my heart. The greatest gift to give you was me. I had never slept with anyone before, but in my heart that night, it felt right. I know it must sound crazy to say this, but I believe I was falling in love with you then. You made me feel special. You didn't pressure me, and I was ready to experience what making love felt like. Your soft voice loving me, kissing me; you just made everything so perfect that night for someone that never had sex with a man. Your kindness, your gentleness, what more could a woman ask for? Being in your arms felt right. Call me crazy, but from the moment I saw you on the beach, I knew you were meant to be together."

Max moved closer and held her hand tighter. His heart went out to her because he felt the same way. This woman was everything to him now.

"When you left, you crushed me. I felt like I part of me was missing. That morning I woke up happy, but then I saw your note and I couldn't believe how blind I was. I believed in you. I never thought that someone could use a person like that. I trusted you! Something in my heart told me you were the one. I was so delusional to think that someone like you would want someone like me. I wasn't myself after that. I walked around like a zombie for months, trying to figure out what I did wrong, but deep down it had nothing to do with me. I know I did nothing wrong to

$$$

deserve what you did. When I got back, you know I tried calling you to see what had happened, but you wouldn't take my calls. I just wanted to know, but the more I thought about it, I told myself that it was just a fling, that it wasn't serious."

Max felt her pain. His heart ached to know that he had hurt her so much. He never took a woman to bed without her knowing the outcome. It was just sex back then. Megan was different though. She made him feel things that he never knew he could feel for another person. "Megan, I was an asshole for leaving you as I did, and I've been regretting it every day since then. I have not been the same without you. I hope you believe me."

She held up her hand to tell him to stop. "I tried calling again, three months after that." Megan held her head low. Her vision started to blur as tears began to run down her cheeks. She couldn't understand after three years why she was still this raw. She had to say it, she had to tell him. Maybe it would finally ease the pain. "Max…" Tears blurred her vision. She couldn't hold it in anymore. "I was pregnant."

XOXO

# Chapter Nine

Megan closed her eyes and started sobbing. All the pain, the hurt, the loss of losing his baby, knowing she wasn't strong enough. She needed a little time to get her emotions under control, so she left Max at the table. She had lost her baby; a baby she didn't expect but grew to love. She would have done anything if only they could have saved her baby boy.

*Pregnant.* Max didn't move; she was pregnant with his child. He just sat there. Did he hear her right? They didn't use protection. He had lost control that night. He had never wanted or desired a woman so much it hurt. He had forgotten his one rule: CONDOMS. He never wanted a woman to have an unexpected pregnancy. He was shocked. He couldn't believe that she had not told him sooner. He would have stepped-up, owned his responsibility of being a father to the child. Be the man that she would have been proud of. Suddenly, the words sunk in: she said *was!* He stood up so fast that the chair went flying against the siding and went inside to find Megan. It crushed him knowing the woman he loved was hurting because of something he did. He wasn't proud that he left her because he was a coward. She was crying and trying to hide from the world around her. Being

XOXO

pregnant had meant something to her, and living it all over again, he could see the turmoil in her shaking body.

"Megan!" he whispered, seeing her there wrapped into herself. It broke his heart. He did this to her; he took away her hope, her dreams, her light, her happiness. The blame was on him alone. He went to the couch and sat beside her. He took her in his arms and lifted her on his lap. He held her tight and tried to absorb her pain without a word, caressing her back as he kissed her on the top of her head. *What a prick I was for doing this to her*, he thought. *If only I would have acted like a man.* "Baby, what happened?" he asked her in a calming, loving voice. He held her tight, trying to calm her shaking body. He let her cry.

Megan took a few deep breaths and leaned her head on his shoulder as she tried to control her tears. "The day you saw me with Luc, was around the time I had just found out I was pregnant. I was so happy about the news and Luc had just returned from his last tour. Luc Ellis was ex-military special forces and he had told me he was retiring, that he wasn't going back. That was the same time everything happened. I was overly excited that day. As months passed, I tried one more time to contact you, but I wasn't able to get a hold of you. I wanted to tell you about the baby and I didn't want to leave you a message about it. When I didn't hear back, I knew that I would be on my own with this child. I had come to terms and financially I knew I would be okay." Megan took a deep breath.

"Then one late afternoon, the weather changed to freezing rain. The roads were slick. I was coming home from work. A driver was going too fast when he saw me and slammed on the brakes, but he hit me on the driver's side. When I woke up, I was in the hospital. Mom was at my side. I was unconscious for a while. Mom noticed that I was holding my belly and that's when

$$$

she told me that I miscarried, I lost our child. They said they tried to save it but it was too late, I had lost the baby, and I knew I would never be the same."

Max held her like she was the most precious person in the world. Even the strongest people can have a weak moment. What do you say to a woman that went through so much pain alone? All he could do was listen. What happened to her was a freak accident. Max could tell she was blaming herself for losing the baby. As he held her tight against him, he wiped away the tears. He couldn't help but feel sadness for losing a child. His heart ached knowing she went through this alone. He could have been there for her. He could have returned the call. He failed her in ways that he would never do again. He kissed the top of her head, trying to calm her down and make her feel that he was there now, that she could lean on him. He would protect her and cherish her, if she were willing to take a chance on him.

"Megan, look at me!" He lifted her chin. "Baby, I'm so sorry! I wish I could have been there for you. I was an asshole for leaving you and an even bigger one for not calling you back. None of the messages you left me said anything about you being pregnant or how urgent it was. So many time I wanted to call you, to beg you to forgive me, but I knew that you would be better without me, or so I thought. I was wrong." Max would take away all the suffering if he could. He had never lost anyone before, but now his heart ached feeling her lost.

"Max, I'm so sorry I lost your baby." She hadn't felt whole from that moment she had lost the child. How do you go on when you've lost something, or that was created with love, on one night of passion? Her heart ached every day for not being strong enough to have a healthy baby, his baby. She wanted it so much because she knew the love they shared that night was magical.

XOXO

"Megan, it was not your fault. How can you blame yourself for this? It was an accident. Now I know why you hated me so much and the reason you stayed away. Nothing I can do or say right now can express how sorry I am for not being there for you." Max held her tighter and took a moment for them to grieve the loss of their child.

"No one in my family ever found out I was pregnant. Mom never said anything. Lizzie and Luc and Mom were the only ones. I hated myself for being so careless that day. I should have stayed home." He looked her in the eyes and tried to wipe away the tears that were still falling.

"The accident was not your fault. You cannot blame yourself, or it will eat you alive. Things happen for a reason, you do not question them. I know it's sad, but God works in mysterious ways. It could mean that something better is coming. You need to focus on that. You survived, that is all that is important right now. We cannot control what life throws our way, but we can learn from it and move on. I only wish I could have been the man you wanted me to be back then."

"Max!" Megan couldn't hold back any longer. The floodgates were open, and she couldn't control her tears. He just held her. "Your son…" She hiccupped through her tears and felt his hold a little tighter.

He felt remorse for not being there for her, when all she ever wanted was to be loved. She would have raised their child on her own if the baby had survived. How stupid of a man he had been for treating a woman like that.

"I was afraid to tell you. I thought you would be angry with me once you found out, and that you would leave me again. That's why I didn't want you around or even touch me. I didn't want to fall for you again and get hurt. I was confident that once

$$$

I told you, I would never see you again. That night when you kissed me at the fundraiser brought back all the old feelings I had for you, and the only way I could survive was to close you out. I hated you so much for leaving me."

"Megan, sweetheart, back at the house that night, there was no going back. I was fighting for you. I would have done anything in my power to have you back in my life. We can get through this together. I'm not leaving this time. You are the one I've always wanted to be with."

Megan leaned her head on his shoulder. She could feel his warm breath on her forehead. His scent was all around her as she inhaled deeply, trying to control her tears. She just wanted to lose herself in his embrace and sighed deeply. Telling the truth was freeing her of the hurt and pain she had inside for all these years. No words were said as they took a moment to finally grieve the loss of their child. She felt the thumping of his heartbeat against her hand. "I wish he would have survived."

Max lifted her chin and looked into her eyes. The feelings were still there. Behind all that sadness there was still hope, so he took a leap of faith and kissed her gently on the lips. He looked at her as he caressed her cheek. "Me too. I'm sorry. Sweetheart, from the first moment I saw you at the fundraiser that night, I knew I wanted you back. All I can do is ask for your forgiveness. Please give me a second chance. Let me prove to you that you can trust me again." Max had never said those words to a woman before, ever, but telling her now felt right. He did love her, but he wasn't ready to say it just yet. He would move heaven and earth for her.

Megan looked into the eyes and she knew he was telling the truth. She knew how he felt because her feelings for him had not changed. Even if he had not said those three words, she could see

XOXO

it in his eyes. "I never wanted anyone else. Keeping everything locked up inside me for years, I was scared to tell you. Luc once said that the only way for me to move forward was by telling you what happened. If there was any chance for us to make it, we could never have secrets between us. For months, I have been fighting with myself. Staying angry at you was easier." She held his face with her delicate hands as she felt him lean in and kiss her palm. "I was losing the battle that morning when you kissed me. The guilt was too much. I was angry but that moment you kissed me, I knew I would lose. I couldn't fight you anymore. But the night I was attack, all I could think about was you. All I could see was your eyes looking at me. I felt your touch, your warmth. That is what made me fight, knowing that I needed to take a chance, a new beginning with you." She was throwing caution to the wind and hoped to hell that they would both survive tonight.

"Angel, you have me. I promise you, and I will not fail you this time. You have my undivided attention." Max leaned in and kissed her gently. "I'm sorry, baby, for what I put you through." He kissed her again, and this time he didn't hold back.

Megan straddled him and wrapped her hands around his neck. She felt lighter as she looked into those beautiful eyes. She knew what her heart always wanted, and it was Max. She couldn't fight him anymore. Was it a moment of weakness? *Hell no.* She was tired of feeling numb and going through days without feeling loved, because she knew he loved her in ways no other man loved her. The moment he kissed her, there were no more second thoughts. She chose to take a leap of faith, not knowing what the future would hold. She wanted to feel alive again, to be happy, and finally move on.

$$$

## Chapter Ten

The moment his lips touched hers, she wanted Max to take her places that she had not felt in years. Her heart racing, she pulled him tighter against her holding him, deepening the kiss that she had craved for so many nights. Max knew how to kiss and damn if she was not aching for him. She rubbed her body against him as she felt his manhood pressing against her core. His scent was driving her wild, his touch was making her skin burn in need, and all she wanted was for him to be inside her. She couldn't take it anymore. She looked him in the eyes and yanked her camisole over her head. She was desperate for his touch on her burning skin, but yet he was holding back. For one split second, she was going to remove her bra, but he said no. Her chest was heaving so fast. She grabbed hold of him and kissed him with a hunger that she couldn't control. She moaned into his mouth, going crazy with need for him.

Max looked at her flushed face, her hounded eyes, wanting him, begging him. He wanted to take this slow and he wanted to please her. Once they crossed that line, there was no turning back. He took her bottom lip and sucked on it, kissing her face, her cheeks, her neck, licking, biting, kissing, tasting every each of her skin. "What do you want, Megan?" He held her close

XOXO

to him, kissing his way to her ears. Her nipples were hard the moment she took her bra and threw it to the side. Her breasts were perfect. He kissed his way down as he took a nipple into his mouth and sucked on it, then bit down, enjoying her moans as she rubbed herself on his manhood.

"Please, Max," she cried out, wanting more.

"I want you so much. Is this what you want, Megan? I don't think I can hold it anymore. I want you and only you," he whispered. "No turning back. There will never be anyone else." He looked into her eyes, waiting, giving her a chance to say no.

"Please, Max! I want you."

Max lifted her body without breaking contact with her. She was coming alive in his arms. She wrapped her legs around his waist. "Hold on tight, baby!" He walked down the hall as he nibbled on her neck and he could feel her breath on his face. She was pulling his shirt out of his pants as they headed to the bedroom. Feeling her delicate hands on his hot skin made him want her more.

She squealed as he threw her on the bed. Her happiness was making him crazy. She crawled to the end of the bed, kneeled and opened her arms to him. "I should have told you sooner, if I had known. All this time I wasted, I could have been in your arms." Max was a virile man, sexy, beautiful, muscular—the whole package.

"You should have." Max took a stray hair into his hands. "You are so beautiful. No going back, Megan. You are the one I want." He trailed his hand over her shoulder. She grabbed his shirt and ripped it open with all the force she had. Buttons went flying everywhere.

"I'm sure. Now stop talking. More kissing and touching." Megan eased her hands up his shoulder and removed his shirt,

$$$

then she did quick work on his pants and they fell to the floor. He had only his boxer shorts when he crawled on the bed and laid on top of her.

It would take all of his control not to bury himself fast and hard inside of her, but tonight he wanted to please her, pleasure her, build her up so much in need that she couldn't think anymore. All she would see was him. Damn, she was beautiful; her swollen lips, that he just devoured, her flushed cheeks. She was his sex addiction. He took her legs and wrapped them around his waist. He wanted to feel her hot skin on him. She was topless and still wearing her skirt, but not for long. He kissed his way down as he maneuvered to untie her skirt and pull down the zipper. Hearing her moans, her little cries, she lifted her bottom so it would be easier for him. "I could kiss you all night."

"Max, I need you." Every time he touched her, he caressed her body, she ached for him more and more. She wanted him inside her." Damn it, Max, fuck me!" She cried out, needing him.

Max kissed his way up her body, feeling her heating up as he moved closer to her nipples, to her torso, to her collarbone, to her neck, to her ear as he bit down. "Baby, we have all night. I want all your orgasms to be mine because I'm the one that took you there, and just when you think you had nothing more to give me, I will take you there again and again, until we are both sated and cannot move."

"Enough! Please, Max, I need you now."

Max chuckled. "Oh, I will, baby. Be patient my love." He stood up and removed his boxers in front of her. He watched as her tongue came out and she licked her lips, then bit down on her bottom lip. He never had issues with his manhood. It stood proudly in front of him as he held it in his hands. "Is this what you want?" He pulled her by the legs to the end of the bed, then

XOXO

took her underwear and ripped them off her body. He heard her gasp, but something he noticed was never there before. Megan had perfect, flawless skin; it was pale against his dark skin, but soft. There was something different though. She now had a tattoo that wasn't there three years ago. Max fixated by it. He trace it with his finger, the angel wings wrapping a pair baby feet, with the initial DMP engraved on it. He looked up and could see that Megan was looking at him as a tear ran down her cheeks.

Megan didn't pull back but just laid there watching him. When you are in the moment of making love, you don't think; you just feel what that person is doing to you, taking away all the pain, the heartache that was once buried but now set free. She sighed. Watching Max, looking at her reminder, she had engraved on her body. "When I lost the baby, I didn't know how to cope, so I had to do something. I decided to get a tattoo in memory of our child. I didn't want it to be big, just significate to me so no one else would see it." She wiped away a tear from her cheek.

"It's beautiful. What does the DMP mean?" Max traced it with his finger.

"Dylan Max Pierce. I had to name him even though there was no burial. To me it meant something." She touched his hand, and he took hers in his.

Max took her lips once again and got lost in a battle of emotions that he couldn't describe. Damn, all he wanted to do was take it slow, but now this changed the beast inside of him. He wanted to brand this woman as his. Max needed her like he needed air to breathe. He broke the kiss and looked into her eyes. "I will make this right. I thought I could take this slow, Megan, but I can't." He wrapped her legs around his waist. She was wet and ready for him. With one quick thrust, he buried

$$$

himself deep inside of her. He heard her gasp as he waited for her body to adjust to his girth and the moment her body relaxed, he began to move again. Nothing was holding him back now. Her whimpers and moans were making him crazy, like a savage man and he couldn't control it any longer. He took her lips with so much force he tasted blood, but he didn't care. She didn't care. They were one as they moved in sync. Her screams fueled him, making him go faster with each thrust.

Shining lights sparkled in her heart, her sweat, her breathing, her screams, all for one man, were making her wild and lost in this moment of passion. Megan couldn't think, she could only feel what he was doing to her. "God, yes!" she whimpered. "I'm going to come, Max, please! Yes…yes…yes!" She couldn't hold it anymore. She could feel the tightness in her belly, the feeling that everything inside was exploding. She arched her back as she fisted the sheets. She heard her name and yelled his. He finally took her where she so desperately needed to go. She had forgotten how good it was with him. She fell over the edge to oblivion.

Max fell on top of her, he felt her arms and legs wrap around him, holding him tight. They were both breathing hard and could almost hear each other's heartbeat. Max rolled over and took her with him as she laid like a blanket on top of him, both sweaty, sticking to each other. As they came down from their high, still breathing heavily, he whispered, "Damn, woman, I wanted to take this slow." He kissed her head and held her tight.

"I'm not complaining. It was never this good." Megan kissed his chest. She snuggled up to him and rested her head on his chest. She could hear how frantic his heart was beating. Her whole body was limp. She felt his soft hands on her back. She could lie here forever in this embrace. "Max."

XOXO

"Yes, baby?" Max kissed the top of her head, enjoying her warm body on his. This was where she belonged. He will protect her from anyone that would harm her.

"I'm sorry for not telling you sooner, and I should have tried harder back then." She looked up and he kissed her forehead.

Max could sense her vulnerability, that rawness in her. Hopefully, this beautiful woman lying in his arms would give him a second chance he so desperately wanted. He pulled her up and took her lips in his. He wiped her hair away from her face. "I promise you, this is where I want to be, with you. I'm not leaving this time. I hate myself for doing what I did to you. I was scared back then about what I was feeling for you. I didn't know how to control the emotions I was feeling. I ran like a coward, but I'm not running anymore. I'm glad that you told me what happened, and I cannot imagine the pain you had to endure. Tonight is real. It's a new beginning that I'm willing to fight for you. You, my beautiful, sexy, loving woman; you're mine now. Thank you for sharing the past with me, but tonight we move forward—no going back. No more sadness in those pretty eyes. Is that clear?"

Max kissed her again with such tenderness, hoping that she could feel how his heart was raw and open. They finally spooned each other, her back to his front. He held her, not letting her go, as they both fell into a peaceful slumber.

$$$

## Chapter Eleven

"Well isn't this cozy! I left for three days, but I seriously thought you would be back at your place by now!" Lizzie snarled at him. At first, when Joe told her that he had everything covered, she would have cancelled her trip to make sure someone would be with Megan, but never would she have thought that he had assigned Max as her protector.

Megan and Max were lounging together on the lawn chair. Max was all wrapped up and snuggling with her, whispering in her ear. She was leaning against his chest, holding hands and giggling. Megan looked up and saw that Lizzie wasn't too happy.

"Looks like you kissed and made up," she said in a harsh tone. She was tired and wanted to spend time with her best friend, but having Max there was setting her off-kilter.

"Lizzie, how was your conference?" Megan looked at her and knew that she didn't approve of Max being there.

"Long and exhausting. It's good to be home again." She watched Meg and Max being all cozy. "Meg, can I talk to you? Alone?" Last time this man was in her life, it destroyed her. That crowbar must have given her more damage than she thought.

XOXO

Megan rolled her eyes and looked at Max, then leaned in and kissed his lips. "I'll be right back!" She walked into the kitchen and looked at Lizzie. "What's up?"

"You tell me. Why are you all cozy out there? You kissed and made up? Need I remind you what happened the last time? I know he looks like a hero to you because he's the one that found you. I was so happy that Joe got a swing at him. But Meg, I need to know where your head is. Was that bump on your head more serious than we thought?" Lizzie was tapping her foot in frustration. She did that only when she was tired and exhausted.

"I know you have my best interest at heart, and I love you for it, but Max and I have worked things out."

"What do you mean you worked things out?" Lizzie couldn't believe what she was hearing. Yes, she defended him at the hospital, but she never thought this would happen. *Ah hell, this is not going to be good.*

"Let me finish. I finally told Max the truth about everything—the accident, the baby, and how I feel." Megan sighed and got that far-away look. She couldn't help but smile.

"So, let me get this straight. You're telling me that he's been here since two nights ago?" Lizzie knew she should have cancelled that damn conference, but she couldn't help noticing that her friend was glowing. She didn't want to give her a hard time, but she had to. She had to make sure where her head was.

"Yes Lizzie, he has. I told him everything."

"Everything? And you're telling me that he apologized to you for what he did?"

"Yes." Megan took her friend by the hands. "It's okay. We talked about everything last night, I swear. We still care about each other. He loves me."

$$$

"Whoa! Seriously, the love word?" Lizzie didn't see that coming. "You must have hit your head harder than I thought!" She didn't trust Max Pierce; he did it once, and in her opinion, he would do it again.

"Lizzie, I love him," she whispered. "I never stopped loving him. He feels the same way, but I haven't told him in so many words because I'm not ready yet. He made a mistake, and I believe with all my heart that he does love me. We realized that we are happier together than apart. Can you not be happy for me?" Megan wanted her best friend's blessing because, in the end, they cannot lose each other.

At that moment, Max came in from outside and looked at both girls. He stopped beside Megan. "Ladies, is everything alright?" He backed up a little as Lizzie approached him.

"Listen, you piece of shit. If you ever, and I mean ever, hurt Megan again, I swear, you'll have to deal with me. Trust me, it will not be pleasant!" Lizzie got into Max's face and poked a finger in his chest. She feared no one, especially some arrogant, selfish billionaire.

"Lizzie! That was uncalled for!" Megan grasped her arm as she looked at Max apologetically.

"It's okay, Megan." Max loved the spunk in Lizzie. "She says what she means and is only protecting the people that she loves."

"No, it's not! Lizzie, please apologize." Megan gave Lizzie a stern look and got between them.

"I understand your concerns," said Max. "I swear; I have her best interests at heart. What happened three years ago will never happen again. She has my undivided attention, and I will treat her like the goddess that she is. I will do everything in my power to make sure she spends the rest of her life happy. I'm the lucky one. She's giving me a second chance. Believe me, I don't want to disappoint her ever again. I love this woman, and I will give her the moon if she wants it.

"Tell you what, let's all go out for a nice dinner and get better acquainted. You can ask me any question you want. I'm an open book." He could call Josh to this get-together, but he decided against it. He needed to know that Megan's best friend was okay with this. He needed to fix what was broken. When had he become relaxed, smiling, no stress, this was so unlike him. It was all about getting the woman he loved back in his life.

Lizzie turned and went to the cold room, took a bottle of wine, walk back, and said, "Okay, then. Let's get better acquainted!" Lizzie handed him a glass of wine. "A toast, to a man that finally got his brain in check." She lifted her glass and waited as they all clinked together.

Megan hugged her best friend. She knew that no matter what, she would always have her back, and she loved her for that. She watched as Max and Lizzie started to talk about business. This was Lizzie's way of getting information from him. After all, the man was a genius when it came to business. Megan finally relaxed and enjoyed the evening with her best friend and lover.

They entered the restaurant, and Max wrapped his arms around her waist, as they waited to be seated, and lean in and whispered in her ear; "I called Josh, I hope you don't mind." Megan looked back and smiled, knowing that Lizzie would be surprised. She knew her best friend was fighting the attraction they had, but to her it was all about sex. Max saw Josh approaching from the back of the restaurant. He had to secure a booth where they could talk privately.

Megan couldn't stop laughing as the night went on. "Oh my God, you didn't do that as a child." She looked at Max, eyes wide open. She held her stomach because she was laughing so much.

$$$

"It was all about being the master pranksters. Brandon never knew what hit him until it was too late. The moment that door opened, all the honey and feathers stuck to him like glue, but what we didn't know is that there was a bee's nest near the old shed. The moment everything came crashing down, bees came out and swarmed around him attacking him. He ran towards the pool, and Josh and I were hiding at the other side. Man, mom, was so upset with us. Who knew he was allergic to bees? He blew up like a balloon." Max and Josh were laughing so hard. "Let's just say my father didn't take it kindly and we were grounded for two weeks after that."

"Bro, I think you're getting old and your mind is slipping. It was a month, but it was worth it. Brandon always had the upper hand, being Mom's favorite." Josh shot back the rest of his beer and couldn't help but give Max a high five.

Megan loved watching him with his brother, relaxed, enjoying a night with friends. He was outgoing, caring, funny, and sexy as hell, with a smile that could make a woman do whatever he desired. She would be crazy not to give him a second chance or even trust him. Life was a risk, but her heart knew what it wanted deep down. She thought back to how Max had never left her side once they had left the hospital. Yes, it drove her crazy, but he proved to her that he was in this relationship for the long haul. Just that alone made her happy, and she couldn't help but smile about it. She watched Lizzie and Josh's exchange looks from time to time. She could only hope that Lizzie would find that kind of happiness. Lizzie protected her heart, and didn't let many people in, if just once she would let her guard down. Megan was finally at peace with herself. She felt Max's hand on her thigh, and only that little touch made her want him even more.

XOXO

His touch was gentle, but it made her stomach flutter. The need for one person was compelling, those small contacts were more intense now than before, and it made her brain fuzzy. Her heart floated away as she concentrated on his hands on her thigh. She watched him smile as he leaned in and kissed her in front of everyone. She loved the way that his affection didn't faze him in public. Yes, Max Pierce was known to be a selfish bastard in business, but not many people knew this soft, sweet, attentive side.

They said their goodbyes to Lizzie and Josh. Megan felt him take her by the waist and kissed her neck. "What would you say to a stroll down at the old port? I have a surprise for you." Max felt her lean into him, and she held his hand.

"I would say lead the way. The night is still young, and it's beautiful out." Megan turned in his arms and lifted on her tiptoes to kiss his lips.

Max opened the door and let her in. He made sure she was secure, then leaned in and kissed her gently. His smile was infectious, but as he made his way to the driver's side, he stopped as he noticed an enveloped wedged in his door. He looked around and didn't see anything. Max had no reason to call in his security tonight, was he wrong. But he couldn't help the feeling that someone could be watching from a distance. He looked inside and cursed. He took out his phone and turned around so Megan wouldn't see. "Pierce, I need security at the pier on the yacht, secure the area. Be there in half an hour." Max took a few minutes to calm himself before getting behind the wheel. He tilted his head to one side, then the other, and pocketed the envelope. *Dammit, this needs to stop. We need to find these bastards. They are not just coming after me now, they are eyeing Megan, and like hell, if I will let anything happen to her.* Once he knew he had everything

$$$

under control, he turned and got behind the wheel and closed the door. He could see her looking at him but knowing someone was watching didn't make him feel any better. He started the engine and looked into his mirrors as he eased out of the parking lot towards the downtown Montreal pier.

XOXO

## Chapter Twelve

From the moment Max sat behind the wheel, Megan knew something was wrong. That flirtatious man in the restaurant, the one that was telling jokes from his childhood, the easy-going man enjoying the evening with his brother Josh and her friend Lizzie, was no longer. Now he sat behind the wheel tense and alerted about his surroundings, watching in every direction and not saying a word. "Max, is everything okay?" Megan leaned in and put her hand on his thigh. She could feel how tense he was.

"Yes, sorry about that." He took her hand and kissed it. He gave her a reassuring smile. "Now for the surprise."

Megan knew without a doubt that he was hiding something, but she would give him the benefit of the doubt and let it pass for now. She watched him navigate the SUV into private parking down at the Old Port of Montreal. He handed his gate pass to the guard and the gate opened. "You have private parking? You're full of surprises, aren't you Mr. Pierce?"

"One of the perks of being CEO. We entertain a lot of customers. Besides, I was thinking after our walk, we could go on the yacht and sleep there. It's a beautiful night." Max was relieved when he spotted his bodyguard in the distance. He cut the engine and took Megan's hand and kissed her. "I'm a lucky bastard to have you by my side finally."

Megan took his face and brought it closer, wanting to feel his lips on hers. "Did you say you have a boat?" She looked at him and saw the twinkle in his eyes coming back.

"Miss Harrison I need to correct you; it's not a boat, it's a yacht that can sleep, ten people. I thought you knew." He smiled at her. "Shall we explore?"

"I think I would have remembered if you told me you had a boat or yacht or cruiser whatever the term is."

"I was distracted lately. We also have a cabin up north! I'll have to take you there one weekend, so I can pleasure you and hear you scream for miles." He reached up and caressed her cheeks. "I would do anything for you, Angel."

"You know, Mr. Pierce, you keep surprising me. We seriously need to talk. I know that the sex is fantastic, but we need to learn more about each other. What else don't I know about you?"

"Baby, there may be times when you may not understand my decision. I like control, and like getting what I want. I do things sometimes on impulse without thinking of the consequences, especially when it comes to your safety. Megan, there are people out there that are out to get me over my business actions. Anytime you feel that being with me is too much, tell me, okay? You are my priority. All I ever want is for you to be happy."

"Oh Max, I can put up with your controlling matters, because I know." Megan touched his chest where his heart is. "I know how you feel here in your heart, that is the person I adore." She looked at him. He was so close she could kiss him, she inhaled musky scent of his cologne, and that alone made her tingle all the way to her core.

$$$

"Then let's go have some fun. I know this little jazz place just up the street." Max opened the door and ran around to open the passenger door. He held out his hand and helped her out of her seat, and closed the door, then caged her in. He touched her cheek, then rested his hand behind her neck, and pulled her in for a scorching kiss that would leave her breathless. She moaned into his mouth as he leaned into her body. Her hands went into his hair. He wanted her right there. He broke the kiss and leaned forward and rested his forehead on hers. "I have plans for you, but first I promised you a little jazz." He took her hand and started walking toward the exit, knowing his security team would not be far behind. The feeling of someone following them was still there.

As promised, they enjoyed the Jazz Pup on St. Paul Street and had a few drinks while listening to some local band. They walked along the shore of the St. Lawrence River, and by the time they made it back to the marina, it was already late. Max noticed a guard approaching. "Everything secured, sir." The guard went back to his post.

Megan looked at Max then looked over her shoulder as the guards walked away. She didn't say anything because she knew Max was cautious. She still had the feeling something was bothering him. He wasn't relaxed like he was at the restaurant just a few hours ago. She also saw him exchange an envelope as the guard walked away. He pulled her along, holding her tight against him as they passed every boat you could imagine—small ones, medium ones—but as they reach the end of the dock, there was the biggest one she had ever seen. The lights were on, and she could see two bodyguards awaiting instruction. Max pulled her along, and he stopped just before the plank, letting her walk in front of him. She was excited. She loved being on

XOXO

a boat; the freedom of the wind blowing through her hair, just being on the open water away from all her worries. Her dad used to take her now and then when he decided that everyone needed to stop and enjoy the small things in life. But this boat, or should she say yacht, was more significant than she had ever imagined. She had only seen this size in movies, never up close. She had noticed as they were walking up the name on her was *My Angel II*. Something inside squeezed her heart a little more, and she choked up.

"Mr. Pierce, everything is secured, sir. Will there be anything else?"

Megan felt Max's lips on her head, and she looked up at him in total awe. "This is yours, isn't it?" Megan watched him with a smile, and he kissed her nose.

"Yes, she's mine. Welcome aboard, Angel! Thank you, John. Miss Harrison and I will be below deck for the night." John left them as he walked away towards the front. "What do you think? I bought her a few years ago. It's a great way for me to lose myself when I need to get away." He held her from behind as he nuzzled her and gave her little kisses on the neck.

Megan giggled as she held him tight against her. "She's beautiful. Do I get the tour?" She looked over her shoulder as he took her in a kiss that made her head spin. She turned in his arms as she wrapped her hands around his neck and pulled him down. Feeling his tongue fueled her desire for him. It dueled with hers in a battle of control. She moaned in pleasure as he caressed her ass. She felt him hard against her, and right now she just didn't care about the tour. She wanted him inside of her. They broke the kiss as he leaned his forehead on hers. She was gasping, trying to control her heavy breathing. "I want you," she whispered.

$$$

"And I you. You undo me, Megan. Your smile, your passion that reflects back at me… It humbles me. You make me want to be a better man." Max looked deep into her half hooded eyes. He had never had this chemistry with any other woman, only her. "Now, before we get arrested, let me show you our yacht." He kissed her gently on the lips and opened the glass door.

The moment they walked through the glass doors, it was breathtaking. The place was huge, able to sit at least twelve people comfortably. It had a mahogany bar, a built-in sound system, and a remote with one button that would pull out a fifty-five-inch TV. The blackout windows for privacy you could see out but not from the outside looking in. They walked through the kitchen, well equipped with everything you could imagine. As they descended the stair to the left, there was a full guest bathroom, twin beds, and a laundry room. She looked at him. "Do you take her out? Impressive, I've never been inside a yacht this big. I cannot believe you have this." She looked at him in awe, and all he could do was smile. They made their way down a couple of other stairs to the master suite. It had a king-sized bed and a closet to the left. To the right was a lounging area with a full bar and TV. They walked through one more door and entered the master suite bathroom. It had a full-sized shower, big enough for two. The countertops were granite with a full-sized mirror and all the necessities. She knew Max was wealthy but never in her wildest dreams did she think of this being his.

"So, what do you think, do you like it?" Max watched her through the mirror as he moved her hair and kissed her neck. "Captain is on standby if you want to take her out tonight or tomorrow." His eyes never left hers.

Megan turned and watched him. He looked like a little boy that just showed off his new toy. "Max, she's beautiful. When

XOXO

do you have time to enjoy it? You seem to be the kind of man that is all business. I cannot imagine why you would have such a beautiful yacht." She held him by his forearms as she looked at him, feeling all that desire still building in her.

Max leaned into her as he rested his forehead on hers and trapped her as he held her against the countertop. "She reminded me of you. I called her *Angel II*. She called to me, and I had to have her. I couldn't help myself. I fell in love with her the moment I stepped on board. Like the moment I met you, I knew that I might never have you again, and I lost the chance with you. I named her after you, Megan. The yacht would never be the original angel, but at least I felt at peace when I was here. I've never brought anyone on board except for my family and some close friends. I want to take her out. I want you and me to go somewhere together, and try every surface, so when I'm here, I know you are with me."

"Oh, Max!" She raised her hand and touched his cheek. "I love her; she is beautiful. I was thinking, does that shower work?" She gave him a wicked grin.

Max looked at her, and a smile spread across his face. "Of course! Want to test it out? Then we can test the bed, the galley, the guest room, and any other surface you want. You know, she has not been officially christened."

"Well, Mr. Pierce, I hope you have enough stamina. You can start by taking me here… there… and up there." She leaned up and kissed him. The next few hours passed as they tried every surface they could imagine, and by the time the sun was rising, they were both sated and exhausted. They finally fell asleep in each other's arms.

$$$

## Chapter Thirteen

BOOM, SHE'S DIED. WATCH YOUR BACK, ASSHOLE. WE ARE COMING FOR YOU!

Max saw red. The only thing that could make his blood boil was a threat against Megan. He swore as he took his glass and threw it across his office. He heard it shatter. *How can this happen? Why the fuck hasn't my security found who is sending these letters? For weeks now they have been sending the same goddamn note. If they want me, come and get me. Don't involve Megan, you fucking asshole. Who can it be? My gut is telling me that Mariotto has a vindictive side. I don't have proof though. They are good, whoever it is.*

They reassured himself he had bodyguards watching Megan, because if anything ever happened to her... Max watched the traffic below, so deep in thought. He didn't hear his brothers come in, so when a hand touched his shoulder, he went swinging.

Josh and Brandon stood there as they looked at the shattered glass on the floor. They looked at each other and walked up to Max's desk; Max had no clue they were in his office. Brandon approached Max and put a hand on his shoulder. He moved just in time before Max's fist collided with his face. "Easy, brother. What's up your ass?"

XOXO

Max watched Brandon duck and saw Josh from the corner of his eyes. "Dammit, Brandon, you have a death wish or something. I could have hurt you."

"You wish. You know I'm younger and faster than you are, old man." Brandon moved away as he took a seat in front of Max's desk.

Max watched as Josh poured himself a glass of bourbon and two others. "Help yourself, Josh. Don't mind me."

Josh handed one to Max then one to Brandon. He sat down on the chair next to Brandon and kicked his feet up on Max's desk, then shot back his bourbon. "What's up your ass, anyway? It looks like your fine crystal hit that wall back there."

Max watched his brothers. He took his glass, shot back the amber liquid, then went back to the bar and poured himself another. He shot it back once again, feeling that burning sensation all the way to his stomach, and slammed the glass on the counter.

Josh looked at Brandon. He knew something was wrong but didn't know what. Max never looked this angry, and the last time he had seen his brother this upset is when they were young. Max always knew how to control or challenge his anger. Out of the three of them, he was the one in control at all times. "Max, what's going on?"

Max took a deep breath. His brothers, the ones that he trusted more than anyone else. He knew that no matter what, he could count on them. These last few months, Megan was his whole world, from the moment she told him about the baby she had lost, fighting the attraction they had, and the attack, that left her unconscious. He thought he had lost her but that night changed everything for him. He loved her. He would make sure that from that night forward, he would protect her. But the

$$$

letters still came. At first, the threats were about him, telling him that they were going to take back what belonged to them, but the game changed that night when he found another letter telling him they knew his weakness now. From that moment on, he knew that he would always have someone near her.

"Bro, what is going on? We've never seen you, so lost in thought that we feel that you are not even with us." Josh looked at Brandon with concern, as they watched Max brace himself against the counter on the bar, still in deep thought.

"Whatever it is, you know we are here for you. What is going on?"

Max turned and walked to where Josh was. He looked at his feet on his desk and growled.

"Sorry man." Josh put his feet down in defeat.

Max leaned on his desk and took a deep breath. "Six months ago, I started to get threats now and then, saying to watch my back, I would receive them, when I least expected it, nothing unusual we get them all the time, nothing ever comes of it, well not until recently."

"This is nothing new. We always have these threats, and they die down after a while. Mergers and takeovers never go easily." Josh said.

"I know, so I wasn't paying much attention. I knew it would die down, but it didn't. The letters were coming more frequently, but about three weeks ago, something changed." Max looked at his brothers.

"What do you mean?" Brandon asked. "Wait, didn't Megan get hurt around that time."

"Yes. I thought she was just in the wrong place at the wrong time, but that night while I was waiting in the hospital, I received another letter. Everything was happening so fast that I didn't know who was around and I found a note saying, 'We know your weakness.' I didn't know at the time how it got in my pocket. So many people were around me that night, but I knew that I needed to protect her. If it were only me, I wouldn't care, bring it on, but now they are coming after Megan. She is my weakness, and like hell, I will let anything happen to her. But I'm not sure how to protect her either. I have guards following her every move. She doesn't understand it yet because I have not told her the full story. All I said to her was that it's needed because of who I am." Max reached out and showed his brothers the latest letter.

"Damn, bro, what can we do?" Josh said. "I know how you feel about her and I know how she feels about you. You should tell her the truth. That woman will chew your ass off if you are hiding anything from her."

"That's the thing. I wish I knew why our security team hasn't found anything conclusive yet. Our team is good, but our security team is not the best that is out there. We need someone that can get the job done. I've checked out all the past mergers and everything, and everyone checked out. My gut is telling me that it might be Mariotto boys, but we have not turned up anything yet."

"Max, they have the motive after what the old man did, but we cannot be going around and poking the bear if we do not have the information." Brandon said. "What has our security team come up with?"

"Absolutely nothing. They security team is worthless right now and I'm thinking about finding someone, with more experience. I need someone, better, someone that can track whoever is doing this to us and pinpoint a location and end this before someone gets hurt." Max said. "I'm open to suggestions if you have anything. I cannot lose Megan."

$$$

Max watched his brothers rise and looked them both in the eyes. He knew he trusted his brothers, they had a way of calming him, so he could focus on the matter more clearly. "I need you to promise me something."

"Anything," Josh and Brandon said in unison.

"Promise me that if anything happens to me, that you will both look after Megan. I want to know that if something ever happens, she will have you both on her side. I have this trip that I need to do and will not be back until the end of the week. I wish I could bring her with me, but she has the complex to finish, and she's stubborn and will not take time off."

"We will watch her, I promise," Josh said. He put a hand on Max's shoulder.

"Promise, we have your back." Brandon said. He hadn't been involved much with the complex that Harrison was building, but he had heard great things about Megan, and he knew how his brother loved her. She had changed him in a way. Brandon put his hand on his shoulder also. "We will find those bastards, Max, and they will pay for what they are doing."

"I agree with Brandon. They are messing with the wrong brothers," Josh said in a stern voice.

"Thank you for having my back." Max looked at his watch and knew he had to leave soon, but first, he had to call Megan to make sure she was okay. "Okay, now get out. I have unfinished business before my flight." Max hugged his brothers and slapped each on the back.

"Sure you do, brother. Don't let us stop you." Brandon made a sound like kissing as he walked out.

"Grow up, Brandon. One day you will get what's coming to you," Josh said. He slapped his brother on the back as they

xoxo

walked out of Max's office. "I'll tell Julie to get cleaning up here to pick up the mess, Max," Josh shouted as he walked out.

$$$

## Chapter Fourteen

"Joe, I need help. I need a ride." Megan called her brother because Max was out of town and she didn't know who else to call when she felt this scared.

"Baby girl, what's going on?" Joe could hear from the tone of her voice that she wasn't herself and that something was wrong.

After she woke up, she must have blacked out for a few seconds. She was holding back tears, but she couldn't stop her hands from shaking. "Joe, please come and get me. Max is out of town, and I cannot reach Lizzie. I'm scared, Joe." She whispered to him, as she closed her eyes, trying to gain some composure on what had happened. The police and emergency response units were there when she came to. She couldn't remember how long she was out. Why does this keep happening to her? She recalled driving home from the complex after a long day. She was listening to her music singing out of tune; thinking about Max, his earlier message stated he was flying back tomorrow. She was happy. For once in her life, she really felt that everything was just right.

"Megan, where are you? I will come and get you." Joe was running out the door to his truck. He could hear Megan asking someone where she was, but couldn't hear anything. "Megan, who is with you? Give the phone to the person you are talking to."

"This is Officer Malone."

"Officer Malone, what is going on with my sister, and where is she? What happened?" Joe waited to find out what was going on as he tried to calm himself.

"Mr. Harrison, your sister is at Station Four on Source Blvd. She was in a minor accident." Officer Malone didn't have time to say much more and the line when dead.

Megan just watched as the officer gave her the phone back. She took it but couldn't control her hands from shaking. She told the officer all she knew, but all she could remember was a black Hummer pulling up beside her, not paying attention, and the next thing she knew, there was a hand. That is when she saw the gun. They were aiming for her but then the gun moved, and they shot the tires. She heard the first shot go off and served. She downshifted her Audi to pick up speed, but she wasn't fast enough. The Hummer was just too big of a vehicle against her small car. Her front tire blew as the bullet connected, and the Hummer tried to push her off the road. She went into a tailspin and hit her head against the glass, trying to keep control of her car before it hit the side rail. That was all she remembered. She had a cut to her forehead from her head hitting the glass before the airbags deployed.

Megan held her head low and linked her hands together trying to control her shaking. She closed her eyes, trying to think of something else, anything but what had happened tonight. She felt a hand on hers as she looked up into her brother's concerned eyes.

"Megan, I'm here. Let me take you home. Are you okay?" Joe watched her as he took her shaky hand in his. They were

$$$

cold, and he could see that she was freezing. Her whole body was shaking. "What happened?" He looked at her scared eyes, knowing that she was about to cry. "Officer Malone, is that right? Can you tell me what happened? My sister is in shock."

"Mr. Harrison, could we speak privately please?" Officer Malone asked. "I just have a few questions to ask."

Megan looked at Joe. "It's okay, Joe. I will be okay now that I know you are here."

Joe gave his sister a reassuring hug. "I'll be right back." Joe followed Officer Malone outside the room, down the hall to another office. They closed the door behind him. He watched the officer as he offered him some water or coffee and sat down behind the desk.

"Mr. Harrison, your sister, told us what happened and we believe that she could be a target. The people that did this knew what they were doing. They were sending a message."

Joe looked at Officer Malone and knew what he was saying. *Someone was out to get Megan because of her involvement with Max. He was keeping those threats to himself because Max said that he had everything under control and that his security team would be watching. Where in the hell were they today? Why weren't they watching his sister? Ever since her attack a few months ago at the complex, the threats were coming more and more. It had to stop. They almost got her tonight, and there was no one there to protect her.* He decided he would call Luc Ellis Security. He was the only one he trusted with Megan's life.

"Mr. Harrison, do you have any information on who might be doing this? Today's message was clearly to show that they could have killed her. All it took was one shot to her front tire. You know how accurate you need to be on a moving vehicle at close range?"

XOXO

Joe knew someone was after Max, but he just didn't know who yet, so unless they had concrete evidence that he could share with the officer, he would rather not say anything at all.

"Mr. Harrison, if you know anything, you need to let the police handle it. You need to give us that information so we can do our job. Is your sister in trouble?" Officer Malone kept his voice calm and watched Joe reaction. He knew he was hiding something.

"Officer Malone, if I knew I would share, but I don't. The only thing that I can say is that my sister was attacked a few months ago in the complex we are building. They left her for dead. She hasn't regained her memory from the night of the attack yet, so there is not much I know. We still haven't found Chris Sutton, who was our night foreman." Joe didn't give a rat's ass what this officer was telling him. They haven't found anything about that attack or who else was in the building that night.

"Very well, Mr. Harrison, you may leave, but if you remember anything that might help us find who did this to your sister, here is my card. Call me. We believe that this was a hit, and the reason is as yet unknown. Your sister said that the vehicle was a black Hummer, which should mark it down. If we find anything, we will reach out to you." Officer Malone stood and extended his hand. "Thank you for your time, Mr. Harrison. You are free to go. Take care of your sister."

Joe left the office without a second thought. He walked down the hall to the room where he had left Megan. He watched her from the window as she rested her head on the table. He walked in and said, "Let's go, Megan. Let me take you home."

$$$

## Chapter Fifteen

Joe had said that he didn't have to come in this morning after last night's accident. *Yeah right, something is going on.* Once the cobweb cleared, she knew deep down that someone was after her. Joe insisted for her to stay home but what good would it do? She had a building to finish. She missed Max. She had tried calling him just to hear his voice, but all she got was his voice mail. It was only six days since he flew overseas for business, but it's funny how a person can become so attached. It was late when they got back from the police station, so she texted him saying that she missed him and wished him a good night.

When morning came, she had still not heard from him, so she buried herself in work. Timing was everything right now. This building had to finish on schedule, and it was crucial she had to stay inside the budget. The supplier for the countertops was not working for her right now. She had to stay inside her guidelines, and this asshole was not giving her the price she needed. "Come on, Jack," she barked back. She was getting nowhere fast; she only had a few more weeks till her deadline. She was talking with Jack Cadieux from Granite Top and Kitchens, and he was not complying to her price.

XOXO

Frustrated, she leaned her head back against her chair and rolled her eyes, knowing that he was taking her for a ride on the price. She took a deep breath, and she knew the moment he walked into her office. Her heart speeds up just knowing that smell of his cologne. God, she missed that smell. She looked up and saw him leaning on her doorframe with the most incredible smile. That just made her heart pitter-patter faster.

A few months ago, she told him everything—about the car accident, her pregnancy. She thought once he knew the truth he wouldn't want her. She was wrong. That night changed everything. Besides the odd business trip, he had to take; they were inseparable. Even though they had come clean about their feelings, she still had not told him she loved him. Last night scared her, knowing that she would never have the chance to say to him *she loved him* if something terrible happened.

Megan hadn't realized how much she missed him until he was there in front of her. Who wouldn't want a virile man, tall, dark hair, muscular body, and a smile that just made her weak? The desire that he had for her reflected from this eyes and fueled hers. She looked at him knowing what was beneath that suit. She couldn't help eyeing him like he was naked. She bit down on her bottom lip. Her body heated up picturing him naked and inside of her. "Jack, I'm sorry, someone just walked in. Revise those prices for me. I will call you back." She hung up the phone, not giving him time to say goodbye.

Max watched her finish her call. He knew he did the right thing. When Joe called telling him that Megan was in an accident, he knew he had to fly home. He called his pilot to fuel up the jet and headed back. It was the longest twelve-hour flight he had ever had. He couldn't text her or call her due to turbulence and god he wished he could have been there for her last night.

$$\$\$\$$$

He walked into her office. She hadn't realized he was looking at her. She looked tired and exhausted, but she was his breath of fresh air. That moment when she realized he was in the office; the time had stopped. Max closed the door and watched her say goodbye to whomever she was talking to. As she approached, he took her in his arms and held her. Her almond scent; her delicate body against his; damn he missed this woman. One week without her was too long. Max took her face with both hands as he looked into those hazel eyes and felt relief that she was safe. Her expression haunted him; he knew she had not slept in a week. So many questions were running through his head. Why weren't the bodyguards with her? He had left specific instructions before he went overseas, to his security team. Someone would get his anger as soon as he was back in the office. He just needed to see her first. He traced the scratch on her forehead and leaned in and kissed it, then her eyes, her cheeks, and then he kissed her mouth gently, feeling her warm lips on his. "I'm sorry, Angel. I should have been here. When Joe called me, the moment I got your call, I was heading to the airport, I just couldn't get back to you fast enough."

 Megan pulled him in, feeling him against her, his scent, his strength, his warmth. God, she missed him. When she couldn't reach him, she knew there must have been a good reason. She pulled away and looked into his eyes. "Who would do this, Max? Why would someone deliberately hurt me? They had a gun. They could have shot me last night." Megan was trying to hold everything in but couldn't. She tasted salty tears on her lip. She was scared, thinking that she might not see him anymore. That is what scared her the most.

XOXO

"Oh baby, I'm sorry. We will find them, I promise you." Max held her even tighter against him, knowing she had to let everything out of her system.

Megan took a few deep breaths, relishing his scent and his strong arms cocooned around her. She hadn't realized how much she missed him. He was home, and that was all that mattered to her. All the fear she was holding back, she finally let it go. Then she realized she hadn't expected him. He was only supposed to arrive tomorrow. Then she finally realized what he had said. "Joe called you? Oh, Max, I'm sorry. You shouldn't have cancelled your business trip." She wanted him there, but she didn't want him to cancel any deal that was going on because of her.

Max couldn't believe what he was hearing. How can someone this beautiful and tenacious and loving think he wouldn't be there for her? "Babe, you are my priority before any business deal I may have. You come first. I just needed to see you first making sure you were okay."

God, she missed him. "I've missed you." She kissed him gently and felt his hands pulling her closer to him. That gentle kiss turned into want, and she wanted more. She wanted to feel his hot skin against her. The kiss deepened, and as she tasted his tongue, their teeth clicking against each other, she felt his powerful pull that only he had on her. All thought of being scared vanished. She knew that nothing would ever happen to her when they were together. They broke the kiss, and she felt Max lean his forehead against hers.

"Damn, I've missed you. Tonight, my place? I want to strip you naked and taste every each of your body and be inside of you." Max was breathing hard, knowing that he couldn't control his erection around her. He knew she was safe now and that Joe would not let anything happen to her, but still he didn't want to

$$$

leave her. He cupped her face, knowing how aroused she was, as much as he. Only Megan could make his heart race like he had run a marathon. He was just about to throw caution to the wind and take her right here on her desk. That is when they heard a knock on the door, then Joe's voice on the other side.

"Max," Megan whispered. She was still in a haze of lust, and so turned on that she felt the pressure building. She wanted more. She wanted his touch, and she wanted him to take away the ache she was having in between her legs. Her core flooded with heat. She squeezed her thighs together, hoping to relieve the pressure that was building inside of her. But just like that, he pulled away and opened the door. He left her needing and wanting more.

"Joe." Max took Joe's hand as he watched Megan still in a haze of desire. "What do you know? Any word yet on what they found?"

*How can he do that?* Megan thought. Being with Max, she was in a world of her own, where there was no one else around but them. She was now needy, aroused and wanting more, so how can he do that? The moment he opened the door he was all professional like nothing ever happened. She saw it then, just a quick look of worry, but just like that, gone in a blink of an eye. Now he was all business, and that hard shell was up. No one could sense what he was feeling.

Megan watched the exchange of the two men she loved. Something was wrong. Someone shot at her, and it wasn't random, and she knew it. Then it came back to her, at the time she thought nothing of it, A few weeks ago someone sideswiped her but she managed to stay on the road. Something was going on, because her brother and Max were exchanging looks, hoping that she didn't notice. "What's going on, Max? Joe?"

XOXO

"Nothing is going on, sweetheart!" Max knew better than to lie to her, but until he had all the details, he didn't want to say anything.

Megan looked over at Joe, then back at Max. She knew they were hiding something from her, and like hell, if she was going to stand there and brush it off. "Either you both tell me what is going on, or I walk out of here, and we are through, Max. I do not like being lied to. We have an agreement: no more secrets."

"Megan, sit down. You are overreacting. Nothing is going on," Joe said. He hated lying to her but the less she knew, the better.

"I'm calling it bullshit, Joe. What are you both not telling me? Has it something to do with yesterday?" Megan looked at Max knowing that if he wasn't going to say anything to her, she would not put up with his secrecy. It felt like he was lying to her. She was not going to put up with it. "Max, if you are not going to tell me what both of you are hiding, I want you both out of this office. And Max, you know I will not put up with lies. Either you tell me or leave, and we it's over." Megan was getting angry as she faced the two most influential people in her life.

Max walked up to her. He didn't care if Joe was standing there or not. He raised his hand to her face and watched her slap it away. She told him not to touch her. She had the power to bring him down. "Fine. It all started right after your attack. We started to receive letters, threats that they were coming after me. The easiest target is through you." Max watched her as she looked at him in confusion. "Last night was a warning. They could have killed you, but they didn't."

"Why didn't you tell me this? Don't you know that we are in this together? Who is doing this? Why now?" Megan looked over at Joe, knowing that he knew and didn't say anything to her. She was not a little girl anymore and dammit, they should

$$$

have said something. She would have watched her back, been more careful.

"I'm sorry, baby. We should have, but I didn't want to worry you." Max took her hand and looked into her eyes. "We do not know who they are yet. We haven't figured it out. Joe and I knew about the threats but they were never serious."

"Are you kidding me? You have known for weeks that someone was after you, and you didn't think this would concern me?" Megan looked up at those eyes and knew that she was doing the right thing. She raised her hand to his cheek and caressed him so gently, feeling his heat, and she felt his lip on her palm as he held her hand in place. "Max, don't you know you are my world? I love you, and if anything would ever happen to you, I would rather die with you than going on living." Megan kissed him. "Please don't hide things like this from me again. We can fight this together." She looked up at him, and he held her tight.

"I'm sorry. You're right, and I promise I will not hide this from you again, but you have to understand now that your life is in danger. You will have bodyguards following you moving forward. Your life is worth more than any business deal. You are the most and only important person in my life. Without you, I'm nothing, and your love will make me slay all enemies who dare to hurt you." Max leaned in and kissed her. He knew this wasn't the place to take what he wanted, but damn did he want her. He released her, trying to catch his breath because that is what she did to him. "I missed you so much. Tonight, seven o'clock. We will finish this tonight Megan." Max turned and walk to the door, but before he left he looked at her; "Angel."

Max told her about the threats; her life was in danger as his. *I cannot stay made at him.* She knew the moment that Max kissed her, Joe left her office as she heard the door close, behind them.

XOXO

Max took her in his arms, and the world around her no longer exists. The kiss was a promise of what is to come. She watched him walk away, feeling his lost once again. When she heard her endearment name he called her, that she loves so much.

Max walked back to her and lifted her chin. "I'm sorry I kept this from you, but I will not put you or your family in harm's way. Tonight we will talk. But there is one request I want."

"What's that."

Max leaned in as he nuzzled her neck, kissing her, licking her particular spot that drove her crazy. He whispered into her ear; "No underwear," Max heard her gasp, at the request. Gave her one more kiss on the lips, and left without a second glance at her.

$$$

## Chapter Sixteen

Megan watched him leave as she held her neck where he nipped her. Her inside where like jelly, her heart was racing so fast. *Damn him he knew what he was doing to her.* She heard him laugh as he exited her office. How could she work now when she was so turned on? She wanted to run to him and *say fuck it, let's get naked.* But she had a call to finish.

The day couldn't end fast enough. Megan left the office thinking of Max's last words. *Since when did he become so demanding, and what was up with him telling me no underwear? What the hell was he thinking anyway, I've never done that before. Seriously, who goes commando these days?* She checked the clock, and the damn traffic was at a standstill. She would never make it at this rate. She honked, as someone cut her off, she just wanted to get home. *Don't they know time is the essence here?* God, she missed her Audi, this rental was brutal! After those assholes shot her, she lost control of her car, and it had to be towed away. The more she waited in traffic, the more her brain went wild. She was thinking of what to wear. Two can play his game, and she knew what to wear.

It was six thirty when she finally pulled into her parking lot. She had no time to spare. Thank god she always had a bag ready,

XOXO

because these last few months, she was living in both places. She hurried to change and grab her bag and out the door she went again. She heard a ding from her phone and read the text.

**Don't be late,** Max wrote.

Megan smiled. **What are you going to do, spank me?** She smiled back at her phone, feeling naughty, especially with what she was wearing.

**Don't tempt me, Angel, I just might,** Max wrote back.

Megan looked at his text. *He wouldn't, would he?* She hurried out to the elevator to her car as she texted back. **Leaving now....xxx**

Megan look at his text: **Oh and Angel, don't forget, no underwear.**

Oh crap! He was serious about that! She bent down and took her underwear off. She stuffed them in her bag. She wiggled from side to side and could feel the cold air under her skirt. She made it to Max's just in time, before seven. She walked up the path to the front door when it flew open. Only then her core heated up seeing him in a pair of jeans and a t-shirt. You had to love Max in a suit, but when he dressed down, he was even sexier.

Max knew she just arrived as he opened the door and grinned at her, if there was one thing he knew about Megan, she was never late. "What the hell are you wearing? Holy shit! Jesus, woman, get your ass inside before a neighbor calls the cop." He pulled her in and shut the door. He looked her over, and damn was she hot. Her skirt was so short if she bent down you could see her ass and pussy. He could see her nipples playing peek-a-boo through the holes in her tank top. She had black stilettos on, at least four inches high. "Damn woman, you're sexy as sin. What you're wearing should be illegal, but I'm not complaining." Max grabbed her by the waist and pulled her forward and kissed her.

$$$

Megan knew she had him, and the kiss did amazing things to her core. She felt the heat almost dripping down her inner thigh. She wanted to get back to him about the no underwear. With everything that happened over the last twenty-four hours, her man was back and she desperately needed him. That kiss was meant for sinful things. She was breathless as she smiled up at him and turned in his arms. She felt sexy. She thought that she could do anything, knowing that Max was affected by her outfit, she could feel his evidence in the lower of her back. He was kissing her neck as she rubbed her ass again his erection. She knew she had him. She felt his breath against her ear as he groaned. She bent down and looked over her shoulder, and the beast was there, ready to explode. His eyes were dark with a hint of green, and she knew her man was losing his control. "What are you going to do, big boy, spank me?" Megan teased him as she wiggled her ass, against his jeans, she felt the roughness against her skin.

"Fuck!" Max groaned as he watched Megan bend down in front of him and knew he couldn't hold it any longer. He was so hard looking at her like that, bent over, ready for him. He lifted her so-called skirt and smacked her hard on the ass. He heard her yelp. He loved seeing his mark on her lovely ass.

"Oh, Angel! Is this what you want? You want me inside you, fucking your sweet pussy?"

"Please Max!" Megan looked over her shoulder and knew she had released the beast inside him. She never thought that spanking, could be such a turn on, and the caress that came after the sting, just that small touch meant so much more, she knew he would never hurt her, but damn was she not affected by it, and wanted more. Now she was desperate to have him, for him to fill her. She had never wanted someone so much.

XOXO

"Lean forward and hold on to the wall, baby! That's it. Damn your beautiful when you're turned on. Now spread your legs. That's it. You like this, don't you? Say it.

"Yes, God Max, please."

Max slapped again and then did the same to her other cheeks. Max heard her moan every time he slapped her. He slid his hand and found her clit. "God, you're soaked. My Angel likes being spank, it turns you on, doesn't it? I'm going to take you hard." He couldn't wait any longer. He took his cock out. It was so hard and standing straight out. He pulled a condom from his back pocket, ripped it open, and sheathed himself. No more foreplay; he thrust himself inside her, waiting for her to adjust to him, and that small cry from her mouth made him harder.

"Sweet love you're tight. Damn, it feels so good being inside you, Megan!" Max felt her move and that is when he moved. He took her fast and hard, every thrust harder than the next. "I just lost it when you bent down like that, all exposed. I could see how turned on you are, wanting me to take you." Max rested one hand on her back, and the other held her hip as he thrust into her.

Megan bit down on her bottom lip, tasting blood. She wasn't complaining. He filled her completely. "Fuck me, Max! I want this as much as you do." She wanted him like this, out of control. She felt him moving, and when he pinched her nipple, she felt herself building, the heat of both bodies colliding together. Thrust to thrust, she wanted more, but she knew it wouldn't last because as one orgasm hit, Max didn't let go. He moves faster knowing she was close, as her wall grip around his cock. When he reached down and touched her clit, she lost it. "Oh god Max, I'm coming. Oh god, yes… yes … yes."

$$$

"That's it, baby, let it go." Max held on to her and kept thrusting. Sweat started to come down his face, and he felt the tightness building inside him. He knew it wouldn't be long as the pressure grew. He felt her wall squeeze his cock like a glove. "Megan, I'm going to come! Come now with me, baby! He thrust hard then took his finger and circled her clit and rubbed her little nub as he heard her scream. Max gave one last thrust and grunted as he reached his release.

Megan felt her leg give. She couldn't stand. She felt Max lift her and back up and they sat on the stairs waiting for their breathing came back down to normal.

Max cradled her and kissed the top of her bare shoulder. Damn, did he miss her. "Wow, just wow! I was not expecting this! What's with the hooker look? Don't get me wrong, I love it, but it's for me only, Angel." He kept kissing her as he could still sense she was coming down from her high. He knew he didn't have much time but this moment with her, he just didn't want to let her go. She laid her head back on his shoulder, leaning on one side. He felt her sweet lips on his jaw.

"You started it. You told me no underwear, and I might have overdone it but I felt sexy doing it for you. Beside, this got me all horny!" She smiled into his neck and kissed his pulse.

Max laughed out loud. "Did you bring a change of clothes? If you leave those on, I'm not going to be able to control myself."

"I have a bag in the car. I'll get it?" she tried to get up.

"The hell you will! Give me your keys. This," Max pointed at her, "is for my eyes only. No, go upstairs and take a shower. Mom and Dad are coming tonight. Even though I love smelling sex on you, it's for me only." He kissed her lips slowly. "I'll be right behind you."

XOXO

Megan watched him leave and she couldn't help but worry that she was meeting his parents for the first time. *What if they do not like me? What if they see me and think that I'm just some gold digger after his money?*

Max took her face into his hand and looked into those worried eyes. He knew she was second-guessing herself. Megan didn't hide her emotions; you could read her like a book. "Relax. Everything is going to be fine. They're down to earth, my parents. They will love you, because you are the most important person in my life and just that alone is the reason I know they will adore you. Now go upstairs and clean that lovely body of yours. I will be right up with your bag." She kissed him and ran upstairs as he walked away to retrieve her bag.

When Max walked into the bedroom, he could hear the water running in the shower. He stripped down in record time so he could see her naked beauty, and he wanted to join her. The steam hit him when he opened the shower door and walked in. Just the thought of her made him hard again, and his cock was standing proudly in front of him. He could never get enough of her. She made his body ache so much.

"Get that away from me, or we'll never get out of this shower!" She looked up and smiled at him.

He laughed and held her tight. "Oh baby, I can't stop. I want you again. See? I'm all hard for you again!" Max growled in her ear. Just the small touch of her hands made his cock jump in front of him.

"We don't have time for this!" She turned to get out of the shower but before leaving she hugged him. The stream of hot water cascaded down their bodies. She leaned in a bit, just enough to move the handle and turned off the hot water. Before he realized what she had done, she took off laughing. She hurried

$$$

out of the shower stall before he caught her. All she could hear was Max swearing as the cold water hit his hot and steamy body. "There, that should cool you down!" She leaned in and kissed the glass of the shower, and she couldn't help but giggle as she walked away.

"Oh shit! I'll get you for that, Angel!" He couldn't help himself. He loved to hear her laugh.

She ran out of the bathroom wrapped in a towel and laughing. By the time Max came out of the shower, she was fixing her hair when she saw him standing there with just a towel around his waist. Even naked, the man showed power. She loved to watch him. She couldn't help but stare, devouring him. She could look at his naked body all day. He was lean, with dark skin and just a little hair on his chest. His stomach was tight, showing off a six-pack of abs and the perfect v below his towel.

"What are you looking at?"

"You, you're beautiful. I could look at you all day and still not get enough of you!"

Max walked towards her and kissed her nose. "That's where you are wrong. You're the beautiful one!" Max winked at her and then kissed her forehead. Then he went to his walk-in closet to get dressed.

Meeting someone in-laws for the first time, was not what Megan expected tonight. Yes, she was nervous; *worried that she wouldn't be good enough.* She had doubts, yes, but what she learned was that Helen and Douglas Pierce, loved their sons. Yes, they were wealthy, but that didn't change them. They believe in helping others, and never forgetting where they came from, loyalty, trust, love and respect went a long way in this family. Megan saw how Max adored his mother and father. Besides the comments of having children and getting married, they were as laid back as her mom and dad. She fell in love with them instantly, and they had accepted her from the moment they had opened the door. Helen embraces her as Douglas, and she finally felt like she belongs, that this was her home now, and what more can a girl want.

$$$

## Chapter Seventeen

Finally, she laid her head on the desk and just wanted to sleep. Megan only wished she could be excited. She was, but her heart was just not into it. After nine months, getting hit on a head unconscious, being run down, being shot at, and working twelve to fourteen hours a day on this building, she could finally say the word; done. The Pierce Complex was finished ahead of schedule, with two weeks to spare, and she was happy that her crew would get the bonus they deserved.

Megan was proud of the job she did. This was her most significant project for Harrison Construction ever. She wished she could do the happy dance, but she just felt miserable. She had just signed off on the final papers so she could turn everything over to Joe, her bossy brother with the attitude of a pig-headed mule. Today they were turning the ownership over to Pierce Enterprises, once they do the final inspection. She took the documentation and walked to her brother's office. She opened the door without knocking and slammed them down on his desk. "Done. I'm out of here." She had an appointment with her comforter and pillow.

Joe looked at his sister, about to tell her to knock the next time, but the moment he saw her, she looked worn down and exhausted. *Bastard.* He felt terrible that he had pushed her so much, but they had a lot going on with this building complex. He wasn't going to say anything. Joe knew he worked her hard. "Go."

"Planning on it. Don't expect me back until Monday. No, wait, I'm taking the week off. Don't expect me back until the following Monday." She reached the door when Joe called her name.

"Megan, baby girl." Joe realized that he could be arrogant son-of-bitch most of the time, but he knew Megan was a perfectionist. She had a passion for building things, and watching everything come together, as their grandfather and their father had, and he couldn't be more pleased with the accomplishment. He couldn't be more proud of her.

"What, Joe? I'm tired and want to go home."

Behind this mahogany desk, he was the boss, but he was also her brother. Joe knew she didn't want this project, but in the long run, she was the best person for it. He had doubt about Max Pierce, but he proved him wrong, and he could see that she was happy even if she looked like hell right now. "Baby girl, I'm sorry if I was a hard-ass on this, but you did an excellent job. I'm proud of you. You work hard, and because of you, our men will have a nice bonus before Christmas. Now I want you to take two weeks off, and I do not want to see you here until December. If I see you here, I will drive you back home myself." He looked at his sister, and she was barely standing up. He touched her face, and she was burning up. "Damn girl, you're burning up. Are you sure you're okay to drive?" He looked at her with concern. Why hadn't he noticed how sick she was before?

"I'm fine, and thanks, Joe, I appreciate it. Now if you'll excuse me, I'm going home to bed." She hugged her brother and left. She needed to rest up to see her lover boy tomorrow. This flu

$$$

was wearing her down, nothing that she ate would stay down these days, that is why she felt so weak.

The next day, Joe, Josh, and Max were walking through the complex and making sure that everything was to their liking before Joe had to sign off on the documentation. "Love what you did, Joe. Having the security guard in the front will make every unit in this building feel safe. We love it, right Max?" Josh said as he looked at his brother. Josh knew Max had flown in late the previous night from the west coast, but as he watched him, he wasn't paying attention to a word he was saying. He looked troubled and concerned. Josh knew it wasn't like him, Max always had the final say on the inspection.

"Max? Are you okay?" Joe asked

"I'm not sure, Joe. Have you heard from Megan this morning? It's not like her not to answer my calls or text messages." Max gave Joe a look of concern. Ever since they had been back together, she had been his priority, his world, and they never missed a call or text message from each other.

"Megan hasn't been feeling well the past few days, so she signed off on the papers, and I gave her two weeks off. She might still be sleeping," Joe replied.

"What do you mean she's not feeling well? She didn't say anything about it yesterday morning when we talked." Max thought back to see if he could remember any signs of illness. "She was a little pale before I left, but it's not like her not to answer her cell phone." Max started to worry. What if something happened to her? He knew the threats were still coming, but until his security team found something, and per his knowledge, they weren't doing the job he expected, he needed to find someone that could.

"Max, maybe she just turned off her phone. She looked exhausted; maybe she's just sleeping it off right now," Joe said,

xoxo

but still he was concerned. He knew that Lizzie would call if something wrong.

"Bro, you worry too much." Josh looked at his brother. *He's fallen hard for this woman.* "You're worried, aren't you?"

"Yes, I am. It's unlike her not to respond to my texts or calls. So call me crazy, but I need to know she's okay." Max looked at his phone for the million time.

"Go, then. I'll finish this with Joe. Do you have any questions or concerns?" Josh asked.

"No, I'm sure you can handle the rest. Joe, this looks amazing she did a great job on this, and your men have earned their bonus." Max extended his hand and gave Josh a brotherly hug.

"Go, I'll finish up here. Call us if you need us. I'm sure Megan is fine, bro."

"Thanks, Josh! Joe…"

"Max, let me know if there is anything wrong with my sister. I know she was fighting a nasty cold, and I know she wasn't looking good when she went home."

"I'll call you," Max said.

Max couldn't get to the condo fast enough. Thankfully, Megan gave him a key to get in, so he wouldn't have to worry about waking her up if she was sleeping. Still, his gut was telling him something was wrong. As he raced through traffic, he noticed that his bodyguards were following. Ever since those threats, security was never far away. He tried to calm himself; he felt that something was wrong with Megan, but he brushed it off. Max believed that it was just someone trying to scare him, and he didn't give into threats. The only thing that made him nervous was that something might happen to Megan, so he had security follow her every move. He pressed his hands-free button. "Has she left the building?"

$$$

"No, Sir," the man on the other line said.

"Make sure you have someone on her at all times." Just like that, he cancelled the call.

Max finally made it to the condo. He parked, and headed upstairs, taking the stairs two at a time. He didn't want to wait for the elevator. He opened the door and his heart was beating so fast he had to take a breath to calm himself. He needed to see her. Being protective of her maybe drove him a little wild sometimes, but it was in good faith.

The place was quiet. He took in the scent lingering in the air: the fresh smell of lavender and just a hint of vanilla. He could hear the humming of the refrigerator in the distance. He knew that if anything happened, she or Lizzie would call. Megan wasn't in the living room, so he headed down the hall and turned the corner towards her bedroom. That's when Max saw her lying on the floor, just in front of her bed. "What the hell?" He kneeled down and moved her hair away from her face. She looked pale and thin. He was going to talk to her about her taking better care of herself. She just looked so fragile. "Megan? Honey, wake up!"

She moaned, and a feeling of relief came over him. "Baby, wake up!"

Max lifted her off the floor and put her on the bed. One of his friends was a doctor, so he didn't hesitate to call. "Ed? It's Max. I need a favor. I'll pay you double for a house call. It's Megan. I'm not sure what's wrong with her. I just found her passed out on the floor. Please hurry."

Max stayed by her side until he heard the doorbell. She regained consciousness, but she kept falling back asleep. "Megan, this is my friend Dr. Edward Bouchard. He's going to check you out, okay? You do not look good, and I'm worried. I'll be right outside if you need me."

xoxo

Megan looked at him with hooded eyes; "Max, what are you doing here." She whispered.

"Don't worry Megan, Ed, will take good care of you, ok?" Max leaned in and kissed her forehead, she was still burning up.

Max paced the living room. He'd been waiting for thirty minutes and he kept looking at his watch. It must be worse than he thought. He heard the door open and turned to see Ed walking towards him. "Ed, tell me what is wrong with Megan. Will she be okay?"

"I gave her something to sleep. You will have to talk to her to make sure she rests and drinks a lot of fluid. I took some blood samples. It could just be the flu, but bring her to my office tomorrow. I will run more tests. I will send you my bill." Ed put a hand on his shoulder. "She's fine, Max, just dehydrated and tired. For now, she should sleep."

"You wouldn't lie to me, would you Ed? You sure there is nothing wrong?"

"Take care of her. As I said, I will run more tests tomorrow. She needs to sleep right now. She's burning up so I gave her something that should bring down the fever. Take care of your girl."

Max understood that Ed was just doing his job, that whatever conversation they had in the room, he wouldn't say a word unless he heard it from Megan. "Thank you, Ed. Let me know what I owe you, and I'll see you tomorrow." Max said his goodbyes and he knew what he had to do; he was going to take care of his girl.

$$$

## Chapter Eighteen

Megan woke up in darkness. Whatever the kind doctor gave her, she felt a little better. At least the nausea had stopped. She knew she hadn't dreamt about Max being there. She could sense him even if he were not in the room with her. She took a deep breath trying to calm herself. All those feelings were coming back now that she was awake. She felt scared. She didn't want to keep a secret from him. She had to come to terms to what the doctor told her. They say love can overcome anything and also change everything. She loved Max with every fiber of her being, with every breath she took. No one had ever come close in the past. Her heart knew, and she felt it every time Max was around, that pull that two people have. But had the man she loved really changed, and was he willing to sacrifice everything for a child? How did this happen? They were careful, but they said it was not one hundred percent full proof. Sex was always amazing with Max. How many times had she lost it with him, just by one touch, on kiss, her body responded so fast? Only just a few months ago, after the attack, in a moment of weakness, she came clean about her attraction. He came after her, begging for forgiveness. He proved to her time after time that she could trust him, but there was still that doubt in the back of her mind.

XOXO

Her heart knew what it wanted, and it was Max, but her brain was always second-guessing, fighting the urge not to reveal too much. She was exhausted; maybe it was time to let go and embrace the love for this man again. She should listen to her heart. Deep down she did trust him. He was always there, protecting her, caring for her, loving her. What more could a woman want? They had this connection that she couldn't explain. They could feel if the other person was hurting, or needed them, or just knew when they wanted to be held, like now. At that moment, she felt him. She heard the door open, and she slowly opened her eyes to see the most beautiful man that God had created, and he was hers. She couldn't help feeling those butterflies in the pit of her stomach. That is what he did to her, when he was in a room. He made her all gooey inside and made her heart beat faster with just one look. She couldn't help but give in to that shy smile as he approached her. She could see the love reflecting back at her, and she knew now without a doubt that this was going to work. He loved her, and that was all that mattered.

Max leaned in and touched her forehead. She still felt a little warm, but he could see that her color was coming back. "How are you feeling?"

"Better, still tired though and hungry."

"Good, I have some soup ready. Do you want to eat in bed, or do you feel strong enough to make it to the living room? I have a nice fire going. I can set you up on the couch." Max sat down on the bed beside her and gently touched her cheek.

"Max! I'm not that weak!" Well, maybe she was, but she felt stronger as she leaned into his touch.

"I know, baby. I just want to make sure you're okay. Joe called asking how you were feeling."

$$$

"What did you tell him?" She wanted to snuggle and fall asleep but this time she wanted Max holding her.

"Not much to tell. I just told him the doctor looked you over. And you were resting." Max caressed her face with his hand.

"Thanks for letting him know. Joe has always been overprotective of me since my parents' death last year."

"I just told him what happened when I showed up and that I'm taking care of you, that you weren't feeling well." Max looked at her, knowing he did the right thing. He saw her relax. "I cancelled all my appointments, and Josh and Brandon will take care of business, and I can take care of my girl." Max saw a smile spread across her face, but he also knew her strength wasn't there yet.

Megan decided to get out of bed. She couldn't lay there any longer and needed to move. He was taking such good care of her, and she felt guilty about keeping this secret to herself. She could sense him as she paced the floor, making sure she wouldn't face plant. She needed to tell him, but the doctor told her he wanted to run more tests first. What if something was wrong with this child and she loses it? Would she be able to come to terms with the idea of losing another child, his child? She didn't want to hide this from him, but she needed to be sure about this before saying anything to him. Just a few days, that is all she needed. Just a few days then she would tell him. Megan didn't like feeling weak. She was a survivor, but her body had completely shut down on her. Her head was spinning again, and as she braced herself on the bedpost, she felt light-headed. She felt his arms around her, lifting her up. "Put me down Max, please."

Max watched her sway a little; then she composed herself. He didn't wait. He lifted her into his arms and sat down on the bed. "Baby, what's wrong? You seemed to be in deep thought

xoxo

just now." He caressed her hair and held her tight against him. "Megan, sweetheart you're pushing yourself. The doctor said you need to rest. I love you, Angel. Let me take care of you." Max knew there was more, he could sense it, but he also knew she would tell him when she was ready.

Megan leaned her head on his shoulder as she sighed and calmed herself down, feeling his embrace. She looked at him from under her lashes. How did he become so in tune with her thoughts and concerns? "Just hold me. I just need this right now."

Max kissed the top of her head. "Megan, I love you. I'll keep saying that to you until it finally sinks in. Whatever is bothering you, and I know there is something wrong, you can trust me. You're stuck with me."

Megan giggled as she wiped away a tear she hadn't realized was running down her face. "Nothing is wrong; I'm just exhausted again." She lied, but she just needed to make sure before saying anything.

Max lifted her off the bed and walked to the living room to settle her down on the couch. He wrapped her in a blanket and stuffed a few pillows behind her. "When you are ready, I hope you will trust me enough to tell me what is bothering you because I know there is something wrong." He leaned in and kissed her. Max could feel her melting into his embrace. "Now, wait here, and I will get you some food."

Megan watched him leave and went into kitchen, and she couldn't help herself but sighed. Yes, she was doing the right thing. First, she needed to know for sure that everything would be okay with the pregnancy. Second, when she was ready and strong enough to clear her head of all the doubt, she would tell him. That was the plan, and she was going to stick with it because it was the only way she could handle it right now. They

$$$

were going to be parents. Will he marry her? She didn't want to force him into marriage. Being pregnant was an accident, it happens, and he was doing all the right things to make her feel that they were in for the long haul.

XOXO

## Chapter Nineteen

Megan rested her head on the pillow listening to the music, and she couldn't help but smile, feeling happy and content. She knew things would work out. She hadn't told him anything yet but would soon. She just wanted to make sure everything was okay. She knew it sounded crazy, but as she rubbed her belly, she felt life growing inside of her, a life she had created with the most wonderful man. While Max was cleaning up the dinner dishes, Megan took the time to kick back and enjoy the music. Her strength was coming back, and she felt much better. She looked over the couch and could see him in the kitchen, with his broad shoulders and his perfect waistline, in his black dress pants that showed his perfect ass. Max's attentiveness to her needs overwhelmed her, and while she could get used to this, she knew it would come to an end. The thought of Max leaving her side and heading back to his home, made her heart beat a little faster. She was enjoying being pampered and besides, she never knew the man could cook. He was a genius in the kitchen. How could a person know someone so well? Max knew her weakness as she watched him sit at the end of the couch. He took her feet and started to rub them. He paid homage to her feet as she moaned with pure joy escape her lips. "That feels amazing; don't stop." She smiled back at him.

Music playing, talented man, massaging her feet, the light smell of lavender lingering in the air, hearing Max's sweet voice as he explained how he wanted to whisk her away to the cabin on the weekend. She heard the buzzer and looked at Max. "Are you expecting anyone?"

He put her feet down and smiled back at her. "Just a friend of yours."

"I wasn't expecting any of my friends to stop by. Lizzie is working late again tonight. Who could it be?" She heard someone knocking at the door. She watched Max open the door and saw Luc. She jumped up from the couch and ran into Luc's arms. "Oh my God! Luc, what are you doing here?" She hugged him.

"Hey, gorgeous! Didn't you know I was coming? Lizzie said you were sick, so I had to check up on you." Luc looked at Max.

"Apparently not! But I'm happy you are here. When was the last time I saw you? That doesn't matter, you are here now." Megan turned to Max, knowing that they had not met officially yet. She took Max's hand. "Max Pierce, meet Luc Ellis, one of my good friends. Luc, this is Max." Megan couldn't help but feel giddy inside knowing that her two favorite men in the world were finally meeting.

"I've heard a lot about you, Mr. Pierce." Luc looked Max in the eyes, knowing he had to say something. "Let me get one thing clear: you hurt her, you will have to deal with me." Luc held on to his hand with a firm grip—maybe just a little too hard—but the man didn't flinch. He knew that he could sometimes be intimidating and he didn't care if Megan was there. He hurt her once, so he wanted to make sure that he understood where he stood.

$$$

"Understood. You have my word. Please, call me Max. We're all friends here, aren't we? That Mr. Pierce is for the office." Max respected the man that protected his friends.

"Come in, Luc, have a seat. Would you like anything to drink?" Megan asked.

"Beer would be okay unless you have that fine whiskey I love so much." Luc smiled down at her.

Max didn't hesitate. He went to the kitchen and came back with two glasses of scotch and glass of iced water for Megan as they all sat down. "So Luc, I've heard a lot about you. I told Lizzie that it was time for us to meet. Any friend of Megan is a friend of mine, or I hope they will be." Max knew that Megan had two best friends who stood by her: Lizzie, who proved more than once where she stood if he hurt her again, and didn't want to get on her bad side, and Luc, whom he still didn't know anything about him. He did his research of course, like anyone that comes in close contact with him or his family.

Megan watched the two men who meant the world to her. She thought that Max might be jealous, but the man was confident and she knew that not much would scare him, especially Luc Ellis. The man was a beast at six-four, ex-military. His looks were beautiful, but there were also shadows there. He seen a lot in his military days and to someone that didn't know him, he was hard to approach. There were a few scars on his face, but that didn't take away his beauty and kindness for the people that he loved. Now Luc had his own security firm, which was doing remarkably well. Megan watched the two powerful men talking about business and being so comfortable with each other. Max listened to Luc as he explained what he did, from high tech security to personal bodyguard you name it Luc Ellis Security did it. There wasn't anything his team couldn't do, including tracking down

XOXO

someone missing or escorting the elite stars or businesspeople. As Megan listened, they seemed to have the same interests in sports and leisure. When they turned to business, Luc explained what he did, and something seemed to catch Max's attention.

Megan watched Max and knew his brain was thinking about something. He didn't think people noticed it. When he was interested in something, you couldn't tell by looking at him—but she knew. Max was always cool, calm, and collected. He always sat with his left leg crossed over his right, and his right hand was resting on the armrest. His palm was flat, but his thumb always moved up and down. She knew that he was thinking fast. Megan had learned a few things since she had been with Max, like how he thinks while he listens to other people talk, or their body language. She couldn't help but smile at him as she grabbed his arm. "Max, maybe Luc can help?" She took his arm and looked at him as he smiled back at her and kissed her forehead. "He's the best, and I'm not just saying that because he's my best friend. He knows his stuff."

Max smiled, reassuring her, and held her a little tighter to his side. "Luc, would you consider meeting with me next week? The security I have right now, well, I thought they were the best, but lately I've been second guessing myself. They work for Pierce Enterprises, but I believe there could be a mole inside my firm. I will need someone from the outside to oversee this if my guess is right."

Luc Ellis was the owner of Luc Ellis Security. They provided high profile security down to the installation of anything to do with home and office security and more. There was no one higher than him; they were the best. Luc noticed the worry in Megan's eyes. He knew something was wrong, but he wanted to hear it from Max. He was grateful that Max was offering to

$$$

meet with his team because he only hired the best. But tonight was about friends catching up, nothing more. "Thank you for the offer. We are always looking for new contracts, and I appreciate it." He shot back the rest of his scotch and put his glass down. "Well, it's time for me to go. You look tired, Megan. I promise I will not take so long to come and see you again." They walked to the door as he took his jacket and scarf, he said, "Max, it has been a pleasure to meet you." He took Megan in for a hug and kissed her forehead. "Take good care of her, Max, she's an extraordinary lady." He said his goodbyes as he closed the door behind him.

Max looked down at her. "Luc was right; you do look tired, baby. Let's call it a night, but first, dance with me?"

Megan watched him go through the music on his phone and link it to her speakers. He dimmed the light and clicked play. She watched him extend his hand to her.

"Dance with me."

Megan put her hand in his and Max pulled her close to him. The comfort of his arms felt like home. They swayed to the music as he leaned into her. She could hear the piano in the background as the tempo eased its way to the vocals. She recognized the song from the first keys played on the piano. She couldn't help but smile as it brought memories flooding back. Then, just when she thought that nothing else could surprise her, Megan felt his lips kiss her neck, then her ear as he pulled her closer, and they danced around the living room. But the moment Max began to sing, emotions overwhelmed her. How did he know the lyrics that she knew so well?

> *When the road gets dark,*
> *and you can no longer see,*

XOXO

*let my love throw a spark,*
*have a little faith in me*

He sang the song perfectly, word for word, as they glided to the music in the middle of the living room. Tears ran down her cheeks; she couldn't help it. She was stunned. She had not known that he could sing so in tune. His voice was mellow, and it was the sexiest thing that someone had ever done for her.

Max lifted her off the floor and let the music play as he kissed away her tears. He walked with her to the bedroom. "Why are you crying? I didn't mean to upset you." He sat down on the bed. "Megan, tell me?"

Megan took a deep breath. "Dad used to sing—off key of course—that song to my mother. I remember as a little girl; my parents never got upset in front of us. Dad knew that this song would always make my mom happy and he would play it and then dance with her in the living room. No matter what happened, I knew Mom would always kiss him, and they would fall more in love. We used to think they were silly grown-ups, but hearing it now just made me realize how much I miss them. How did you know? Max, you sang to me. I didn't know you could sing, and why that song?"

Max kissed her gently on the lips. He was dealing with his own memories of that song. "A few years ago, I had come home early without telling my parents. I heard that song coming from the living room, so I walked toward the music. I knew Dad loved Mom, and I could hear my mom giggling. You meet my mom, she laughs, she doesn't giggle, but with my father, she looked so happy. Just watching them dance, and dad dancing and singing off key as well, I've never seen Mom glow so much with so much love for one person. Seriously, my father was tone-deaf, but that

$$$

song made my mother happy. Then a few weeks later, I asked my father why. He told me that it was because my mom had always put her faith in him, no matter what. It wasn't always happy times for them growing up, but Mom had loved my father that much and trusted him with all her heart. So when that song came around one day, he stopped what he was doing and took her in his arms and danced with her. He said when they first got married, in the beginning, life wasn't so easy, but things turned around for him. It was the little things that my mom cherished the most. Megan, I'm not perfect, and I will screw up maybe more than once, but I do know that you are my world now, and I want to be happy. I'm sorry if it upset you, I won't play it again."

"Don't you dare! I love it, and I love you. Thank you for sharing this with me." She leaned in and kissed him. "Thank you for tonight. I have wanted you to meet Luc for the longest time. I trust him, you know, and I believe he can help." Megan touched his cheeks and kissed him slowly. She looked into his eyes and knew this was her forever; it had to be. "Max…" she whispered.

"Sleep, Megan. You need your rest. Tomorrow we have plans." Max undressed her and then stripped down himself and pulled her near, spooning her against him. "Sleep, baby." He heard her yawn and the next thing he knew; she was sound asleep.

XOXO

# Chapter Twenty

The weekend had passed in a blur. Megan knew it was time to go back to work. December was around the corner, and they had lots to finish. But as she laid in bed, she couldn't help but remember the most romantic night. 'Marry me,' he had said. She had looked at him with pure joy and screamed, 'Yes!' She stretched out her arm as she looked at the beautiful ring on her finger. She could still hear the music in the background as the song "At Last" came to an end. Max went down on one knee and opened the box of a beautiful platinum solitaire diamond ring. The night was perfect, from the dress he picked out, the shoe, underwear, right down to the jewelry, to the limo ride. It was everything a woman could dream of having. But the best part was not a dream, it was real and it was her future. Even though she knew the night was flawless, they were both keeping secrets from each other.

Megan walked into the kitchen smelling the aroma of fresh coffee. God, she loved the smell of fresh coffee. Her stomach growled, knowing she needed food. She noticed the toast, fresh fruit, and peanut butter waiting for her on the table. She heard Max talking with someone as he stood near the patio door. She sat down, waiting for him to turn. She heard him say, "I will, and yes, make the appointment." Not knowing what or with whom he was talking too—hopefully, nothing major—she noticed how tense his body was. The moment he turned and saw her there, time stood still. Their eyes connected and Megan knew that her feelings for this man would never change. Still, something was wrong, she could see it. He didn't smile at first, and then she heard him say, "Ten o'clock, Julie." Megan watched him come towards her, lifted her chin, and looked into her eyes, then kissed her with so much passion it took her breath away. The kiss was slow and demanding, and it just made her weak at the knees.

"Angel, finish your breakfast, and I will drive you to work." Max watched her as he went to the counter and poured himself another coffee. He leaned against the counter as he debated telling her. Joe had called earlier saying that Megan had to go down to the station to identify her attackers. After all these months, they finally had them. Now hopefully the bomb threats would stop.

"Max, I love the idea of you being my chauffeur, but you are a little protective right now. I'm a big girl and I can drive myself. But there is something wrong, I can tell. Is there something going on at work?"

"It's settled, I'm driving you."

"What's going on, Max? What are you not telling me?" Megan looked at him, and she knew she was not leaving this place without an explanation. Something was wrong. Whatever that call was about, had him thinking and she knew something was about to happen. Max was concerned about something. He was trying to avoid it, but his body language didn't lie if you knew him well enough. His composure wasn't the same; he had this intense look, like he was far away planning something. His jaw line was tight, and she could see the frustration in his eyes.

$$$

Megan knew he tried to hide behind that persona, he builds around himself. So whatever that call was about, it was giving her an uneasy feeling inside. Was he changing his mind about the proposal, now that she had said yes? "Max, what's wrong?"

He arched one of his brows and looked at her. "Nothing's wrong! Why do you think something would be?"

"Don't tell me nothing's wrong!" Megan got up, walked around the island, and face him. She leaned into him and wrapped her arms around his waist. She could feel him relax a little. She looked him straight in the eyes. Something was bothering him, and it had nothing to do with business. She felt his arm come around her waist. "I know something's not right because right here," She put a finger over his eyebrows, "is your worry line. So tell me, what is going on, Max? I do not want there to be secrets between us." She was keeping one from him, but she had a good reason—she needed to make sure and she needed more time.

He sighed. He did not want to tell her, but he had to, because as soon she arrived at the office, Joe would be taking her to the station. "The police caught your attackers. They have been in contact with Joe and I. We tried to hold them off as long as we could, but they insist that you come down to the station for identification."

"Is that all?" Megan blew it off. "It's about time they get what is coming to them. They left me to die, Max. They are going to jail and I have no issues with going. Is that all?"

"Joe and I didn't want to get you more involved because if they are the ones coming after me, they are coming for you also. We just want to protect you."

"Max, nothing will go wrong. I'm fine now. I'm marrying the man that I love, and nothing will happen to me. I will go down

XOXO

there and do what is right, then tonight you and I will have romantic dinner."

"Romantic, huh! Well, Miss Harrison, what are you not telling me?" Max leaned in and kissed her nose."

"Good. Now let's go. I need to stop at the condo after work to get warmer clothes. These clouds out there don't look good, and it's supposed to snow." She looked into those beautiful eyes. "Don't hide things like this from me. I love you, and it goes the same way. I do not want anything to happen to you either." She leaned up and kissed him ever so gently on the lips.

Max opened the Range Rover, and when she was secure, he closed the door. Megan watched him walk in front of the vehicle and then open his door and slide into his seat. *Am I crazy to think that such a man could have such profound feelings for me? But this goes deeper than anything I could ever imagine. I remember how Dad would look at Mom, as if she were his whole world. I can see that look in Max's eyes when he looks at me. I know that, no matter what happens, our love will always come first. We come first! How I love him more and more each day. I was crazy to fight him for so long, and now I have to fight for my family and for my unborn baby. If they do not want to think outside the box, to figure out if someone is coming after me, maybe I should call Luc. He and his team will find a way to get these jerks. No one will mess with me if I get my hands on them. I have too much to lose now.*

Megan sighed, turned her head, and looked at Max. Yes, this was moving fast, but now she just couldn't picture herself without him. She had a lot to process, from bad guys willing to hurt them to a merger. Apparently, her brother Joe and Max were in discussion about merging the companies. Max believed that it was the right thing to do, and Harrison would have exclusive rights to anything Pierce Enterprises required, from

$$$

restoration, new building. It was a shock at first, but she knew Max was thinking of the future. They rode in silence, but she still felt his hand on hers, and she knew Max would never let anything hurt her.

"What?" Max smiled at her as he held her hand. "What is that beautiful brain thinking?"

Megan sighed as she rested her head on the headrest. "Things are moving fast. It feels surreal, and I have to pinch myself."

They pulled into the parking lot of Harrison Construction and parked the car. Max took Megan's hand and squeezed it tight as he turned and looked into her eyes. He leaned in just enough that their lips were touching and said, "Yes, no regrets. You are my future." Then he kissed her. He felt her body melt into his as she opened up to him. The kiss deepened and the world around them faded, leaving them in their little bubble. He loved how Megan pulled on his coat like she couldn't get enough of him. Max pulled away first. He loved seeing her freshly kissed lips reddened by him, her flustered cheeks. She opened her eyes, and he could see the passion and the desire that she had for him. "I love you. I don't like to fight with you, Angel. I want you safe, and until we can find out who is doing this, I do not want you alone. Please promise me you will always be with someone. I hired a bodyguard for you, although I know that you are going to hate it. Until then, please promise me that no matter what, someone will be with you."

Megan looked at him and felt a shiver run through her body. All this overprotecting, overbearing alpha male thing overwhelmed her. She needed to get used to it, but she didn't want to harm herself or put her baby in harm's way, so there was nothing else she could say. "I promise, Max, that no matter what,

XOXO

someone will always be with me. I love you too." She kissed him one more time before she opened the door and walked inside.

$$$

## Chapter Twenty-One

Max knew Megan was home and safe, and he would meet up with her later, but he could not keep his mind from worrying. Another bomb threat was given to Megan this morning, and she reassured him that she was okay. He needed to find these people. His damned security was doing nothing, and he believed that there was someone on the inside, but who? This morning, he fired them all, except for a few that he trusted. Now he was hiring the best. All morning, L.E.S. was there changing everything, from cameras to keypad entries to the building, to background checks on all his employees. He was not taking any chances. However, from the moment that Joe and Luc Ellis entered his office, he knew that something was not right. If something had happened at the police station, Joe would have said something, and so would Megan, for that matter.

She was requested to identify her two attackers, and after months of searching, they had finally caught them. The bastards could rot in jail, for all he cared. The threat that Megan had received earlier that morning did not sit well. They were after her, and it pissed him off! They wanted his attention, and they had it now! That is why he had called Luc Ellis to meet with him. What he didn't expect was Joe walking in with Luc. Max

XOXO

watched as Joe and Luc took a seat in front of his desk. He knew he was not going to like the outcome by the way that Joe was looking at him. His expression was cold and hard. Max knew enough to know that Joe was pissed off. He was not the type to play guessing games and beat around the bush, so he had to ask. "What's going on, Joe? You wouldn't be here if something weren't wrong."

"Mariotto, that's what's wrong! The other guy with Chris Sutton was none other than Angelo Mariotto. Megan did not recognize him, or else she would have told us who he was. So tell me, Max, before you signed the merger documents, did you not have Mariotto Construction under contract? Why in the hell is he targeting us?" Joe glanced at Luc and then at Max. When looking back at him, Max did not show anger. He was always in control of every situation. Fear was not in his vocabulary, and he did not show his feelings. Joe saw the businessman, the controlled, arrogant asshole. When he mentioned Mariotto, he didn't flinch. Yes, Pierce had lost money in the deal, but he had gained it back within an hour. Joe was pissed off, but he was keeping it under control. He needed answers if his family was in danger, and he needed to know how to protect them. Did he not hear what he was telling him? Could somehow Mariotto be out to get him because of the bankruptcy? News on the street said that Mariotto lost everything—business, home, car. Everything he owned was gone. The bank called in the debt. Could Max Pierce be behind it all? He was powerful, that much Joe knew, and people did not cross him.

"Are you sure about this, Joe? If you are, I want full security on her, on everyone. Do you hear me?" Max slammed his hand down on his desk and looked at Luc. "Damn, I should have known not to trust them, but they never did anything wrong

$$$

in the past. The old man had gambling debt, that is how he lost everything. It had nothing to do with Pierce Enterprises. We only took back what they owed us, and we still lost thousands of dollars. Luc, whatever the cost, I want someone on Megan until we know who is behind this. If Angelo is involved, I know that Marco is not far behind. They are tight, those two. Do whatever you can to track them down. I want answers, and I want them today. Do I make myself clear?" Max was standing because he couldn't bear to sit anymore. He paces the floor of his office. If Mariotto was behind this, he was not sure how far they would go. He watched as the snow kept falling and covering everything like a blanket. "I don't like this, Joe!" He tried to control the anger inside him. He needed to stay calm and not lose focus.

"Max, trust me, I will have someone on it right away. Can you tell me anything about the deal? I've heard that name before and it's not good. Nothing was proven, but I heard they were responsible for bombing some retail stores," Luc said.

Max turned and looked at the man sitting across from him. Harrison trusted him, so he also had faith in him. Max knew that Luc cared for Megan like a sister and that alone made him trust the man, so he reached out and pulled open a drawer. He threw an envelope in front of him. He watched Luc open the file and look through it.

Luc whistled and showed it to Joe. "Damn, that is a lot of money."

"Yes, the old man was deep in debt. We found out too late, so we tried to get as much of the money back as possible. However, we did lose a few thousand on this deal. Apparently, he was good at hiding it."

"I will get O'Neil to work on this. He is the best at tracking people," Luc said. He trusted Henry O'Neil. They were best friends and had served together in the military. They were the best sharpshooters in the Canadian Forces and served their country for as long as the passion was there. The moment they decided to leave, Henry and he started LES, but he was a silent partner. "I will have an answer for you in a few hours, and even if I don't, I will still call you with an update." Luc extended his hand. "Max, always a pleasure." Just like that, he left with the file in hand, without looking back.

"Max, if Mariotto is behind this? Our families are in danger. They have mob connection, in some way, and Marco will not let this go. Who's to say that he won't come after Maggie or Ethan or even your brothers?" Joe was worried. He had his family to protect. He didn't know how brutal Marco could be, but his gut was telling him it wasn't good.

"I'm sure, but I do not believe it's the old man if Angelo is in prison, and I hope he rots in there for what he did. All I can say is that I know they are coming after me. Right now, the easiest way to get to me is through Megan. I promised you, Joe, I will kill the bastards if they put one finger on her. I will let Josh and Brandon know about this. If they want me, they will come after my family, but until Luc can get back to us, I don't want Megan to know about this. She may ask questions, but I will explain to her how serious this is."

"I agree. We may regret it, but I have your back on this. The less Megan knows, the better. Once she finds out, she may be on the warpath, but there is nothing I will not do to protect my family," Joe said. He stood. "Max, I need to go. I have a few meetings this afternoon, but we'll keep in touch." He turned and walked out the door.

"Julie, can you come to my office, please?" Max knew the moment she arrived without looking at her. "What I need to ask

$$$

you has nothing to do with business." He looked up at her, and she nodded. "I need your help on something. It's a personal favor."

"How can I help you, sir?" Julie loved her job, and she loved working with Max. He was demanding most of the time, but it was nothing she couldn't handle. He was a great boss that took care of his employees.

"I asked Megan to marry me on the weekend, and she accepted."

"Congratulations, sir!"

A smile spread across his face just thinking about her. "Thanks. Here's the thing. I want to plan this wedding for December 23. Megan doesn't know about this. Find a hotel that has a reception hall big enough to hold the ceremony and reception party afterward. Do you think you can help me out with this? There's no price limit. If you manage to find one, there will be a big bonus for you. Here are a few contact names of people I deal with who have hotels in the city. Can you check with them as to what they have available? My guess would be a hundred to a hundred fifty people. See if they can give you a deal on a room as well. I want this to be a day she will remember."

"I'll get right on it, sir." She took the list and headed out of the office with a smile on her face. She knew most of the men on the list, and believed that she would have no problem finding a place.

XOXO

## Chapter Twenty-Two

"I remember, I remember everything." Megan watched Max walk in the room as she was fixing her bag. Max had called her saying that they were going out tonight, and to pack an overnight bag.

Max walked up to her and took her hand. "Baby, what do you remember?"

"At first I knew it was Chris Sutton and the other guy. I remember now. I don't know why I had blocked it out, but it was Angelo Mariotto. Max, they are dangerous people. If Angelo was there, that means Marco was also. I know they are in prison, but I'm scared. What if something happens to you? What if..." Megan looked up into those green eyes she loved so much. "I cannot lose you, Max. They are dangerous people."

Max took Megan into his arms and held her. "Everything will be okay. I promise you nothing will happen to you or me. You have my word." He felt her sorrow, knowing everything from that night came back to her. She was shaking in his arms. "Sweetheart, everything will be okay. Luc will make sure that nothing happens to us."

"Oh Max, how do you know this? Those men came after me, they shot at my car, they could have killed me, but they didn't. How do you know?" Megan was feeling the anxiety, knowing that this was not good for her. The moment that Joe left her, everything from that night came back. Seeing Chris Sutton and the other guy with the crowbar, she knew him but she never could put a name to the face—until today. That fear of running, that if she didn't make it to the end of the hall, they would get her. She never knew why, but now she did. It was to delay the progress of the complex.

"Megan, listen to me. No harm will come to you. I will make sure of it."

"Oh God, I'm going to be sick." Megan ran to the washroom. Her anxiety was getting the best of her today. She made it just in time before all her lunch came up. Max was on her side holding her hair up. "Leave me, Max. I don't want you to see this, please."

When she stopped heaving, Max looked around the bathroom, trying to find a cold face cloth. He opened the cabinet and grabbed a towel. He hurried but just then a package fell to the floor. Not thinking anything of it, he dampened the cloth and wiped down her face. "Baby, what's wrong? You are white as a ghost." Max knelt down in front of her. "You're shaking, baby. I promise no harm will come to you."

Megan looked on the floor at the box laying there. She knew she had to tell him. It was the fifteenth time she had taken the damn test, even after Dr. Bouchard told her she was pregnant. She needed to tell him. She watched him get up and rinse the cloth again, but just as he turned and bent down, he saw the box and looked at her.

"Megan, what is this?" He knew what it was, but did this mean that she was pregnant? Why would she keep this from him? "Megan, sweetheart, are you pregnant?" Max knelt again as he took her cold hands in his. "Megan, no secrets, remember? Are you with child? Are you pregnant?" Max knew he wanted

$$$

children one day with her, but he never thought it would be this soon.

Megan looked at Max as tears started to run down her face. She wasn't sure if he was angry and happy. He was calm and his voice was soothing. She watched him as he put a hand to her face to wipe away the tears coming down her face. She had to tell him. She had to let him know that it not just her anymore. Would he want this baby as much as she did? It wasn't in the plans, well not yet anyway. First, they wanted to get married, then children would come later. She couldn't speak. Her voice had gone dry, but her heart was racing out of control. She could only answer him in a nod.

"Oh baby, you're pregnant! Why didn't you tell me?" Max looked at her as her color started to come back. "How long have you known?" He lifted her up. He didn't want to have this conversation in the bathroom. His girl was pregnant; it all made sense now. She wasn't drinking any alcohol or having her regular coffee in the morning. Everything she was eating was healthy. He didn't think about it, but now that she told him, it made sense. He walked down the hall to the living room and gently sat down with her on his lap. "My sweet Angel, talk to me."

Megan looked into Max's green eyes. She didn't see anger or fear; she saw love, joy, and passion. "I found out when Dr. Bouchard came over. We passed another test but I wasn't ready to say anything because I was scared. What if something happened? They say the first three months are crucial and maybe I just didn't want to get my hopes up again. I'm sorry I didn't tell you, but I just wanted to be sure that I was out of danger." She felt guilty.

"This changes things! We will marry, and not because you are with child, but because I love you. You are the person I want

XOXO

to be with for the rest of my life." Max placed his hand on her belly. He smiled at her and kissed her forehead. "How did this happen? Well, I know how it happened, but we were careful. How far along are you?"

"Dr. Bouchard says that I'm about nine weeks. He's going to do an ultrasound in two more weeks. Are you okay with this? I'm sorry I didn't tell you, but I just wanted to be sure first. After the first baby, I just didn't want to get my hopes up."

"Yes, I'm pleased you're pregnant! I'm going to be a father. You're my beautiful girl. I'm going to take you away this weekend to the cabin, just you and I, a getaway from all this craziness." Max held her tight. It was time to celebrate. He thought about calling an emergency meeting with both families. "Megan, do not worry about a thing. I will take good care of you and our child, but we need to let the family know, don't you agree? This is big news and they need to know. I have put out a warning to everyone today about what is going on. Extra security will be with you; Luc said he assigned Henry O'Neil to you. Trust me on this: nothing will happen to you."

Megan looked at him. She wasn't ready to tell everyone. Being unmarried and having a child, her parents would not have approved, and she wanted to marry before the child was born. She needed to tell people. Maybe it would be for the best. "Okay, but just the immediate family."

"Agreed." Max reach in his pocket and took out is cell phone. "Josh, get everyone together for me at the house. Yes, Mom and Dad also. This news is going to please them. Yes, Brandon too. Let's say at eight o'clock. Thank you." Max handed the phone to Megan. "Your turn."

She took a deep breath and dialed Joe's number from Max's phone. "Joe, it's me. Can you come over to Max's house about

$$$

eight o'clock? We have some news." Megan listened for a moment. "No, nothing wrong, we just want to get everyone there. Can you get Maggie and Ethan? Oh, can you call Luc? I want him there." She listened to what he was telling her. "Everything is fine, Joe, I promise. Max and I have some news to tell everyone. Please be there. Thank you, Joe. See you later. Yah, love you too." Megan hung up and looked at Max. "We are really doing this, right?"

"Damn right, woman! You're my life and there is nothing I will not do for you."

xoxo

## Chapter Twenty-Three

Two weeks ago, Maggie found out she was going to be an auntie. Her baby sister was going to have a baby. She also knew that Max was pulling out all stops to make this wedding work. That was his surprise to his soon to be wife, which of course she didn't know. Max had decided the same day she told everyone that she was pregnant, so he started on his plan for the wedding ceremony. Joe was in charge of the arches, Lizzie and she were in charge of the family and guests, with the help of Max's mother. He was doing this all without her knowledge. In the meantime, Max gave Megan a date that he wanted to get married to keep her busy, so she wouldn't collide with his plans.

Max swore everyone to secrecy. She hated the idea, of course, but she went along with it. Maggie could hear Megan's frustration as she slammed down the phone one more time. Maggie hated to see her sister angry and frustrated. She was pregnant for Christ's sake. *Doesn't he know that he shouldn't play with a woman's emotions like that? It's not okay for her stress level.* Maggie walked to Megan's office. She leaned on the door frame and couldn't help but smile at her, but she couldn't give it away. Megan was banging her on her desk. "Stop, Megan. You will give yourself a headache doing that." Maggie walked in and lifted Megan's head.

"I can't do it, Mags. What was I thinking to say yes to this? I love him, but this is impossible to plan in less than four weeks. Everyone I called either tells me good luck, or dies laughing at me. I give up."

Maggie came around her desk and knelt in front of her. "Listen to me. Don't stress out on this, okay? Lizzie and I will put our heads together and we'll come up with something. Everything will be all right. Even if we have to do a home wedding, I'm sure Mrs. Pierce's house could accommodate. Have you seen that house?" Maggie smiled at her.

Megan hadn't realized that a tear escaped as she listened to Maggie. Could there be hope? "Really? Do you realize we only have twenty-three days to plan this?" With everything else around them, so far she hadn't heard about any demands or more threats—unless Max wasn't giving her the information. Still, there was always that concern in the back of her mind.

Maggie wiped the lone tear from her face. She needed support; she needed her big sister to give her the strength to pull this off. "I'm always up for a good challenge, aren't you? We'll call Lizzie and have a girl's night tonight. What do you say? Mom always said three heads are better than one. Now clean up this mess. Let me finish the design and we will leave around seven. What do you say?" Maggie watched as Megan smiled back at her, giving her hope. She knew she could rely on her.

"Okay, let me call Max and let him know so he doesn't worry about me." Megan picked up the phone and dialed Max. She watched her sister leave and heard Max's voice on the other line.

"Hello, beautiful!" Max could hear she was hesitant on the line. Something was bothering her. "Everything okay at work?"

$$$

"Are you sure we can pull this wedding off by December 30, because I'm not getting anywhere. I'm at a roadblock, but Maggie believes that we can pull something off if we put our heads together. Why can't we wait until after the baby is born? Please." *There, I said it. Does this make me a coward?* Megan heard him take a frustrated breath from the other end of the line, but when he spoke, he was sweet and calm.

"Angel, I don't want to wait. You and I should be married before our child is born. Do you need help? I can make a few calls if you like."

Megan closed her eyes and listened to Max's baritone voice as he hummed the song she loved so much, which eased her tension. "Max, I give it one more week. Promise me that if I cannot find a hall, we'll fly to Vegas."

Max laughed; "Baby, don't tempt me, because you know I will."

"I know you would. I just wanted to tell you that Liz and Mags will come to the condo tonight. Maybe we can figure something out. So see you later, okay? I love you." Megan could finally breathe. This man eased her tension and she felt much better talking to him.

"Love you too. Drive safe, Angel." He hung up the phone and couldn't help but grin at the thought that she would never know what hit her. He looked at the text that he had just received from Maggie: **She's panicking. We have to pretend to secure something.**

Max replied: **Everything's under control. I talked to a buddy of mine. He's calling her shortly to tell her they have an opening on December 30.**

Maggie texted back: **You're a cruel man, Max Pierce. You do know she is carrying your child, right? She doesn't need the stress of planning a wedding. But I know what you're planning will be the most romantic thing my sister will ever have, and for that, I will forgive you.**

XOXO

Max couldn't help but grin and replied: **Only because I love your sister to the moon and back.**

"Maggie, it's done, I just received a call from the Ritz saying they have an opening on December 30. Now the hard part, getting everyone there; so much to do with so little time." Megan walked in all dressed and ready to go. She sat down in the chair in front of Maggie's desk. "I'm ready to go when you are."

"See? You worried for nothing. I knew something would come through. Now, let me start my car because it's cold outside. Winter came early this year, give me the warm summer months, compared to the cold winter one anytime." Maggie closed everything down and put her coat on. "Why is it that we are always the last two people in this office? Come the New Year, we must leave earlier." They walked toward the front door, punched in the security code, and locked the door.

"I hear you, sister. Once the baby arrives, it will be fewer hours and more home time."

"Let's ride together. We can pick up your car tomorrow when I drive you back, but I'm sure Max will give you a ride." Maggie looked around the parking lot again. Joe said to be on guard in case they left late. Megan's car was at the far end of the parking lot near the field. "Why did you park so far away?" Maggie asked as she was about to get into her car and saw Megan walking toward hers. "What are you doing? Get in the car, Megan."

"I need a folder in the back seat. I forgot about it. It's a guest list." Megan stopped and looked at her sister. "Damn, it's cold out tonight. I should be wearing a parka."

"Megs, let me get it for you. Get in the car. Besides, mine is all warmed up."

Megan didn't hesitate—she was cold. "Back seat, blue folder. I will unlock the car." Megan clicked on the car key to open her car

$$$

door. She tried a few time but the damn thing wasn't working. New car and it's already broken, she presses the button one more time and she heard a click. She looked up at her sister halfway across the parking lot, and next thing she knew, her body was thrown against her sister's car and she fell to the ground. An incredible noise echoed in the air. She blinked then looked up to seeing her sister flying through the air, as she hit the cold asphalt. Megan covered herself with her arms, as she heard the noise of glass cracking and her car lifted through the air, then landed back down on the ground with an incredible boom. The look of horror spread across her face and she screamed. "Maggie!" The loud noise deafened her. She watched her car blow up into a thousand pieces, with parts flying through the air. The smoke made dark clouds rise into the night air as the flames burned through her vehicle. Alarms came from inside the Harrison building. She screamed to Maggie, lying on the ground, not moving. "Oh god, this cannot be happening. Why me, dammit?" She mumble to herself. The sound of the explosion would wake up everyone from a couple of miles away. In the distance, she could hear sirens. She screamed out Maggie's name again and started crawling toward her sister. She didn't care about the cold ground beneath her. All she wanted to do was get to her sister. Megan needed to know that Maggie was alright. She looked around, but there was no one. *Where the hell were her bodyguards?* She heard the sound of a vehicle approaching at lightning speed and two doors flew open. Two uniformed guards with the LES logo drew their weapons as they worked together to survey the area.

Megan heard them yell, "Stay down." She watched one man run in Maggie's direction. He carefully checked her out, making sure nothing was broken. He yelled, "She's okay." He lifted her

XOXO

into his arms like she weighed nothing and cradled her towards the vehicle. Megan recognized the guy; they called him as Sanchez, one of the Luc Ellis Security team. He was a beast and very scary looking, the kind of guy you didn't want to see in a dark alley. Megan looked at Henry kneeling in front of her; "Henry, Maggie, oh god, please tell me she's okay."

"Megan, are you hurt?" Henry looked her over making sure she had nothing broken.

Megan heard Sanchez scream she was okay; "I'm fine, why does this keep happening I thought everything was okay they were still in prison?" Megan looked at Henry O'Neil was Luc's best friend and partner. She had talked to him a few times over the years. Henry lifted Megan into his arms as he ran to the SUV and secured her inside.

She looked at Henry, and shook her head. *How can he be so calm, when everything around her was on fire, glass cracking, things exploding?* The man showed no fear, and he did everything fast and efficiently. As panic started to consume her, all she could think about was her sister. She hoped she would be okay. Megan took a deep breath trying to keep the tears at bay as reality finally overcame her. She realized that tonight, she could have died!

$$$

## Chapter Twenty-Four

Megan hadn't said much. She looked at Henry as he got behind the wheel and reversed the SUV. Megan looked at his eyes through the mirror. Her hands were shaking, and her heart was beating so fast. Megan knew that she needed to calm down. She needed to make sure that the baby was okay. Megan felt a pain in her left shoulder, and it hurt like the dickens, but she was alive. She couldn't calm herself; her body was shaken up. She looked at Maggie then at Henry again. "Henry, we need to call Max and my brothers." She turned her attention back to Maggie. Megan saw Maggie stirring and finally opened her eyes. "Thank God. Don't scare me like that, Mags!" She held on to her for dear life as Henry maneuvered the vehicle out of Harrison. He headed west toward the highway, and the man was driving like a madman, passing cars left and right.

Then she heard Max yelling through the speakers of the vehicle and the words that he was barking were not pleasant. She listened to the authority in his voice. She knew deep down that Max didn't like to be given bad news, mainly when it concerned her safety. Megan knew she needed to calm him down. "Baby, I'm here, I'm fine, but I think Maggie's hurt. We need a doctor. We need to get her to the hospital. Please, Max, I need you. That could have been me. Maggie was heading to my car, but it blew up before she reached it. She's hurt, Max!" Megan was breathing hard and fast. She felt her heart racing. She knew that she should take a few deep breaths to calm herself, but couldn't get her heart to calm.

Just like that, she heard Max's voice change. He was no longer the arrogant businessman barking orders to everyone; he was now her Max. "Listen, Angel, Henry is taking you to the hospital. Stay with Maggie; I will be there shortly. I will call Joe and Ethan. Henry, do not leave her side. Glue yourself to her if you have to. Stay by her side until I get there." Then the phone died. Henry looked over at Sanchez. He knew that this should not have happened. As they drove toward the hospital, they could hear the sirens in the distance; fire trucks and police were heading to the site.

*Why does shit like this happen to me?* She thought. *When is this going to stop?* Megan looked at her sister and took her hand. "Mags, are you okay?" Maggie's face had a few cuts but nothing deep enough to scar. One of her arms looked limp, and she could have broken it, but she couldn't tell under her coat. She watched as her sister started to come around. She was laying on her back as she held her head on her lap. "Maggie, please do not move. I'm not sure if you broke your arm." She tried to reassure her, but as she watched her face, she knew she was hurting.

"What the hell happened?" Maggie was looking at Megan as she bit back a sharp pain in her right arm. "And who are those guys? Where are we?" Maggie was unsure of what had just happened. She remembered walking to Megan's car and then nothing. Maggie looked at Megan as another pain ran through her. She waited for her sister to answer the question. "Fuck, Meg! What the hell happened?" As she looked up at her, she tried to

$$$

straighten up but she couldn't. It took her a few tries as the car was moving and going through red lights and swaying from side to side. "Hey buddy, easy asshole, I'm hurt here," she yelled.

Megan couldn't help but laugh, even though she shouldn't. The Harrison frustration was coming out of her sister's mouth, and she knew that she would be okay. A few bumps and scratches, but she would be okay. "My car exploded and if it wasn't for you stopping me, that could have been me. Mags, I'm sorry, I never meant for this to happen to you." She held her good hand. "I never knew that they would physically do it. I only thought that they wanted to scare me." Megan kept Maggie's hand, feeling remorse and knowing her sister was hurt.

"What the fuck who would want you dead? Who the fuck are they?" Maggie heard a chuckle from the front seat and this made her more agitated. Hell, she was always the calm one in the family. She knew how to handle Joe and Ethan because god knows those two were more like her father, but deep down Maggie had the Harrison blood in her, and when she wanted answers, she needed them now.

"Ladies, we are here. Don't move!" Sanchez jumped out first as he swung open the back door and pulled Maggie out. "Miss."

Maggie looked at the goon trying to manhandle her. The guy was impressive; built like a brick wall knowing it would take an army to bring him down. He was at least six-three, if not more. "Hey buddy, I can walk. I do have two feet, you know. Let me go now." Maggie screamed in frustration. Yeah, she was mad, but she was still trying to remember what the hell happened. She watched the guy hold up both his hands but stayed close to her just in case.

"Mags, he's only trying to help. Let him do his job," Megan replied.

xoxo

"Megan, who the hell are they, and what job are they doing?" Maggie was frustrated and another pain shot through her. She knew what her sister was doing, avoiding the question, and if she didn't get an answer soon, she was going to hurt someone, starting with the goons that kept touching her. She hit his arm away from her.

"They are my bodyguards. Max insisted on them. What happened tonight shouldn't have happened, and I'm sorry you got hurt," Megan replied.

Maggie inhaled a deep breath trying to contain the pain. "What the hell? Wait a minute, is this what Max was talking about a few weeks ago, about us watching our backs, and extra security?" She kept walking towards the entrance of the hospital with the two goons following behind. She held onto Megan's arm. "This arm is killing me; I think it's broken." Maggie looked at her sister. "Megan, are you okay? Is the baby okay?"

Megan was holding back tears. She looked over her shoulder and found Henry looking at her. She looked at him again, but she couldn't tell what he was thinking. The man showed no fear, he was completely emotionless. Then she looked at her sister. "I'm fine, but I will get myself checked out. I haven't felt any pain or anything."

Megan watched the nurse take Maggie away. She was grateful that she didn't have to wait, even though she was shaking inside. She knew that she should also get checked out. Henry was at her side.

"Nurse, this woman is pregnant. We need to have her checked out, please." Henry looked at Megan as she held on to him.

Megan finally lets out a deep breath. She needed to sit down. She knew she was high on adrenaline. She felt someone holding her elbow and looked up at Henry. "I need to sit down unless you

$$$

want to pick me up from the floor." She knew that it was just a matter of time. She could feel that her nerves were finally letting go and her knees weakened as she held onto Henry for support.

Henry took hold of Megan. "The nurse will be checking you out." He led her to the wheelchair the nurse brought to him and they took her to a room to get her checked out.

Megan looked at Henry as they wheeled her into a room, before the doctor showed up. She finally broke the silence. "Henry, how did they get so close? I usually click my keys just before I reach my car. I could have died!" She looked concerned. "You know Max will want answers."

"I wish I knew. We have not seen anyone come in or out of the area. We have surveillance twenty-four hours. Sanchez and I were just relieving the afternoon shift when we showed up," Henry replied. "I've called Luc in. Whoever it was, you better believe we will find the asshole. There was a blind spot where your car was. The field was likely the entry point. Luc will survey the area to see if he can find anything. You never park your car at the end of the building, why today?"

Henry looked at her with intense eyes. He knew that protecting Megan was his number one priority and he failed her. He watched as the doctor came in and he left the room to wait outside. After fifteen minutes, the doctor came out. Henry showed his security badge and walked back into the room. Sanchez maintained his position at the door.

Megan whispered to him, "I'm all right. I just have a few scratches on my hand, nothing major, and a bruised side. The baby is fine. I want to advise you, Max will be on the warpath when he gets here, and I'm so not looking forward to it. He's going to bulldozer himself in and take over, and I can just imagine how Joe will react. You're in for a long night of debriefing. Thanks for

XOXO

being there." She was tired. She laid her head on the pillow of the uncomfortable bed.

Megan heard him before she saw him. "Where is my wife?" Max had a voice of authority that you didn't want to reckon with, unless you ready for his anger. She smiled at the thought of *wife*. Megan could hear him shouting her name even under that calmness. She looked at Henry. "He's not happy, Henry. I'm sorry." She sensed the panic in his voice. "In here, Max." It didn't take him long to find Megan.

As soon as the door flew open, she sensed the relief in his eyes as he looked at her. She watched him approach. At first, Megan thought she saw fear run across his face, but then as soon as he saw her, it changed to a look of concern. He leaned in and buried his face in her hair.

She loved the masculine scent of him and finally felt his strong arms wrapped around her. Megan knew that nothing would ever hurt her, when she was in his arms He was there with her and tears eventually flowed down her cheeks. She finally let go of the built-up emotions. Megan needed his comfort and strength right now, but most of all she needed his arms around her, to know she was home and safe in his embrace. Megan missed the daggers as he looked at Henry O'Neil.

"It's okay, baby. I'm here. Everything is fine. Are you hurt? Did the doctor check you out?" Max let her cry, but he wanted to beat someone so bad that he was having a hard time controlling his anger. Max would not lose it in front of Megan. "Sweetheart, are you sure you are okay? You're not hurt or anything?"

Megan looked up at those emerald green eyes, and a look of concern ran across his face. "I'm fine, Max. I did fall, but Maggie took most of the blast. I only hit my back and fell on my butt, but nothing hit me, just a few scratches." She felt his strong arms

$$$

wrap around her, holding her tight. "I can't breathe! Too tight, Max." He loosened his hold.

"You are not going anywhere from now on without a bodyguard, do you hear me? I am not going to jeopardize your safety and the safety of our child. If I need to lock you up, I will."

"My overprotective man, I promise!" She took both her hands and touched both sides of his face and pulled his lips to hers. She wanted him. She loved to feel his strength when she was at her worse. Until they found out who they were looking for, Megan would not put her child or herself in any danger. She finally saw Joe and Ethan walked through the door. She knew she could control Max, but the look on Joe's face was terrifying. She knew that world war three was going to happen, but this was not the place to blow up. She had to stop him. "Max, Joe, we are fine. Maggie should be fine. I'm fine."

"O'Neil, Sanchez, stay with her. I will be right back. Baby, do not move from here," Max replied. Max stood and leaned in and kissed the top of her head. She safe, he had all the money in the world, and the one thing he cannot seem to control, is her safety. He will be damn if he's going to stay on the sidelines and wait. Tonight was not just a warning, they wanted to kill her. Max never showed how brutal he can be, in front of Megan, but tonight someone was going to receiving is warp.

Megan watched Max walk up to Joe and Ethan. There were a few harsh words said, but Max stood his ground with Joe. She watched them walk out, knowing they didn't want her to hear what needed to be said. The door flew open when Maggie was rolled into her room. Megan got up and ran towards her as she kneeled in front of her. "Everything's okay. I'm so sorry, Maggie. This should have never happened. Can you please forgive me? I was so scared when I saw you lying there. I thought I had lost you." She looked at her. She had a sling on her arm and a few scratches.

"I'm fine, Meg. A few bruises and a broken arm. I rather it was me than you. Now, you think your goons can take us home?"

"Yeah, I think it can be arranged. I'm sure that Joe and Ethan would rather take you home, they didn't look too happy when they walked in, and Max took them outside. Honestly, Max wasn't in the best of mood right now, so I rather stay clear of them, till this blows over.

"Meg, you didn't hurt yourself, did you? And my niece is okay?"

"I'm all right, and she is holding up also. Just a few scratches but nothing major. I just want to go home and sleep until tomorrow. We can reschedule the planning for another night. I will call Lizzie to let her know."

Megan wanted to put tonight to bed, so she looked up at Henry. All she had to do was send him a signal and he and Sanchez were at her side. Megan watched as they came up to her and Maggie, protecting them and not letting anyone near them. They guided them out the front door of the hospital, where she found four angry men in a heated discussion. Luc had arrived, but right now she didn't care. She just wanted to go home and take a nice long bath. "Max, let's go home, I'm tired."

Megan knew that he was holding back his frustration just by the way his big hand was holding hers. She wasn't about to complain to him because right now she needed him. She knew he wanted to make sure that she was always by his side, but then she watched him stop in front of Luc and Joe.

Max took her hand and walked toward his SUV. He looked down at her, then back at Luc and his team. "I want him found, and fast. This is not over. I want answers by tomorrow. Getting

$$$

that close and installing a detonator to her car... should have never happened. Do I make myself clear?" He kissed Megan's temple and then kept walking until she was safely inside his vehicle under his watchful eye. He looked at her, knowing that he had almost lost her again. She was unharmed, but still, he leaned in and kissed her hard. He wanted to let her know that losing her was not an option. He was breathing so hard as he leaned into her forehead. "Do you know how scared I was? Do you know that losing you is not an option for me? You're my world, Megan. Those bastard got to close tonight! Megan, that should have never happened." He was trying to calm himself, easing the beast that was willing to explode inside of him.

Megan put her hand on his face. "Max, I'm okay. I know this shouldn't have happened." She took a deep breath, embracing his warmth against her skin, his lips on hers, his deep green eyes that she could easily lose herself. She kissed him again and wanted to lose herself in this man's protectiveness. "Let's go home, baby." She watched as he maneuvered the vehicle out of the hospital's parking, and then took her hand and brought it to his lips. *This ordeal was over, or is it?*

xoxo

## Chapter Twenty-Five

Max finished his email as he waited for the doctor to examine Megan. He decided that he was taking Megan to the cabin to get away from the craziness. He sent a message to all concerned: Luc, the security team, Joe and Josh, and Brandon. He read the report from Luc about the bombing.

**EMAIL FROM LUCELLIS@LES.COM**
dated December 8, 2017. 08:00am.

*Max, we tracked it down. The one responsible for the bombing is Marco Mariotto. We were able to get a satellite tracking on the day of the explosion. As you may know, bail paid for Chris Sutton and Angelo Mariotto and will be released. My team is tracking them at this time, but we still have not been able to pinpoint where Marco is. We highly recommend that you stay near and not refuse our team to stand by you. We also found out who the mole was on your security team. He was linked to the Mariotto family. It was Oliver Romano. He is the third cousin of the Mariotto family. We are looking for him as well. That is why they*

XOXO

knew your every move. I will keep you posted as soon as my team has tracked everyone down.

Sincerely,
Luc Ellis

**REPLIED: MAXPIERCE@PIERCEENTREPRISES.COM**
dated December 8 2017 09:00am

*Luc, I'm not taking any chances, but Megan needs to get away, so I'm taking her to the cabin this weekend, before our wedding on December 23. She requires a little downtime. No one will know our location due the remote area. Only my family know about this cabin. Track these bastards down fast and do whatever needs to be done.*

Max

    Megan was lying down as she stared at the ceiling. Today they were going to find out how the baby was doing. This ultra-sound was to determine that everything was going to be okay. She was at twelve weeks. Megan's mind couldn't help but wonder as she thought how grateful she was for being alive. She was lying on a small bed with her legs dangling as she looked at the poster of puppies on the ceiling. She couldn't help but laugh at that. The room was small with minimal lighting, to her right from the ultrasound machine, and to her left was Max. *Why would they give a pregnant woman a gallon of water to take, knowing that she had to pee so desperately? Don't think about it, Megan, think of something else.* Distraction yes, she could do that. She watched her soon to be husband, her fiancé. He was king of his

$$$

world, and when he barked, people jumped. Max was going to be a father, a husband. He looked like nothing ever bothered him. It was his rules and anyone that went head to head against him would lose. Max looked just perfect in his tailor-made suit, pressed shirt, and dark green silk tie. He was the kind of man that GQ magazine would love to have on their cover. His strong jaw and high cheeks bones, his perfect black hair that always looks like he just got up, and those curls she could play with his hair for hours. Messy but perfect. His eyes were like shining emeralds and when he looked at her, she got lost in them. *The desire, the passion when he looks at me makes me all gooey.* Max only showed his real feeling to the people he loved and cared about. The businessman could make anyone crawl under a desk and weep of fear.

Max looked up from his tablet and saw Megan looking at him. He smiled. *God, I would jump off this bed and take what belongs to me, strip those clothes off and taste every part of his body. I love him, and he makes me ache just by watching him. His strong muscles, his perfect abs, his kisses, and oh, those lips of his. Max has the power to do that to me. I can feel my heart racing, and I imagine him on top of me, deep inside of me.*

"Angel, stop looking at me like that. I know what you are thinking, and I want it too, but for now, focus. The doctor will be here shortly." He smiled.

Megan smiled back as she watched him wink at her. Just as she was about to jump off the bed, she heard a knock on the door and the doctor entered. "Later," she said and licked her lips. She knew he was thinking the same thing.

"Good morning, Max, Megan. Are you ready to see your baby?"

"Morning, Ed. We are both ready, yes," Max said.

XOXO

The cool gel that went on her belly gave her a shiver as she watched the monitor. She felt Max's hand on hers as they both watched.

"Would you like to hear the heartbeat?"

They both said "yes" in unison. Tears fell out of Megan's eyes. She was overwhelmed with happiness. The last time, she didn't have a chance to hear her unborn child's heartbeat, but now, her heart was flowing with all kinds of emotions. There was a life growing inside of her. *Our child.*

Max leaned in and wiped them off her cheeks and kissed her. He couldn't believe the emotions that were going through his body: excitement, joy, pride. His father could never prepare him for this kind of happiness. At that moment, he knew that he would do anything to protect both of them, his family. Then, all that went south when the doctor said, "Wait a minute!"

"What's wrong?" Max said with a look of concern on his face. He looked at Megan, who was having the same reaction.

"Well, well, look at what we have here."

They both look at each other. "Ed, is there something wrong with the baby?" Max said as he held onto Megan's hands.

"Megan, Max, you're having twins!"

Max gripped Megan's hand harder. "What?" He could feel his legs start to give and he leaned in and held onto the bed.

"Congrats, kids. You are having twins. Now, do you want to know what you're having?"

They both looked at each other and said, "Yes."

"I couldn't see her at first because her big brother was hiding her. I will print our copy of the ultrasound so you can both have a copy." Ed wiped down her belly and then left the room.

"Oh my God! We're having a boy and a girl!" Max grinned. Love could not explain, how he was feeling right now, so much

$$$

pride and adoration for this woman. He kissed his beautiful bride to be and looked into her eyes. "Angel, we are having twins." Max beamed. He was ready to shout this to the world. "Now, you have given me the perfect gift. There are no words to describe exactly how deep my love for you is. Megan Harrison, I love you."

XOXO

# Chapter Twenty-Six

The moment they left the clinic and told her family, she just wanted to go home, but she needed to finish her work first and the day just dragged. They were prepping to close for the holidays in a few days. There were just a few things Megan needed to finish, but she had a hard time focusing. She couldn't believe she was having twins. Wow! Just a few weeks ago, she was joking, but now reality was kicking in. *Max must have some super sperm or something!* she laughed. Megan waved at the chauffeur so he could drive away, but she knew that he would wait until she was inside. She opened the garage door to Max's house—soon to be hers too. She hadn't been there for over a week now. Why the man wanted a more prominent home was beyond her. This house was big enough to fit a family of ten. As she opened the garage door, she noticed that Max's black Range Rover was already there. Megan touched the hood, and it was cold. *He must have been here a while.* She heard the click of the chain as the garage door closing after she had entered it, knowing that Max's driver must have to press the button. She noticed a new Q5 Audi Midnight blue beside his Range Rover and wondered who was with him.

XOXO

Megan entered the kitchen and turned on the light. Max had a huge kitchen that every woman would dream of having. The kitchen could entertain many guests at once. On the left, he had a French door fridge with ice built in and on the right, the range had two ovens side by side. In the middle of the kitchen, he had an island counter that could comfortably seat six to eight people around it. The black granite counter top with a hint of beige covered the surface, which brought out the ivory cabinetry. It opened up on the side to a dining room that could seat twelve. The dining room opened to a full glass sliding door that viewed a snow-covered deck. The windows at the far end of the dining room cast more sunlight into it, so it had all the natural light possible. Megan turned on the light as she roamed through the house but everything was in darkness. She knew Max was there, but where?

"Max?" she yelled. Still no Max! *Where is he?* She walked down the hall to the office, nothing. She yelled out again, "Max? Are you home? You're freaking me out Max, where are you?" Still no answer! She walked up the stairs and turned left towards the master bedroom. She got closer to the first bedroom on the right. "What's that smell?" she said aloud. She looked down and saw a light coming out from under the door. She called again, "Max, are you in there?" She opened the door slowly. "Oh. My. God!" Her hand flew to her mouth as her eyes opened wide. There he was, sitting in the biggest rocking chair she had ever seen. The painted walls were green and yellow. One of the walls had Disney portraits. On one side they had princesses from Snow White, Belle, Arielle, Cinderella, and Jasmine. On the other, there were Aladdin, the Beast, and Prince Charming. There were also two mahogany cribs, one all decorated in pink and the other one in blue. There was not just one rocking chair

$$$

but two, and two changing tables. There were two of everything, from car seats to strollers. She could feel tears running down her cheek then she looked at Max. He had a smile plastered on his face, knowing what he did surprise her.

"Do you like it?" Max said.

Megan looked at him. *Did she like it? She loved it.* Knowing that he did this for her just made her heart ache for this man she loved so much. "Max, I love it! How did you manage all of this? It's beautiful!"

Max wiped the tears from her eyes and hugged her.

"Isn't it a little soon to decorate the room? Why did you pick this room?"

"After I left you this morning, I got an idea. I talked to Maggie, and she gave me the names of a few painting crews. So I hired a few people, went shopping, and tried to get everything ready before you got home. This room is my gift to you."

"Max, it's beautiful. You thought of everything. I'm so lucky to have you." She raised her hand and touched his cheek, feeling the warmth.

Max loved to feel her hand on his skin. "Well, just how lucky?" He gave her a mischievous smile.

"This lucky!" She pulled him into her and kissed him hard. As they kissed, she roamed his body until she reached his jeans. She could feel that he was already hard. *God, this man is a stud!* She dropped to her knees and released his cock from his jeans and boxers.

"Megan, what are you doing?" He looked down at her.

"Making good on a promise of pleasing you!" She grabbed his cock with her hands and licked the tip with her tongue. He bucked forward.

XOXO

"Shit, Baby! I won't last if you keep doing that!" He looked down at her, and her hair flowed over her shoulders. He watched her take him into her mouth. One of his fantasies coming true; this woman, this goddess, could bring him to his knees.

She took him in her mouth as she grabbed his shaft. She took him deep, sucking him hard and scraping his cock with her teeth. Max held her head as he pumped in and out of her mouth.

"Angel, that feels so good," he said, trying to control himself as a deep moan escaped his lips. She was taking him deeper into her throat, and he pumped faster. He knew he wouldn't last long. Her tongue and mouth were making him surrender and weak. Max felt the end was coming soon as he watched her take him in and out of her luscious mouth.

"Baby, I'm going to come! Jesus Megan! Fuccckkkk!" He bucked into her as his release hit the back of her throat. She drank every drop and licked his shaft until all evidence of his pleasure was gone. He held onto the wall behind her, so he didn't fall on top of her. She got up off the floor. Her lips were red and swollen, and her eyes were darken. He knew she was turned on and that he had to give her the same pleasure. The look of desire and lust shined through her.

"Thank you, my love, for this beautiful room. Our children will love it. I love it." She smiled at him, kissed him on the lip, and left the room.

He was still leaning on the wall, trying to regain his strength. "Where do you think you're going?" She turned and ran to their bedroom. He went after her and caught her. She squealed as he lifted her and dropped her on the bed. He said, "My turn!"

"But Max, I'm hungry."

"Oh, I'm starving too!" He lifted her skirt. "Jesus, Megan! Where's your underwear?" Max would never have known she

$$$

was bare under her skirt, but he loved what he saw. She was so ready for him. He could see her pleasure and smell it.

Megan couldn't help herself but laugh. "I took them off before I came into the house!" There was only one reason she wanted to come home. She wanted Max inside her to complete her, so they were one. Before she left the warmth of the car, she had managed to remove her underwear. Just the thought of him lately made her horny as hell. But Megan wasn't going to tell him that. A girl needs to keep them guessing.

"You're all wet for me already. I need to taste you before I take you." He took her like a starving man. He wanted her so desperately, but first Max wanted to make her come. He knew she was close, and she was as turned on as he was. "Oh, Baby! Your beauty, drives me crazy. You're always ready for me, to sink deep inside of you, your taste, your smell, when you are turned on drives me, and that is all I'll ever need."

Megan knew once Max went down on her it wouldn't take long, that she would be screaming his name. "Oh God Max, yes harder." Megan held his head in place as his tongue did the most amazing thing to her clit. She needed more. She needed him inside her. "It's my hormones! I'm always horny lately! It's like I can't get enough of you. Max, please just take me!" She felt his tongue on her fold, and as he sucked on her clit, she couldn't take any more teasing. She needed him inside of her now. "Inside now! I want you inside me, Max."

Max lifted himself and kissed, little bite, and licked her body as he went upwards. Then he took both his hands and ripped her blouse open. With one pull, buttons when flying everywhere he didn't care. He would buy her another blouse. Right now Max wanted her naked in front of him, and he wanted to be deep

XOXO

inside of her. "Jesus Megan, you're beautiful. I love your breasts." He leaned in and took one into his mouth.

"Arrgggg! She didn't care about the sensitivity of them right now. She wanted him inside of her. The man was a genius with his tongue. He could play with her body and turn her into a raging inferno, ready to erupt. Then she felt him at her entrance. "Take me, Max. Stop teasing and take me."

Max thrust into her with one quick push. She gasped at the size that invaded her. Max waiting until her body adjusted to him. He couldn't believe that he was still hard after that mind-blowing, blowjob, but there was something about her that just turned him on. He felt like a teenage boy around her, always ready. Max pushed in and out and harder each time; then he pulled out of her. He lifted and turned her around. "On your knees. Lay your face down and lift your butt up higher. You'll feel it better this way. That's it, Baby." He rubbed her clit, and she let out a small moan. He thrust back into her, grabbed both sides of her hips, and thrust into her harder, losing himself in this beautiful body of hers. She let out a loud scream; Max couldn't get enough of her pleasure noises. Her moans drove him crazy.

"Oh God, Max! You're so deep! Harder, Max! She felt like a wild animal, feeling him thrusting in behind her. She could feel every thrust. Megan felt his grip on her side as she met him thrust for thrust. She needed to come, so she placed her middle finger on her clit and circled it fast and hard. She felt the burning building inside her, feeling the tightness building, feeling only him inside her. She was close. She couldn't take anymore and wanted to scream.

He got a rhythm going, pumping into her. His heartbeat was increasing, and he could feel the blood rushing to his ears. Sweat was building on his forehead. He noticed she was teasing her

$$$

clit, so he bent down and took one of her breasts in his hand, and then squeezed her nipples. Megan was close. He could feel the wall wrapping his cock like a nice tight glove. He leaned into her and said, "Come for me, Angel, let it go." Then he bit down slowly near her ear, and that is when he felt her milking his cock, and heard her scream out his name.

"Arrrgghh!" Megan screamed as her walls tightened around his cock. "Max!" Her whole body came with a force she never knew she had, but as she milked him with her orgasm, Megan felt him thrusting into her. She dug her nails into his back, holding him. As one orgasm finished, another one was building inside her, if that could be possible. She held on and the thumping of her heart was deafening. She lost herself in the pleasure once more as he kept thrusting into her. She heard him let out a loud growl, and she felt his release inside of her. He thrust two more times and then he fell on top of her just for a second, then he rolled to her side. They stayed there, Max on his back, and took her hand in his. He lifted it to his lips and kissed it. They both laid there. It could have been minutes or hours, as they came down from their high of out of control lovemaking. They both took what they wanted, and she leaned into him, wrapped her arms around his damp skin, and felt his hand caress her back. Megan was in heaven. She had everything she ever needed. No bomb or threats would ever separate them. She loved this man with all her heart and to lose him now would kill any feeling she had.

There was not an ounce left in her to keep her eyes open, and all she could do was embrace the darkness that finally took over and she just fell asleep in his arms.

He just held her as she slept. When he started the road to getting her back, he never knew that it would be so good. Megan

XOXO

was his world now, and he would do anything in his power to protector her. He only wished they would find the asshole that was willing to hurt someone so precious to him. That bomb was a warning that he took personally. He had enemies, yes, but to go as far as to have someone killed as a warning sign—if they wanted his attention, they had it. Luc assured him that the bomb in Megan's car was planted by Mariotto from above satellite tracking, they were able to zoom in. Even with the cameras around the building, there was always a weak spot, and it just so happened it was where the car was parked. He felt it in his bones that the Mariotto family was behind this, and now they have the proof. Old man Mariotto had lost everything. He was a stupid man that made a bad investment but knew how to hide them. Yeah, he was aware that signing with him would be wrong, but he did his job in the beginning and everything was legit. Then the old man got greedy and lost at gambling. He felt Megan stirred on his arm and heard her stomach rumble. He couldn't help but laugh. "Wake up, baby."

She looked up into those green eyes and smiled. "Feed me! Hungry! I need food!" Her stomach growled again.

He kissed her nose. "I'm starving." He hit her ass. "Get up! Woman, let me make you something to eat."

"You ruined my blouse again! Max, you have to stop ripping my clothes off! I won't have anything left to wear!"

"You can walk naked all day long! That would be okay with me!" He watched her move towards the bathroom and followed her.

"Of course it would be! Wait until I'm as big as a blimp. Then you might think differently!"

"Oh no, Angel. I'll just have more of you to look at and love." He slapped her on the ass again as he passed by her to turn

$$$

on the shower. Max could hear her laughing. He adjusted the temperature and then went up behind her and circled his hands around her stomach. He kissed the top of her shoulder then looked at her in the mirror. "I love this belly. Our children! You are amazing, you know that."

She smiled back at him and followed his hands with hers. "I like it when you lose control, Max. You're an animal when you want to be, and I love that I can bring that out in you."

"You do that to me, Angel. You make me lose control. Only you can do this to me. I like it hard, baby, but I also like it slow. Now let's take a shower. Once I feed you, we can start round three. I have a night all planned and tomorrow we are heading to the cabin for a few days to rest up."

"Wow! You're really taking good care of me!"

"I'll always take care of you, Angel."


XOXO

# Chapter Twenty-Seven

"We need to stop at the Pierce estate. I have called a meeting with my family and yours before we head out to the cabin." Max took Megan's hands. "Mom made brunch for everyone, included your friends."

Megan never questioned Max's motive. When Max confirmed that Mariotto was after them and that Chris and Angelo were out on bail, so they were going to be extra cautious. Getting away meant that no one would know where they would be. She still didn't feel comfortable about going to the cabin, with no security, but Max re-assured her that they would be fine. No one knew about the Pierce cabin.

She watched Max pull out of the condo's parking with ease. With all the snow accumulation, she knew that Lizzie would never get out on her own and this would be her excuse for staying home. She knew Lizzie didn't show her feelings very well. She pretty much kept to herself, but Megan could see how tired she was. "Hey girl, how are you doing?" Lizzie hid behind her work. Her spa was her life; she never took some downtime for herself. That is why Megan, decided she was riding with them to the Pierce Estate. She knew that she came back early this morning, and she looked a little hangover.

XOXO

"Well, I got over my hangover. I think that extra bottle of Merlot was too much last night. I'm officially off wine for the next few days," Lizzie said, holding her head.

"Liz, I know we haven't talked much lately, but are you sure you're okay?" Megan knew that Lizzie hated these family reunions because last summer her and Josh had a thing, but Josh did something and Lizzie was not very forgiving.

"Meg! Do you think I'm going to talk about it with his brother sitting right beside you? Seriously?" Lizzie torqued back with a little bitterness in her voice.

Megan knew that subject was off limit. Yeah, they had a fling. Something happened and Lizzie gave him his walking papers. Lizzie didn't feel like talking about it, and sometimes it's just best to say nothing. Megan watched Max glanced at her and gave Megan a reassurance smile. He kept a good handle on the steering wheel on the drive to his parents'. The road was bad enough, and this was no time for speed, yet people were passing them like they weren't moving. Megan knew Max's attention was on the road, and there was something about his posture that worried her. He wasn't his usual relaxed self. He was gripping the steering too tight. He kept watching the mirrors, and he maneuvered the vehicle onto icy roads. "Max, what is it?" Megan couldn't hold it anymore. Something was wrong.

Max glanced at Megan. "I don't want to worry you, but I think someone is following us. I'm not sure, but that black Hummer behind us, every time I move, he moves. If I turn, he turns. But I'm not sure, it could be nothing." He gave her a reassuring smile. Max's gut was telling him something different.

Megan looked at Lizzie. Max was doing his best to keep it steady on the road. She was glad that they had all-wheel drive.

$$$

"Max, he's speeding up and getting closer," Megan said, starting to have a bad feeling.

Max pressed the button of his Bluetooth. "O'Neil, we are being followed. Are you near?" Max had security following them. He knew Luc would have his best guys on it.

"Sir, I'm three cars behind that black Hummer. I noticed as soon as you pulled out from the condo," O'Neil replied.

"You have a take on who is driving yet?" Max asked

"No! Plates unknown. It's fake, sir. I would suggest you take the next exit. Right now he's coming up fast behind you and we cannot see who is inside."

"Max, you're scaring me. Please slow down," Megan asked, then looked at Lizzie.

Max looked at Megan, trying to give her reassurance. "Hang on, ladies. I'm getting off this road. Lizzie, I need to make sure you have your safety belt on. Megan, sweetheart, everything will be okay. O'Neil is behind us. Nothing will happen." Max focused on the road ahead. He had precious cargo on board and wasn't going to let anything happen to them.

Lizzie watched as the Hummer passed beside them and saw it coming into them. She screamed, "Look out!" The huge Hummer sped up beside them and cuts them off.

Megan looked at Max, concentrating as he maneuvered the vehicle under the snow and black ice. Megan had a feeling this would not end well. All she could do was hold on and pray that nothing would happen. Megan wanted to scream as she watched the black Hummer. Max swerved around vehicles trying to get to the exit. Megan's nightmare came back as she remembered that horrible night so many years ago when she lost her baby. The Hummer was still tailgating. This nightmare will not end, just when you think everything is okay. *It isn't. My heart is beating so fast, I think I'm going to pass out, but I don't. I think this is all a dream, but it's not, this is happening again. I don't want to lose these babies. Just when you think you're in the clear, the unthinkable happen, and the* SUV *goes into a tailspin. I closed my eyes, but I just do not want to see, what we will hit, I feel my head turning in every direction, and I held on to dear life.*

Max couldn't lose his focus, he needed to straighten this SUV before someone hit them. The moment he skidded on the black ice, the SUV went into a tailspin; his primary concern was not to flip the darn SUV. They finally came to an abrupt stop leaning against the snow bank, facing the other direction into oncoming cars. Thankfully, the other cars slowed, and no one got hurt.

Megan couldn't move. She couldn't speak and felt the blood drain from her as she watched the Hummer in front of them. It was like the darn hummer was laughing at them. Then another big black SUV pulled up beside them. The security guys in the second vehicle took off after the Hummer. Snow went flying everywhere, hitting the windows and blinding them.

Megan's heart was still beating so fast, she thought it was going to explode. The moment that Max's voice broke through the fog of fear, she turned toward him. She wasn't sure if it was her nerves, but she needed to breathe. Her lungs were burning because of lack of oxygen. Megan couldn't move, but yet she watched Max reach across and unhook her belt. He grabbed her over the middle console, and then she was resting on his lap.

Max, looked over his shoulder, Lizzie was ok his concern was Megan; "Megan, sweetheart, everything is okay. We are fine." He tried to ease her shaking body, as he caressed her and kissed her cheek. Her shaking stopped as she finally took a couple of deep breaths. "Angel, talk to me. Are you okay? Lizzie is safe and I'm

$$$

fine. I want to make sure you are okay." Max was worried that Megan was or might be going into shock.

Megan began to calm down and then panic started to take over again. Her hands were flying, and she was hitting Max in the chest. "What the hell was that, Max? When is this going to stop? I can't take this anymore." Megan was angry now. She was tired of people coming after them.

Max grabbed her hand and tried to calm her down. "Angel, I promise you we will get these people, if it's the last thing I do." He kissed her tears away. "I'm sorry you are in the middle of this." He held her.

Megan looked into his eyes and knew he was telling the truth. She took a few more deep breaths, then looked over his shoulder. "Lizzie, you okay?"

"I'm fine. Your man has some driving skills, by the way," Lizzie told her.

Megan's fear subsided, and she couldn't help but laugh. "Yeah, he does, but he scared me shitless." Megan looked at Max and smiled, then kissed him. She took a few more deep breaths and finally relaxed against him for what seemed like hours, but it was only a few minutes. Megan pulled back and looked into those gorgeous greens. "Let's get out of here, baby." Megan got back into her seat and buckled up. She watched as Max eased forward, making sure that there was nothing wrong with the vehicle, and drove away.

They finally pulled into the Pierce Estate. It was the biggest house she had ever seen, and she didn't know this kind of place existed outside the city. The driveway was about a mile from the main road. It had acres of land as far as you can see. As they approached the house to the left, there was a five-car garage. One of the doors opened, and Max drove in. The main entrance had a full circle driveway, and in the middle, it had a huge water fountain. The front of the house was stone with double doors, two massive columns, with four more on each side. There were triple windows on each side of the main door.

"Wow! Max, your parents' home. I've never seen a house this big before," Lizzie said.

"Yes, it is large. When my dad bought it, he also bought the two lots beside it. It's in the country, but not far from city life. Dad would give anything to Mom, she took one look at this house and wanted it. She's the heart and soul of our family."

As they walked through a long corridor to the main entrance, they could hear voices and laughter. Max knew that she needed a distraction and he needed to make a call to security to see if they knew who the guy was.

"It's about time, Brother! What happened?" Brandon could sense something was wrong with his brother. But he also knew this was not the time to ask questions, with Megan and Lizzie and his Mom not far away. He took Megan in his arms and hugged her and kissed both her cheeks. "I still can't figure out what you see in my brother!"

She laughed. "Brandon! Charming as usual, but I only have eyes for him."

"Too bad! Oh! I see you brought me a gift." He also hugged Lizzie and kissed her on the lips. "Can I unwrap you now or later? Early Christmas gift." He winked at her, being playful.

She slapped Brandon on the shoulder and said, "Behave yourself, and no." Lizzie laughed.

He laughed and wrapped his arm around her shoulder as they walked through the living room.

"Darling, come in. Just set all your coats in the closet. Come, come. Everyone is in the living room having drinks. Megan

$$$

darling, you look beautiful! Is my boy taking good care of you?" Helen hugged her.

Megan was smiling on the outside, but if she could drink, she would be downing a shot of bourbon right now. Should she tell everyone that they were almost in an accident, or should she keep pretending? "Oh yes, Helen. I can't complain." Megan looked over her shoulder at her husband-to-be, but he wasn't paying attention. He was on his phone and he didn't seem too happy about it.

"Lizzie, it's so nice to see you again. You look lovely as always."

"Thank you for inviting me, Mrs. Pierce." Lizzie looked at her with a smile.

"Oh please, call me Helen."

Brandon looked at Max. "Oh, this is going to be fun. We've never had so many beautiful women in one place."

"Behave yourself, little brother. Don't start any trouble." Max slapped him on the back.

"The hell I won't! Josh is already walking on eggshells. Having Lizzie here should make things interesting and fun." Brandon smiled and winked at Lizzie.

"Where is he? I need to talk to both of you," Max said.

Brandon turned, looking at his brother, knowing that something was wrong. "In the den. I think he's hiding. What is this about?" He watched his brother reach for Megan and kiss her. Max said something in her ear. She smiled back at him. Max walked back towards him. Whatever was on his mind wasn't good, and he wasn't sure if he wanted to know. Without another word, he walks beside him to the den as he opened the door.

Max didn't waste any time. As soon as he came into the office followed by Brandon, he said, "I want the fuckers that are out to get me. This stops now. They almost ran us off the road on our

XOXO

way here. O'Neil lost the trail. I don't know how but he did. He found the Hummer abandoned. Megan and I are heading to the cabin today. This is why I wanted everyone in one place, so he could explain."

Josh looked at Brandon. He seemed as clueless as he was. "What are you talking about?" He watched Max pace the room as he went to the liquor cabinet and poured himself a shot of bourbon, and shot it back.

"Max, what is going on?" Josh looked at Brandon like asking him; *What the fuck?*

Max Pierce was always the one in control and didn't let anger control him, but Josh could tell whatever it was, wasn't sitting well with him. He could see how tense he was. He knew about the threats and bombs, and that Megan nearly got shot. Then the car explosion that almost killed Megan. He never seen his brother so lost at that moment.

Max turned and looked out the window. There was something peaceful: about snow-covered backyard, the peacefulness of something untouched, had a way of calming him. "If it were just me, I wouldn't give a rat's ass what they were doing, but these assholes are gunning me through Megan. On our way here this morning, we were being followed and whoever was inside that Hummer wanted to drive us off the road. He didn't care who he hurt. He wanted us to flip. I'm not sure how I was able to control it, but I did. O'Neil was tracking the vehicle, but the license plate was bogus. They tried fingerprinting but got nothing; Hummer was clean."

Brandon and Josh looked at him from behind. They walked to the window to stand by his side, and they both put a hand on his shoulder as support.

$$$

"Josh, Brandon, this is getting out of hand. I don't want to lose Megan or our children because some business deal went sour. We have always done business by the book, and our deals were what was best for Pierces Enterprises. Mariotto is after us, all of us. They want me bad enough, and in the process, they are hurting what is most precious to me. Megan! I cannot lose her; she's everything to me." Mariotto had a vendetta against him, but business was business. This was personal now, and he wasn't going down without fighting back. Max would fight for her and his children. He had the best security that money can buy, but they were always one step ahead of them.

"Max, Luc must be getting close to finding their location. Have you talked to him?" Brandon asked.

He looked at his brother. He swirled the rest of his drink in his glass and shot back the last of the liquid amber. He felt the burning sensation all the way to his stomach. Even that couldn't take away what he was feeling. "Something's coming down, I can feel it. You know how I feel when I get worried about something? I have a family to protect now. I want every resource we have to find them. We need to stop the Mariotto family before someone gets hurt."

"We've done everything legally. Our lawyers approved, and we have never complied with threats before," Josh said. "You know this isn't the first time. These attacks are personal and I understand that."

"Dammit, Josh, these are getting worse. Before it was just threats, now they are coming after us. We need to stop them. Who says they don't come after Mom or Dad, or you and Brandon? We need to up security. I couldn't live with myself if something happened to any of you. I want you to pull all the resources you have to find them. I'm giving you the full authority

XOXO

on this while I'm away. You find something, you call me or text me! Scrap that, call the main line. You know cell reception up at the cabin is pointless. Joe and Luc are working on something, but I did not have a chance to talk with him yet. Megan is always around, and I don't want to upset her. Are we clear?" Max looked at his brothers. This time he was serious. He was angry with himself for letting this go so far.

"Who don't you want to upset?" Joe said as he walked in the den, followed by Luc and Ethan.

"Joe, did you talk to that guy yet? What have you learned?" Max asked. He was tired of excuses, and he needed answers right away.

"Sorry Max, I haven't had a chance to talk to you. Luc still has his tech guy checking on it, but I have no concrete information for you just yet. Angelo was released, and Luc is on his tail, but Marco, his older brother, he's pulling the strings, and he's out for revenge for what you did to his family," Joe said.

"The old man had serious issues. He wasn't pleased with us, but we had to do it. Please keep me posted. I'm leaving this afternoon for a few days, at least for the weekend. Megan needs to relax. Josh will be able to get a hold of me. Understood? I don't want Megan to worry about this after the ordeal we had today. She was shaken up by it. I want her in a stress-free environment." Max eyed everyone in the room one by one. He wanted them stop, and everyone nodded their agreement.

"I heard about it, Luc filled me in, and I agree. I should have more information in the next couple of days. Max, please watch your back. I trust you with the life of my sister, but is it wise to go without bodyguards." Joe replied. "Is it safe to go to the cabin?"

"I've had a tail on Marco, but they still haven't found him. Sanchez has been watching the family, but nothing has happened

$$$

yet. Angelo per my knowledge is watching his back and staying low. O'Neil found the Hummer in question, but nothing came of it. Whoever was inside knew what he was doing. Max, I swear I will find this guy," Luc said. He looked him straight in the eye and then looked at the other men watching him. Luc knew that he had the trust of the brothers and Joe and Ethan, and he would make sure nothing ever happened to Max and Megan.

"Now that is something you don't see every day, "Maggie whispered into Megan's ear.

Megan looked at her sister. "What's that?" Megan watched Maggie turn her head towards the entrance of the living room, and Megan's heart thumped a little faster.

"That, my dear sister, is a lot of alpha male power, and your man is the leader of the pack." Maggie fanned herself.

Megan watched Max at the center of the pack, followed by Josh and Brandon on each side of him, with Joe, Ethan, and Luc. The men were lined up like a football team, and whatever was on their mind, they meant business. "They are hot, aren't they? And my man is the hottest one of the bunch." Megan elbowed Maggie. "Damn, I'm lucky."

"I still can't believe that those three men, look like Greek Gods. Brandon may be the youngest, but I believe that he's the best looking one of them all. I can't wait to see what kind of babies they make," Maggie told Megan. Maggie eyed them and smiled at her sister. "But I got to say, if he's the king alpha of the pack. But something is wrong, I can sense it. Just look at our brothers. The Pierce boys may fool us, but Joe we know too well. Something is definitely bothering him."

XOXO

# Chapter Twenty-Eight

Joe woke up that morning still worried about Megan going to the cabin. Something was telling him it was wrong. He looked out the window at the light snow still falling. Megan had promised him she would call. The last check call was last night when they arrived. He hadn't heard from her yet this morning. The one rule Max promised he would keep. Joe knew something was wrong. It was not like her not to call him. He had tried calling her but got nothing. The line was dead. He had a bad feeling that this was not going to end well. Luc and Josh had both called saying that they were coming over. He finished his fourth coffee that morning. It was not like him to drink that much caffeine, but the alternative, bourbon, wouldn't sit well.

He heard the door open and turned and seen Ethan, Luc, Josh, and Brandon walking in. The expression on their faces said something was wrong.

"What the fuck is going on?" Joe growled, knowing his gut was right.

Josh looked at Luc. "Joe, I cannot reach Max. Julie has tried also. It's not like him. Max always checks in with Julie. I know that the cell reception is no good in that area but the main line should be working and it's not."

xoxo

"What aren't you telling me, Luc?"

"This morning I got a call from my tech guy that is tracking the Mariotto brothers. It's not good. We got a trace on them; they are heading north. They are about three hours ahead of us," Luc said. "But that is not all." Luc looked at Brandon and gave him the floor.

Brandon looked at him. "I did some digging also," he said. "The old man owed a lot of money. Even though Pierce lost a fortune, the old man owes many others apparently. Marco was trying to make sure that nothing happened to him, so he paid off a few of the wages with a guarantee that he would get the revenge on the person that did this to his family. Marco wasn't expecting Pierce to sue them, so there is also a hit on Marco's head, from what I heard. I gave a list of the workers to Henry, and he was going to get back to me."

Luc looked at Joe and Brandon. "Your list got a hit. It was Chris Sutton. He's an old friend of Marco. They went to school together. Angelo was just tagging along to make sure that the project wouldn't get done in time. He had given false information and yet he worked for Mariotto for years," Luc said. "We didn't catch this on our first check because his real name is Christopher Suntan. He somehow changed his name and identity so he would get the job at Harrison."

Joe looked at all the men. "We need to get up there, and fast. I do not like this, Luc, not one bit. If you are saying they are heading north, that means only one thing. Max and Megan are in danger. Dammit, Luc, Max is paying enough money to have surveillance. They are both at risk; they have no bodyguards with them. Max words indicated that no one knew about the cabin, so how did they get that information if the Mariotto's are heading north. God knows where they could be now." Joe slammed his

$$$

mug on the counter. It shattered. Yes, he was pissed. "Why are we still sitting around talking when we should be on our way to the cabin? I will be honest with you: I'm not getting a good vibe on this. I know there is something wrong, I can feel it. It's not like Megan to not check in. We made a promise to each other."

Josh looked at Joe, then at his brother. "Julie called me this morning also. If there is one thing I know about Max, he always calls Julie, every morning at nine. That call did not come this morning. That is when she called me." Josh looked at Joe, then his brother. "No one knows about this cabin but our family, so if they are tracking Max, then you know those guys are heading towards them. We should be heading there now. They have three hours ahead of us, and if my calculations are right, they should be there within the hour."

Joe was listening to everyone. *The hell with it!* He thought. He turned toward the bar. He needed something strong to calm him, and poured himself a shot of bourbon. Then he walked toward the main window in his living room. Joe knew his feelings were accurate. He could sense that Megan was in trouble. He had always had a unique link with her. When she was little, he could sense her pain, her fear, or if something was wrong. "Luc, I don't know what it is, but I have this feeling that something's not right. I can feel it!"

Luc didn't have to think twice. "Joe, my team is outside. We are ready to go. I've reached out to police in the area. They are waiting for my call, but will not do anything until they have something concrete," Luc said. He knew what Joe was thinking, and it was time to head to the cabin.

"Josh, Brandon, we need to go to the cabin and check things out. I'm not staying here hoping that she will call. It's not like Megan not to call. Josh, do we need a snowmobile?"

XOXO

"No, you can get to the cabin from the main road. There is an access road that we can use to be undetected. Not many people know about it. With the snow, you will need proper gear," Josh said.

"We are ready, Joe, but we need to move fast," Luc said.

"Then let's go. Give me five minutes to get my gear." Joe and the others loaded up the SUV and headed out. He looked at the men riding with him. "I know I shouldn't worry, but it's my sister and I want no harm to come to her."

As they drove away, they knew it would take approximately four hours to get to the cabin. Once off the main road, there would be another half hour to the cabin. "We get it, Joe," said Brandon. "Max is a very powerful businessman, and he can be a prick when he wants to. Lots of people hate him. Hell, even I hate his guts sometimes, but I wouldn't want anyone to hurt him."

Josh looked at the text he had received. "Luc just texted me. He says that we should stop at the police station. We need to follow protocol."

"To hell with protocols!" Joe said. "We need to get in and get out."

"Joe, he's right," Brandon said.

"Tell you what. We'll check out the place first and then if we believe we need to the call to the police, we will," Joe said.

$$$

## Chapter Twenty-Nine

Megan has been around construction all her life, but when Max took her away for the weekend at Pierce's log cabin, she fell in love with it. From the moment they drove up to the front door, she entered the cabin and was in awe how beautiful it was. To be honest, she wasn't expecting a log cabin, but she should have known that the Pierce family would never do anything small. The main door was a double oak doorframe, and the frosted glass had a beautiful oak tree design. When she walked into the main entrance, she was happy that it was still daylight. The view was breathtaking. The windows ran from floor to ceiling and side to side, giving them the most fantastic view of the lake as the sun was setting in the distance. The cathedral ceiling made the place look even more welcoming. They went down two steps to get to the living room. On the left there was a huge rock fireplace with a massive oak mantel, and to the right, it opened to the kitchen, then the dining room. The north side was the window from the living room to the dining room. She couldn't help but fall in love with it. The place was so peaceful and quiet; just what she needed. Tranquility. What she loved the most was the bare window that didn't hide the beauty of the lake. When Max promised something, he kept his word. That night they made

XOXO

love in front of the fireplace, in the bedroom, and any other place. He made it special for her.

The next morning, they woke up in each other's arms. They were exhausted due to do the lovemaking and just being together. Megan couldn't be happier to have the peace of mind she needed finally. No bad guys, no traffic. They woke up early and decided on an early morning walk. Even though the weather was cold, she dressed for it. Max was excited to show her around. They knew there was no one around for miles. The snow had stopped, and Max said that the fresh air would do both of them good. They walked hand in hand in silence. The sun was shining, and the reflections sparkled like crystal against the snow. This place was so remote that they could only hear the wildlife around them. As they walked side by side, the ground crunched under their feet. They couldn't hear anything; it was entirely peaceful. The cold north breeze would chill their faces. From time to time, Max would point out where he could see a deer walking by, but then they would get spooked and run away. "Max, this place… I never want to leave. Thank you. You can whisk me away any time you want," Megan said.

"I know, it's one of my favorite places. Neighbors were far from each other. You should see it in the summer time with the lake and the wildlife that surrounds this place. Mom and Dad used to come up here all the time. Now, we hardly ever come up. With business booming, I'm always flying out at the last minute. I guess I just forgot how to take the time to unwind." He held her close and kissed her forehead.

"I sure hope that things will change once the twins come."

"Baby, Brandon, and Josh will get more work, and I'll be working more from home so I can be nearby. I'm planning on coming up here in the summertime for family time. That is a

$$$

promise. The kids will love it here like we did when we were young," Max said.

"Good, cause I like having you around. I would hate for your children not to know you because you were so involved in your work," Megan said.

"Oh Angel, let's head back so I can have my way with you. I still cannot have enough of you—your scent, your laugh, even the way you talk turns me on," Max said.

Megan squeezed him a little tighter. "And ruin this beautiful day?" But she thought of him undressing her and kissing her all over. "On second thought..." Megan released his hand and started to run toward the house as she let out a laugh. "Catch me if you can, big guy."

"Challenge accepted, but take it easy!" He started to run after her. But the next thing Max heard was a hissing sound. He looked up and saw a bird flying away. That is when he stumbled to his knees and felt pain in his stomach area. He looked down and noticed that the bullet had hit him in the lower abdominal area. Blood was seeping from his jacket. He saw Megan as she looked over her shoulder and all he could do was yell at her. "RUN MEGAN! GET IN THE HOUSE! NOW!"

Megan stopped as soon as she saw Max leaning forward. She heard him yell to get in the house. Like hell, she was going to leave him! She raced to him as she screamed out his name, not knowing what had happened. The moment she reached him and bent down to see what was going on, she heard the hissing that flew by her right ear, just barely missing her. She kneeled in front of Max as another bullet hit his shoulder and missed her again. "Max!" *I cannot lose him now after all this.* He raised his head, but she could see the dimness in his eyes. He was fighting to stay alert.

XOXO

"Baby, get inside! Now!" Max screamed out his concern. He needed her inside the house, knowing she would be safe inside once the alarms were on.

"No! Not without you!" Megan cried out and looked at him as her worst fear came true in front of her. She wasn't going to lose him. She tried to pull him up, but his body was too heavy for her small frame.

Max was fighting with himself to get to his feet. He stumbled as he watched Megan trying to help him. The next thing he knew, he felt a sharp pain in the back of his head and heard a loud scream. The last thing Max saw was Megan's terrified face before he fell facedown into the snow. Total darkness consumed him.

"Let me go! Let me go!" Megan cried. "You're hurting me!" She looked at the two men. She knew who they were. *How did they find us, no one knew except the family?* They had no security with them; they thought they would be safe.

"Get him inside," Megan heard one of the men tell the other. She recognized the voice. *It can't be.*

"Why don't we leave him here? He could freeze, and I'm sure my brother wouldn't care." Angelo Mariotto didn't care about Max Pierce. Ending him would be better, would love to watch him die, too bad he missed his shot, but Marco wanted him alive.

"Chris, what the hell is wrong with you? Let me go now!" Megan tried to break free from his hold, but he was much stronger than she was.

"Shut the hell up, or I will shut you up myself. Get him inside now!" Angelo dragged Max's body into the house, leaving a trail of blood in the snow, and dropped him on the floor of the master bedroom.

"Chris, let me go!" He was holding her too tight and she could hardly breathe. Megan was kicking and hitting, trying to

$$$

free herself from his hold. Chris finally let her go once they got in the house. She ran to Max's side in the bedroom. "Are you guys mental? Why are you doing this? You didn't need to shoot him!" She tried to take her coat off and tend to Max.

Chris gave orders to the other guys. "Secure the windows and remove everything electronic."

Megan looked at the other guys as they went to the windows and did something to them. She knew she was on her own, but she had to make sure that Max didn't die on her. She watched Chris Sutton looking down at her, pointing a gun. "Why are you doing this, Chris? What did we ever do to you? Answer me! Max doesn't deserve this." Megan watched them, and when they finished securing the room so she wouldn't be able to escape, they left, bringing with them the phone, computers, and cell phone. There was nothing left to call for help. They had even ripped the phone out of the wall.

Chris looked at her. "If you don't want me to gag you and tie you up, you better shut the hell up!"

She knew better not to say another word. They locked the door behind them. Megan kneeled behind Max, holding his head up. He was still breathing, which was a good sign.

Max was in and out of consciousness. He could feel pain in his shoulder, his abdominal area, and the back of his head. He could hear Megan's gentle voice. He let out a moan of pain but could not manage to open his eyes.

"Baby? Open your eyes. Don't you dare leave me, Max? Open your eyes. Let me see those beautiful eyes of yours, baby. I need you to focus on my voice. Come back to me, Max." Megan could feel she was getting through to him. He couldn't die on her, not now when she needed him the most.

XOXO

Max focused on the sweet voice asking him to open his eyes. He felt the pain, but he needed to fight this, so he did what she told him and slowly opened his eyes.

"There you are. Stay with me, Baby. Don't you dare leave me and your children? We need you, I need you. Do you hear me, Max Pierce?" She couldn't show weakness, not yet. She needed to fight and give him strength. She was fighting for her family. She was fighting for him to stay awake.

$$$

## Chapter Thirty

Max's eyes fluttered as he tried hard to open them. "Megan?" He was trying to catch his breath. "What happened?" He winced at the pain in the back of his neck and shoulder, and lower abdominal.

"Baby, you got shot. I need you to stay awake. I need to do something to stop the bleeding... I want you to stay with me, okay? Don't close your eyes. Keep talking to me. I will be right back." Megan rushed to the bathroom. She needed to work fast on this. She grabbed a few towels and took whatever was in the pharmacy, then ran to the dresser and took a few old t-shirts. She had to stop the bleeding. She had to save him, that was her priority.

Megan kneeled beside him. His breathing was slow but steady. "Baby? Are you still with me?" She heard a quiet reply.

"Yah." He had a hard time keeping his eyes open.

"I'm right here, Baby." She got up again and stripped the bed, removing the sheets from the bed and pillows. *God, I'm not sure what I'm doing.* She had to make him comfortable. "Baby, I need to take off your jacket." Megan looked at Max. She knew that this would hurt him, but she had no choice. "I want you to brace yourself; this may hurt. Okay? I need you to focus on me. Don't close your eyes, stay with me. You have to stay awake." She slowly unzipped his coat and pulled his good arm out of the sleeve. "Baby, I'm going to push you up. It's going to hurt like hell, so take a deep breath if you can."

Max held his breath as she pushed him forward. He let out a small growl. "Jesus, I'm going to kill the bastard that did this to me." He held his breath and closed his eyes. Max tried to control his breathing as he sought to contain the pain in his shoulder and his lower abdominal.

"Max? Do you think you could manage to stay like this? I need to fix you up. I have to try to stop the bleeding, okay?"

He felt her delicate hands over his back. He could concentrate on her touch. He knew that he would get through this, he had to.

"You have a nice bump on the back of your head. I can see two gunshots, one in the shoulder and the other in the abdominal region. They took my cell phone away and ripped the phone out of the wall. They did something to the windows so I can't get out. So we are stuck here for now."

"How many are they?" He was trying so hard not to yell or scream, and talking through clench teeth, was making his breathing difficult at times.

"It's Chris and the other guy, Angelo. How did they find us? Why didn't we know about this?"

"I don't know. Luc said he was tracking them."

"I have to remove your shirt. It's going to hurt. Are you ready? Hold onto me if you need to."

"Yeah. Rip it off if you can."

Megan ripped his shirt off and looked at his torso. "You got hit from the front on this one, but I don't see where it came out, and this one looks like the bullet went through your shoulder.

$$$

I think the other one is still in there. Let me fix your shoulder first." She ripped the bed sheet, then took two facecloths, one for the back and one for the front. "I need to apply pressure, so this might hurt again." Megan wasn't sure where her strength was coming from, but she wouldn't let him die, not on her watch.

She found some tape in the bathroom. She cleaned his wound and then applied pressure as she put a facecloth over it and then taped it down from his back to the front. She heard him suck in some air and clench his teeth.

"I don't know if this will stop the bleeding. Okay, let's finish this up. Hold on." She did the same on his back, but then wrapped the sheet by crisscrossing it around his shoulder blades. She needed to get pressure there so she could at least stop the bleeding somehow.

"Okay. This would have to do for now, it's the best I can do, for your shoulder for now. Now let's try to fix your abdominals. I'm worried about this one, Max. I can't see the bullet. If we don't get you to the hospital soon, this will cause major problems. I'm not sure if it hit anything inside. You could have internal bleeding. The bullet must be deeper. I will tape you up and wrap a sheet around your abdomen."

"Baby? Where did you learn all of this?" Now and then Max would close his eyes as he sucked in air to his lungs, but he knew he was getting weaker. Max loved the way she was handling this. She wasn't freaking out or fainting; she was getting right into it.

"Mom believed that everyone needed a first aid training course if they worked in construction. It's always been mandatory for us, being on job sites and all. I never feared blood like some people. I'm not sure how Ethan would handle this, but I always wanted to be a nurse. I didn't have the patience for the schooling."

xoxo

"Geez, I guess I'm the lucky one. I ended up with a beautiful nurse." Max smiled at her, or tried to anyway. Max didn't want to worry her, he felt weak, and he knew he was losing the battle to stay awake, his body was burning up, as he could feel the sweat running down his face.

"Max, this is not a laughing matter. I'm scared beyond words here. If help doesn't come soon, I'm afraid of what's going to happen to you. This bullet needs to get out, and the bump on your head is getting bigger. How are you feeling?"

"I have a little headache but nothing I can't handle. How long have I been out?" Max felt Megan's delicate hands touching the back of his head. He knew she wouldn't hurt him but the pain was excruciating. "Ouch! That hurts!" Max knew he shouldn't panic, but he also knew as well as she did that he needed a hospital.

"Sorry, Baby." Megan looked at him, and he wasn't looking good. "We haven't been here long, maybe a half hour or so. I'm trying to put as much pressure on the wound as possible. I need to stop the bleeding. Now don't move. Okay, there. Now hold on." Megan could tell what she was doing was hurting him, but she had no choice. He wasn't complaining or anything like that, but she knew if they didn't get help soon, infection would spread. "Max, I'm going to leave your boots on. I need you to stay warm for now. Can you get up? You need to lie down on the bed. I don't want you on the floor. Here, let me help you up. That's it, easy now." Megan held him tight. He was heavy, but she wasn't going to let go. They made it up to the bed, and she helped him rest against the headboard to make him as comfortable as possible. She didn't want him to have any pressure on his back or shoulder, so he leaned back in a sitting position. She covered him up with the comforter.

$$$

Max bit down, making sure his teeth were clenched together, trying to ease the pain. He knew he couldn't fool her. "Baby, I'm all right. Listen to me, Megan. There is a gun above the vanity. Use it if anything happens to me, do you hear me?" Max knew she would never use a gun, but he had to try.

"Shit! You're not fine, and no weapons. I believe we will get out of here. We have to. If I can't get you to a hospital soon, I'm not sure what's going to happen. You might get an infection due to the bullet. Hold on; I'll come right back. You're burning up." She rushed to the bathroom, took a damp cloth, rushed back to the bed to wipe down his sweating face with cold water.

"Well, well, look at this. Loverboy is awake." Angelo Mariotto had no pity for the person that screwed them over, that took everything from his family.

"You fucking piece of shit. What the hell do you want?" Anger filled his body and his nostrils flared. Max wanted to get his hands on Angelo Mariotto and kill him.

"You're dead and your beautiful girlfriend here is too. Because of you, we lost everything! It's only fair that you lose everything also."

"How was it my fault? Your father is to blame for the bankruptcy, not me," Max growled at him, knowing he was not helping the situation. He knew his parents had a gun in the bathroom, if Megan would have listened to him and brought him the damn gun.

"The hell it is! If you think you're going to get out of this alive, think again."

"Max?" Megan gave him a warning. A few months ago, she had been attacked and left on the cold cement floor, bleeding. If it weren't for Max that night, she would have died. Megan had to diffuse this anger between the two men, before someone got killed. Angelo was unstable, and he seem to be trigger happy, itching to put one more bullet into Max, she said a silent prayer, she still believe that help was on the way.

"Get your facts straight, asshole," he said with anger. "How'd you find us? This place is off the grid."

Angelo pointed the gun at him. "Tracking device. We have people too."

"Baby, he believes that I bankrupted his family business. His father was gambling big time and using funds from the company to pay off his debt." Max winced again as he tried to sit up straight.

"Lies, just lies! You screwed us, Pierce! So now I'm going to ruin you and your precious little family. I should have killed you when I had the chance."

"Angelo! Get out!" Chris said, coming up behind him. He had ordered: Marco would deal with it. Angelo was hot-headed and didn't think of the consequences.

"I don't take orders from you. I'll leave. It's just a matter of time anyway. This place will go BOOM! One more thing, if you think you can leave, think again. If you try opening that window, BOOM! If you try to open this door, BOOM! Have fun! Enjoy your last night together." Angelo left the room laughing.

Megan looked at Max. She'd never seen him that angry before. "Max, you need to stay calm. I know someone will come for us, I can feel it. You call Julie daily; she will tell someone, I know it. Plus, I've been calling Joe. He will think something up because I haven't called today."

Max looked at her. "Baby, all I want to do right now is get my hands on this piece of shit out there and kill him myself." He winced as he tried to move.

$$$

"Max, you're burning up, don't move." She put her hand on his face, and he felt warm. Megan went back to the bathroom, trying to find a bucket of something to hold cold water. She opened the cabinet door and linen closet. She finally found what she needed. She filled it up with cold water and returned to the bed. She took a facecloth and soaked it with cold water and put it on Max's face. Megan couldn't think right now, she had to believe that Joe was coming.

Max laid his head back on the headboard.

"Are you in pain?"

"Just a little, but nothing I can't handle."

"Try not to fall asleep, okay? You need to stay awake. Damn! I need to change your bandages again. Max, I'm worried you're losing to much blood."

"It'll be okay, Angel, I promise." He closed his eyes just a little. He started to feel tired, and his eyelids were become heavier and heavier by the minute, but he felt her beside him. "Don't leave me, Angel, I need you." He whispered as he closed his eyes.

Megan watched as he closed his eyes. She knew that he didn't have much time left. She had to do something. He had a gun. Maybe she had to take matters into her own hands.

XOXO

# Chapter Thirty-One

Joe pulled up on the top of the hill, followed by Luc and his team. From there they could see the cabin, but they were also out of sight in case any other vehicle came by the road. All men stepped out of the trucks and pulled out their gear. Josh was right; you had to know where the cut off was. The road curved to the right and if you didn't know there was an entrance there, you would miss it.

They all looked at Luc for guidance and waiting for his instruction, his team is the best, and this takedown was like a walk in the park for them. Joe could see the authority and respect his men had for him. He was aware that Luc, O'Neil, Sanchez, and O'Connell were all ex-military and had seen worse than this. You wouldn't know they were there until the last minute or until it was too late. They had to respect his authority on this and follow his lead. They were going in guns high, and taking down anyone that considers a threat. They didn't want to go down there without a plan. "Joe, Ethan, Brandon, and Josh, let us go in first. We can assess what's going on and talk to you through these. Luc gave an earpiece to each of them so they would know what was going on. "I've already talked to local police. They will be sending backup in about five minutes. Please guide them and give them these when they show up," Luc said. He gave them back up receivers so they could hear the conversation.

"Luc, bring my sister and Max back. Do what is necessary to make sure they go unharmed," Ethan said.

"I will. I need everyone to be on alert and ready in case someone is hurt. We may require a quick getaway." Luc looked at everyone and gave them the signal. "Men, let's move, and keep talking to a minimum." They headed towards the cabin through the snow. The sun was still high in the sky, which made their camouflage gear blend in undetected. They were all dressed in white gear, from head to toe, and their rifles were white as well, they knew what they were doing. His men move gracefully through the woods like they were ghosts. Not even a branch would crack. Joe, Josh, Brandon and Ethan, all looked at each other as they tried to focus them moving in, their gear made it difficult to see them moving in.

"Guys, there are three vehicles on site, a Range Rover, and two unknowns. Please proceed with caution." The four men surrounded the house. "Eastside clear, nothing to report," O'Neil said. "Northside kitchen area, I see two guys. One at the table and one in the kitchen near the stove," Sanchez replied. "Southside, there is one guy in the main entrance on the phone, but the living room is clear," O'Connell said.

Luc rounded the cabin from the west side and saw Megan sitting on the bed. He moved in closer to get a better view through his scope. There was only so much he could see. "Spotted Megan, moving in closer. Standby." Luc carefully check one window and moved to the other. He saw Megan tending to Max. He got a good view so Megan would seem him. He tapped lightly on the window and pulled away is face mask to making

$$$

sure she knew who it was. "Joe, I see her. She's okay, but it looks like Max is down," Luc said.

Megan was tired. Max was unconscious and hadn't woken up. She lifted her head and held out her hand. It was full of blood the bandages were seeping blood. Max was getting weaker. He needed a hospital. There was nothing more she could do. She was running out of time, and if she didn't get out of there soon, she would hate to know what would happen. She thought she heard something coming from the outside, like a scratching sound, but didn't see it. Megan looked outside, but all she could see was white, snow everywhere. She heard another little tap hit the window. She got up and went in the direction of the noise. The sun was out, making the view outside blinding. She hadn't expected to see her best friend outside looking back at her. She gasped with joy and relief. Tears fell from her eyes knowing that this nightmare would finally end. "Oh my God! Luc!" She whispered, trying not to make a sound. She smiled back at him and knew someone was looking out for her.

Luc signaled her to see if it was safe to lift the window. Megan shook her head, indicating it wasn't safe. She gestured with her hands that there was a bomb. She mouthed, "I can't." She pointed to Max, then to his rifle, and told him two shots had injured him. She heard footsteps coming down the hall and ran back to Max to sit beside him. The door opened, and this time it was Marco Mariotto.

"What do you want? I hope you're happy?" she yelled. She was tired of small talk. It was getting nowhere anyway. These men wanted revenge, and she knew that either she did something or Max would die.

xoxo

"Oh! That's where you're wrong, little lady. He's taken everything from me, and now I will take away everything from him." Marco did not pity them. He wanted Max Pierce dead.

"Marco, get your facts straight. He did nothing to you." She held Max's hand, knowing somehow he was giving her strength.

"He took away my father's company. We have nothing left. My old man liked to gamble, but he didn't deserve to lose everything, and your boy there took that away from him. He took everything away from my family and left us with nothing."

"Your father is to blame for your loss, not Max! Your dad was gambling the Pierce money away. Max got back what belonged to him."

"You're wrong!" he said through clenched teeth.

"Your dad only has himself to blame for his bankruptcy. He had no choice but to close everything down. There was no more money." Megan was keeping her breath even, feeling Max's hand squeezing hers, giving her the bravery she needed to stand up to this miserable man.

"The thing is, little lady, that someone needs to pay, because no one messes with the Mariotto Family if they know what is good for them. Because of this man, no one will trust us again. Let's just say it's an eye for an eye. But don't worry, you will not survive this either." He looked at her with a grin.

"So you included one good man in your rivalry. It wasn't Max's fault. I saw his business transactions, Marco. Your father was in debt over his head. Pierce Enterprises had to take back what was theirs. The bank took over."

"You're lying! To be honest, I'm tired of this conversation, and I just have to put everyone out of their misery." Marco lifted the rifle toward Max.

$$$

"No Marco, please! I'm sure if you talk to Max, he can help. This will not bring back your company. Please don't do this!" There was only so much Megan could do. As she watched him raise the rifle, Megan couldn't help but scream. She lay on top of Max and her only wish was that she would survive this ordeal. She whispered into his ear, "I will always love you, Max." She held his hand and wrapped herself around him.

The next thirty seconds were a blur. Megan heard glass breaking. She heard rifle shooting and a loud noise behind her. She raised her head and to listened a few more shots sounded off in the front of the cabin. She just stayed on top of Max, not moving. Two police officers came in, assessing the room. One bent down to see if there was still a pulse on Marco's body. She looked in horror as Marco was lying face up with a bullet in his head.

"Ma'am? We need to get you out right now!"

Megan looked up. This was not happening. She didn't wish death on any one, and seeing it with her eyes was surreal. She wanted to scream, and escape this never ending nightmare. Megan watched as a police officer approached in full combat gear and face mask. She finally heard what he was saying to her. "I'm not leaving him; he needs care now." She finally snapped out of it and focused on Max.

"Coast clear! Megan? Where are you?" Joe yelled. He knew she was in there, he just needed to find her.

"Joe! In here! It's Max! He's shot! I can't leave him, Joe, he needs help, and he's unconscious."

Joe, Brandon, and Josh came running in, followed by Luc on their tail. "Luc, take Megan. I'll get Max," Joe said.

xoxo

"Joe, be careful. He's lost a lot of blood. He's burning up. We need to bring him to the hospital and fast." Megan watched as all the men lifted him quickly off the bed.

"Move, Megan! We need to get out of here now!" Luc said. He wasn't wasting time. He knew that the cabin would detonate. Everyone had to get out now.

"Baby, hang on okay? Don't you die on me, Max. Joe, Josh, and Brandon are going to lift you." She heard him make a small moan. "Guys, be careful."

"Megan, you need to leave now! Max will be right behind us." Once again, Luc was tired of waiting. They needed to move. He lifted her in his arms and headed out the door.

Megan watched over Luc's shoulder as they carried Max behind her. She looked in front of her when they cleared the hallway and noticed there were three other guys dressed in white with rifles and two other police officers. Right before she stepped outside, she saw two other men on the ground. Just before leaving the cabin, she looked behind her to make sure Max was following.

Joe, Brandon, and Josh carried Max out. They reached Luc and Megan, followed by the others right behind them. Just as they were putting Max down in the back seat, they heard someone yell, "GET DOWN!"

"Hang on!" Joe got behind the wheel of the Range Rover, put it in reverse, hit the gas pedal, and backed up at full speed. "GET DOWN, MEGAN!" he yelled at her. He cleared the driveway. As everyone ran for cover, the cabin exploded. Wood and glass shattered everywhere.

Luc had covered Megan from the blast with his body. "Megan? Are you okay?"

$$$

"I'm all right, Luc. Can we please get Max to the hospital now? We don't have much time." She was high on adrenaline. All she could think about was Max. He hadn't regained consciousness, and she didn't want to think the worst.

The police cleared the way and took the lead, followed by Joe, Luc, Megan, and Max. Josh and Brandon took Joe's truck. They headed to St. Jerome Hospital because that was the closest. The emergency staff took Max right away. She watched as they wheeled him away from her, not knowing if she would see him again. She had to pray that miracles happen every day.

Joe watched his sister as she stood still. Then she collapsed into his arms. She looked exhausted. "Megan! Nurse!" He looked at her. "Megan, you need to be checked out."

Megan was fighting everyone. Even though she felt weak, she needed to stay awake for Max. She needed to be there for him.

Brandon was watching and listening to Joe, understanding his concern, so he approached her. He towered over Megan. He was the same size as Max in height. He knew that if anything ever happened to his brother, he would want them to take care of her, to be there for her through this ordeal. Brandon looked down at Megan. He raised his hand and lifted her chin, so she focused on him. "Megan, please listen to Joe. I'm sure Max will be okay, but you need to think about the babies. Max would want this. He would want us to take care of you and make sure you are all right. Let me get the nurse, okay? We just want to make sure you are alright."

Megan looked at Brandon's beautiful turquoise eyes with a spec of purple surrounding his pupil. They were so caring and warm, and filled with concern for her. She knew she had to sit down. Megan knew her legs would not hold her up much longer; the last twenty-four hours was finally catching up to her. Joe was

xoxo

right, Brandon was right, she needed to let go eventually, and let the men take care of her. She was exhausted and she didn't know how long it would be until she heard news about Max. She didn't want to give up, she needed to be strong, she needed to know that he was going to pull through. She was doing this for him. Megan raised her hand with the strength she had left and touched his cheek. "I'm fine, Brandon! I just want to make sure Max will come out of this okay."

"Baby girl, you're stressed out right now. Please do this for me. Max is in surgery, and we do not know how long it will take. Brandon is right; Max would want to make sure that we take care of you. Please, baby girl, do this for us. We are here for you, and we will make sure that nothing happens to you or Max," Joe said. "Here, sit down. You're going to pass out you are shaking so much." He held her by the elbow and made her sit down.

Megan sat down and looked at all the men standing in front of her. She remembered what her sister had said about the alpha men. She had to choose her fights, and right now she didn't have the energy to fight them. "Okay, okay already. I'll do it to make you all happy, but I don't want to leave Max. There is no way I'm leaving this hospital." Megan looked at everyone in the eye. She meant business. The next thing she knew, the hospital staff was taking her into a private room and the doctor on duty was looking at her chart. "Miss Harrison, your blood pressure is high. You're exhausted and dehydrated. You need rest. I'll give you something to help you sleep. It will not harm the babies, but you need to make sure you stay in bed." The doctor on duty admitted her for twenty-four hours. Megan knew that the guys threaten the good doctor, knowing that she wasn't helping herself by fighting exhaustion but still she didn't want to sleep.

$$$

She refused to sleep until she knew Max was out of the woods. "No, not until I am aware that Max is out of surgery."

"Miss Harrison, I strongly suggest you rest. I'll only give you a small dose. He'll be in surgery for a while. You should wake up when he's in recovery."

"No, I don't want to. What is wrong with everyone? How can I sleep when I know that Max is in surgery, not knowing if he will wake up? I couldn't live with myself. Why don't you understand my concern?" She was angry.

"Meg, please think of the babies. They've been through a lot these last twenty-four hours. You need to keep your strength up for them. You being ill over this could affect your pregnancy," Joe said.

Megan took a deep breath and looked at him. She knew he was right. What good would she be if she had a complication with the pregnancy? "Alright! But Joe, you need to promise me you'll wake me up as soon as Max comes out."

Joe stayed by Megan's side while she slept. Josh, Brandon, and Luc joined him. Ethan was sent home get a change of clothes and make the arrangements because they all knew it was going to be a long night. As he watched Josh enter the room, he knew that there was nothing to report. He had to ask just the same. "Have you heard anything yet?"

"No. Max is still in surgery, and they're not telling me anything. I left messages with the nurse to come to this room if there's anything. I can't understand why it's taking so long. He's been in surgery for almost three hours now."

The next thing they knew, the door opened and all four men stood. They watched the surgeon walk through the door. Without a word, they waited for him to speak.

XOXO

"Gentlemen, well, it was touch and go for a while. One bullet was lodged deep in his abdomen, and he lost a lot of blood. We were able to remove the bullet, but it did do some damage. We were able to stop the internal bleeding. The next forty-eight hours will be critical. He has a high risk of infection. We have him sedated. We'll be watching him closely next twenty-four. We relieve the pressure on the back of his head."

"When can we see him? That will be the first thing his wife will ask when she wakes up," Josh asked.

"Right now he's in ICU recovering, I'll have a nurse come in and give everyone an updates, and you should be able to see him tomorrow." With that, the doctor left the room.

"Joe, thank you. I might have lost my brother today. He'll be mad as hell when he wakes up, especially if he doesn't see Megan," Josh said.

Joe replied, "I hope this nightmare is finally over!"

"Not yet, Joe. The sergeant will need a full report from both Megan and Max when they wake up. I'm just happy we got to them before anything bad could happen. When I saw that guy lift the rifle, I had to take the shot. When Megan's head went down, I took him out. He was ready to shoot them," Luc said.

"You did the right thing, Luc. The rest of us just followed your lead. I don't think the Mariotto brothers will cause any more harm to anyone. It's sad that two brothers had to die," Josh said.

"Damn! I need to call Mom and Dad. They'll kick my ass if I don't let them know what happened."

Joe asked, "Josh, can you call Lizzie also? You still have her number right? Luc, will you handle Maggie, tell her where we are? Brandon, can you stay here with Megan in case she wakes up? I need to talk to the police; they are waiting."

"Sure man. I won't let anyone near her," Brandon said.

$$\$\$\$$$

## Chapter Thirty-Two

Brandon watched the snow drift from the window as the wind picked up. The weather can change in an instant; he couldn't help but wonder what the hell this world was coming too. He had almost lost his brother today. He felt angry about how people would do anything for revenge, but he knew that Pierce had done nothing wrong in the process. At least the bastards got what was coming to them. He knew that when Max woke, he would be mad as hell that someone got this close to him and Megan. He turned as he heard Megan whisper Max name. "Hey beautiful, how are you feeling?"

Megan heard nothing. She opened her eyes to a dim light, disoriented, but then it all came back to her. Her head was still feeling dizzy. "How long have I been asleep?" Megan looked at Brandon with half-closed eyes. She was having a hard time focusing. It must have been the medication.

"About four hours. You were exhausted, and you needed the rest, Megan." Brandon moved toward her.

Megan stretched her arms over her head, then touched her belly to make sure that she could still feel them. There was only one person she wanted to see right now. "Brandon, I need to see him."

XOXO

"You can't, Sunshine. No visitor is allowed in his room until tomorrow morning." He walked to the bed as he looked down at her and gave her the most incredible smile.

"What do you mean? Is everything okay? Brandon, did he pull through?"

Brandon came closer and moved a lock of hair out of Megan's face. "He's out of surgery; it was touch and go for a while. They were able to remove the bullet, he will be sleeping till tomorrow, they gave him some kind of drug so he's in lalaland right now. He lost a lot of blood, Megan. The doctors have someone watching him around the clock. We will be the first to know if anything changes."

"I knew he was losing too much blood. I tried to contain it but without the proper bandages..." She closed her eyes and sighed as she wiped a tear from her cheek. "Brandon, I tried so hard not to think about... the what if… I couldn't give up; dying was not option for me, I had to do everything in my power to keep him alive. I was so scared of losing him. Those animals refused to help. Please tell me he's okay. I can't lose him, Brandon." Megan looked him in the eyes. He looked so much like Max, but different. His features were similar, but Brandon was easy going. He had a kind face, always smiling, not that hardcore look that Max had.

"He's going to be fine, Megan, I promise. You know it will take a lot for my brother to go down. Besides, I don't think that he would want anyone else to touch you. In his eyes, you are only his, and I know he would never leave you. Be prepared, though, when he wakes up, security will be up, and Max will be an even more pissed off arrogant son-of-a-bitch than he already is." Brandon laughed.

$$$

"Oh Brandon, I just want him to be okay. I can't lose him. The babies can't lose their daddy." Megan felt weak but better knowing that Max was out of surgery.

"Sunshine, ever since you came into his life, he's been a different man. I've never seen him act this way before. Only you can bring him down to his knees. He adores you, and I know that he's fighting right now, but give him time. What you did back there may have saved his life. But right now my concern is you."

Megan heard a knock and saw the doctor walk in. "Do you have any news on Max?" She held onto Brandon's hand.

"His fever is breaking, so that's good news. The medication we gave him is working. He's still sleeping. Right now we do not want him to put any strain on his wounds, so keeping him asleep is best." The doctor looked at her chart, and everything seemed stable.

"Can I see him?" Megan asked

"Until his fever is completely gone, I don't want anyone to go in. He's still at high risk of infections, but I will instruct the nurse to keep you posted. You rest up, Ms. Harrison. You went through quite an ordeal, and we want to make sure that you and the babies are doing well. Tomorrow morning, I will personally come in, and take you to see him."

"That is our cue. We are all staying across the street. There is a guard outside if you need anything? Sleep, sunshine, and we will see our Max tomorrow." Brandon kissed her forehead and squeezed her hand.

Megan watched as Brandon left and drowsiness overwhelmed her again, and she fell asleep. Later, she gasped as she opened her eyes. She kept having the same dream, hearing the hissing, the buzzing, the gunshots, but in her dream, she had lost her one true love. She realized that she was still in the hospital bed. She could see a dim light from the doorway, then she concentrated on the man sleeping in the chair. Luc had come in during the night and she had not noticed his arrival. She slowly got out of bed, making sure that she didn't wake him. Megan walked down the hallway to the nurse's station. The lights were dim, so she didn't have to adjust her eyes too much. She whispered to the nurse so knowing how quiet everything was, it was still early and people were still sleeping. "Good morning! I would like to see Max Pierce. I'm his fiancé and I want to know how he's doing. Could you tell me which room he's in?" She gave them a reassuring smile.

"Morning! I see that you have your color back, and you look rested. Would you mind if we went back to your room so we can take your blood pressure? Then we'll go check on him."

"Look, I've been waiting patiently and obeying everyone, but right now all I want to see is Max. Please, I need to see for myself that he's okay. You don't understand, I can't lose him. I'm nothing without him."

"I'll take you, but first please follow the nurse's instruction." Luc stood beside her.

"You know where he is?" Megan saw relief in his eyes.

"Yes, now be a good girl and let the nurse take your blood pressure. We will walk down together." Luc smiled at her as she hugged him back, knowing he would keep his promise.

An hour later, Luc was walking Megan to Max's room, and she couldn't help but notice that there were two guards at his door. Luc was not taking any chances. The head nurse walked over to her before Megan entered and explained, like the previous nurse did, that the fever had broken, but he was still on alert. The doctor would come in later to check him out. Megan looked at her and she apparently told her that she had five minutes,

$$$

nothing more, just to ease the anxiety that she needed to see him. Megan thanked her and had her hand on the door, ready to push through.

Megan looked at the guards and smiled, then at Luc. "I'll be okay. I just want to make sure he's okay." Megan took a deep breath and slowly opened the door. She looked at him and felt a tear running down the side of her face. He's alive. She felt a pain that wasn't there before. She couldn't describe it. It gave her a chill all over her body. She walked to him on shaky legs, knowing that she needed to touch him. She needed to feel his warmth. As she approached and looked at his full beard and his dark skin, his body was motionless. She would give anything to see those emerald eyes.

She touched his face with her cold hand. He felt cold. "Oh my God, Max! Baby? I'm here. I'm not leaving your side. Please wake up for me." Megan took his hand and lifted it to her mouth and kissed the inner palm. "Max, please don't give up, because I'm not giving up on you. I need you too much. We have a wedding coming up. From the moment you ran into me on that beach, you owned me, you stole my heart and my soul, as I yours. We are partners, and we do not give up on each other. Do you hear me? Fight, baby fight for me, for our children, we need you." Megan whispered to him, hoping he could hear her. She leaned in and kissed his lips, lingering there, feeling his warmth. She closed her eyes, giving him strength, showing him she wasn't giving up.

XOXO

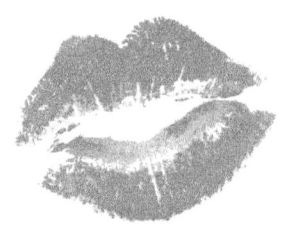

## Chapter Thirty-Three

(BACK TO PRESENT)

*Three days. That is how long I've been waiting to see those eyes. Three damn days. The doctor said that they reversed the medication so he would wake up, but that was yesterday. I know I should be patient, but who is to say that complications might happen? They don't tell me anything, all they say is to be patient. The body needs time to heal, from the moment they transferred him into his room, I have not left his side. Joe is forcing me to get some rest, but I will not rest until I know Max is in my arms again. Is that so hard to understand?*

"Baby girl!" Joe watched Megan. She hadn't left Max's side. "You cannot stay here tonight. We have rented a room for you across the street. They will call as soon as he wakes up." Joe touched her shoulder, giving her a reassuring squeeze.

"I don't want to leave him. What's going to happen if he wakes up and doesn't see me? He's going to think that something happened to me and he's going to freak out. He needs me here to reassure him. Can't we break the rules just once?" Megan watched Max sleeping. Megan looked at him; yes, his face had more color under the growth of facial hair. His heartbeat was

XOXO

steady, and she knew he was fighting his way back to her. So she needed to be here, she needed to make sure that it was her, he saw the moment he woke up.

"Megan, you need your rest. Please do this for me. Come to the Hotel; I'll leave a note with the Nurse to call me right away if there are any changes. You can't stay here all night."

Megan gave a deep sigh. She held his hands and kissed the inner palms, now feeling his pulse. She leaned in close to his ear and said, "I love you, Max. I won't be far. Please come back to me." Megan leaned in and kissed his lips gently, holding her lips to his. "I love you." She glanced at him one more time before leaving the room. She held onto Joe as she exited the hospital.

Joe hugged her goodnight and opened the door for her to make sure she walked into the room. She looked around the room and knew it would be a long night. She wouldn't be able to sleep, or if she did, it would be dosing off only for forty minutes or so at a time. Her mind was too worried about Max. She didn't even bother undressing. She laid down, but when she looked at the clock indicating three am, she had had enough. She walked across the parking lot and took the elevator to where she knew Max was sleeping. She still felt the chill in her body. So no matter how warm Megan dressed, she could never be warm enough. She looked around to see if there were any nurses on duty but they must have been doing their rounds or on a break. She didn't care. She walked to the where the guards were still standing. She approached the door and looked up. "Don't say a word." She smiled. "I just need to be with him."

"Yes, ma'am." The guard held the door for her.

Megan put her hand on his forearm. "Thank you, Henry. I'm glad you're here." She walked in without looking back. The room smelt like cleaning products that tickled her nose, but the light

$$$

was dim with the monitors still beeping low. She took off her coat and pulled a chair close to Max's bed. She held his hand in hers as she kissed the center of his palm. "Come back to me, baby. I miss you. I cannot sleep without you. I need to feel your strong arms around me, holding me. I need to listen to your breathing. It calms me. I miss the warmth of your body lying next to me, your hands that caress me as you rub circles on my belly. Oh, Max, I know I fought you for a while, but now I cannot seem to live without you. My heart aches for you. I can't seem to think straight if you are not there to ground me, to push me to be the best that I can be." Megan laid her head down on the mattress. She knew it wasn't the most comfortable position, but feeling his hand relaxed her. He was her home now. Megan pulled his hands close to her face. It gave her that solace she needed.

***

The beeping gave Max a headache. Pain that is what he felt. The humming of something he didn't know. Max's eyes fluttered, then closed again. He wished that they would turn the damn thing off. He tried again to open his eyes, slowly focusing to where he was. The room was dark, except for a light over the door. He tried to move his head, but the slight movement made it worse. He could see by the corner of his eyes where the beeping sound was coming from—it was him, the monitors hooked to his arm. The back of his head was hurting, and every time he moved, the pain worsened. His right shoulder felt tight, and his lower abdomen. For someone that was in good physical shape, his muscles felt like he was sore everywhere. He had to bite down on his lip because the pain was running through his body like a freight train. His mind was still in a fog as to why he was in this bed. The smell of cleaning product lingered in the air.

Max was trying to remember why he was in a hospital bed but he had to close his eyes again. Wishing his memory would come back to him. *What the hell happened?* All he could remember was seeing the fear in Megan's eyes as he looked up at her. Running, screaming. "Megan," he whispered. That startled him. His eyes opened again, and he felt the weight on his left hand. He looked down to his left and there she was. Megan was sleeping in the most uncomfortable position, sitting in a chair with her head leaning into his hand. He could see the dark circle under her eyes. He flexed his thumb to touch her. He traced the contour of her lips. He felt her warm breath on his thumb. He noticed her brows frowning together, and then he was looking into those beautiful crystal eyes of hers. A tear ran down her cheek, and she whispered his name. "Max!" He looked into those sleepy eyes and whispered, "My Angel."

Megan thought she was dreaming when she felt the smallest caress of a thump on her lips, but then she opened her eyes and saw that Max was looking at her. Her heart stopped for a minute. He was awake. "Oh, Max! You're awake!" More tears started running down her face. "Finally!" Megan sighed.

"Baby, what happened?" His voice sounded a little groggy and dry like he hadn't had water in a month. He licked his lips, and they also felt dry. Max closed his eyes, trying to hold back the discomfort. He held his breath as he tried to adjust himself.

"You're in the hospital, Max. Someone shot you. Do you remember?" Megan stood up and then went nearer to him as she held his good hand in hers. She felt his warmth, his strength, and knew how much he was hurting right now.

"All I remember is us taking a walk around the cabin, then nothing. Are you alright?" Max looked at her with concern. *She seemed to be okay*, he thought, but yet she looked tired.

$$$

"Oh honey, words cannot express how happy I am you are awake. You were coherent for a while after they shot you, but not long. I tried to fix you up, but then you went unconscious again. Let me get the nurse." Megan rushed out the door and ran across the hall to the nurses' station. "He's awake! Could you page the doctor right away?" She slammed her hands on the counter. She knew she shouldn't, but she wanted the doctor there immediately.

Max watched the nurse enter the room. "Welcome back, Mr. Pierce. You gave us all a good scare. You were in pretty bad shape when you came in. How are you feeling? My name is Isabelle Lapierre."

"My throat feels like sandpaper, and I think I could drink a gallon of water," Max replied.

"That's normal. As soon as the doctor finishes examining you, we'll get you some water. Your vitals are good. How is your head?"

"Good morning, Mr. Pierce! I'm Dr. O'Brien. You are at the St. Jerome Hospital. We removed the bullet, and you are recovering well." He flashed a light into his eyes and took his pulse.

Max cleared his throat. "So I heard. How long have I been out?" He watched the doctor, then found Megan still leaning against the wall.

"You've been here for four days. Let's just say you are lucky to be here. Your Ms. Harrison handled herself amazingly."

Max looked at Megan. She hadn't moved since the doctor arrived. Max was absorbing her reaction, and she seemed to be holding herself together, but he knew better. She was caressing her belly, but the look in her eyes was distant. "Four days, huh?"

The doctor did a few tests and checked his shoulder and abdomen, making sure that the bandages were holding. He checked the back of the head. The swelling was down, which was a good sign. "Do you remember anything?"

"All I remember is our walk at the cabin. After that, it's a blank," Max said.

"Well Mr. Pierce, you'll feel some soreness in the shoulder and lower abdomen. We'll be changing your bandages today. We'll do x-rays and a few more tests, but you should recover. Everything looks good, but please, you need to take it easy." The doctor gave his instructions to the nurse on duty and left the room.

Megan stood against the wall, hoping that her knees would not give out on her. She could hear the doctor talking to him, but she couldn't look away. As soon as their eyes connected, she felt the pull that only he had on her. Megan's heart was like a freight train that was going full speed. She could see him nodding, but he wouldn't move his eyes from her. She felt the longing, the hunger in his gaze. She couldn't describe it. Knowing you love someone that deep that you would die for that person. The connection of two people, knowing that your other half, your other soul, was hurting. She could feel that love, that pain, that sorrow, that happiness just by one look. Megan lost herself in those emerald eyes. He was holding her in place with only one look. Megan didn't realize that the doctor had left, that is how far gone she was, but yet she would hear a whisper of her name. Megan felt a sharp kick and held her stomach. She looked down and smiled, knowing this was the first time she felt it.

"Angel?" He looked at her. She hadn't moved. "Angel? Come here, Baby, let me hold you." Max raised his good arm, extending it to her. He wanted to reassure her that he was okay. "Megan?" He smiled at her.

$$$

Megan could feel the tears finally rolling down her face as she watched Max extend his hand to her. The stress from the last few days was finally letting go. She just couldn't hold it anymore. She eventually made her legs go forward. She reached his bed and took his hand in hers. Megan felt the warmth of his masculine hand and lifted it toward her face. She felt his thumb caressing her wet face, and she couldn't hold back any longer. He gently trace her lips with his thumb. She hadn't realized how much she missed this little affection, his touch, his caress. "Oh, Max, I was so scared. I thought..."

"Shhh! It's okay, Baby. I've got you now." It's all he could do to reassure her that he was going to be okay. He wiped away her tears.

"It's not okay, Max. Don't you ever scare me like that again! I can't lose you. I kept talking to you, asking you to fight and not to leave the babies and me. We need you. I could not live without you. I'm not sure where my strength came from; all I could think about was you. I didn't know what more I could do. They wouldn't do anything for us. They wanted us dead." Megan was rambling, not holding anything back, as the tears wouldn't stop.

"Shhh, it's okay, Angel. You made me fight. All I could think about was you, your beautiful face, your soothing voice, and knowing that you were with me. I sensed your presence, my love." Max looked at her with longing, with love. He would fight all her fear and destroy all her demons. He hadn't realized is that she had the same strength and would slay anyone that would hurt her family.

"Oh, Max."

"Come here. Lie down next to me. I need to feel your body close to me. I need to hold you, baby."

XOXO

"I don't want to hurt you. Max, you've been shot, and you are injured."

"You won't hurt me, and not having you beside me will hurt me even more. How long have you been here anyway? Tonight's your lucky night. Sleep now, Angel."

Max felt some discomfort but knowing that she wasn't sleeping was enough to keep his pain at bay. He held her on his good side and caressed her hair. After a while, they both fell back to sleep, just listening to each other breathing. They didn't need words, only each other.

$$$

## Chapter Thirty-Four

A few hours later, the door opened. Josh and Brandon both looked at each other. "Well, this is something we don't get to see every day! What do you think, Josh? I think our brother is not wasting any time." Brandon smiled at his brother with a twinkle in his eye.

Max opened his eyes and looked at his brother grinning back at him. He couldn't help but give them a look that could kill. They had disturbed their moment together.

"I guess our brother has finally come back among the living. He's not wasting any time with his girl." Josh couldn't help but grin back.

"Yeah! Didn't take him long to get her back in bed with him." They smiled at what they were seeing in front of them: a man all bandaged up holding a beautiful pregnant woman with her hair covering her face and part of his chest as she lied on his right shoulder.

Megan finally opened her eyes as she heard a growl coming from Max and laughter a little further away. "Hey! Good morning you guys!" She slowly got off the bed and kissed Max. She could sense how bad he was hurting. "I'll be right back. Boys, go easy

XOXO

on him, he only woke up a few hours ago." Megan looked at Josh and Brandon with a smile.

"Oh, we will. Don't worry." Brandon smiled back at her with a twinkle in his eyes.

"Don't make him laugh or he'll be in pain, and whatever you are thinking about, just forget about it. Your brother needs his rest. Do you understand me?" Megan's voice was clear and assertive. "I do not want anyone to stress him out."

They looked at each other and smiled back at her. "Scout's honor!"

"Oh come on, you guys, you were never Scouts!" Megan couldn't help herself. She knew they meant well; after all, they were brothers, and as far as she was aware, they stood together.

Josh held his hand to his heart and gave her those sad eyes. "Oh, Meg! I'm hurt!"

Megan rose on her tiptoes and kissed Brandon's cheek, then leaned over and kissed Josh's cheek. "Be nice, or you'll both have to deal with me! Am I clear?"

Max chuckled. "I wouldn't mess with an angry pregnant woman if I were you."

"We promise, Meg." They grinned at her as she left the room.

Megan left the room and held herself up against the wall. She raised her head to the ceiling and said a silent 'thank you.' They were going to be okay. Now it was time to tell the others. She lifted herself from the wall and walked down the long corridor to find her family.

"Nice to have you back with us," Brandon said. "That woman is a fighter, Max, and a keeper."

Max looked at both his brothers, and he wanted answers. His memory was coming back to him, but slowly. "Can someone tell me what the hell happened? I'm so pissed off right now." He

$$$

tried to raise himself as he grimaced at the pain in his lower abdomen. He took a deep breath and closed his eyes, trying to control the pain. "I need names!"

"You were right. Marco Mariotto wanted revenge on you. He believed that you bankrupted his father and because of that, he lost the business. We know that it's not true, but apparently, he didn't," Josh said.

"Find him!" He held his breath as he tried to find a comfortable place, but nothing was comfortable. His shoulder hurt, his abdomen hurt, and he had a headache the size of Houston.

Brandon looked at his brother. "You've been out for four days. When Luc and his task force and the police raided the cabin, Marco was about to shoot you. If it weren't for Megan, jumping on top of you, Luc would never have been able to make the shot. He killed him with one bullet, straight to the head. There's no reason to pursue revenge; he's a corpse now," Brandon said. He felt no remorse. The man deserved what happened to him. Pierce Family did nothing wrong.

Max looked at his brother. At least he wouldn't have to search for him. "Good."

Josh looked at him. "Oh, there's more, big brother. The two guys that were in prison, it was Mariotto that posted their bail. They were helping him and unfortunately for them, they also got hit in the attack. These two guys were Chris Sutton and Angelo, Marco's little brother. They all left the cabin in body bags—or maybe in pieces."

Max raised his head and looked at Josh. "Explain." He took a few good breaths and leaned his head on the pillow.

"There's one more thing." Brandon looked at Josh, then and Max.

XOXO

"Brandon?" Max said. He wasn't happy, and it wasn't time to play with his nerves.

"I hate to tell you this, but it's our cabin. When all this was going down, we just barely made it out. It went KABOOM!" Brandon made a gesture with his hand, emphasizing the explosion. "There's nothing left but the foundation. They rigged it from all corners."

"Brandon, I don't give a shit about the cabin. It can be rebuilt." Max leaned up and rested his head, trying to control the pain to his side and shoulder.

"The morning after you left for the cabin, Luc and Brandon received a call. They got a trace on Mariotto, and they were heading north. They had a three-hour lead on us, but we got there in time," Josh added.

"Just so you know, Mom and Dad should be here today. We had to tell them," Brandon said.

"Brandon, you didn't! You know how she gets when one of us is hurt!" Max growled as he grinded his teeth together, trying to re-adjust again. "Damn, this bed is not comfortable."

"We had to! Mom would never have forgiven us; you know that." Josh said

"I will see if Mom and Dad have arrived. Josh will wait here with you." Brandon made his way back to the waiting room. Due to restrictions, his family and Megan's family were there with close friends, waiting for good news. "Hey, guys! Good news!" He saw his family and knew that Megan had already advised everyone. "They just need to run a few more tests, but Josh is with him." Brandon approached his mom and dad and hugged his mom.

$$$

## Chapter Thirty-Five

Megan couldn't believe how two weeks passed by. Max was doing well and was out of the hospital. It was a roller coaster ride these last couple of weeks. The wedding was coming up and Max didn't want to postpone it. She kept the plans intact. She couldn't say no to him, no matter what. He was alive and back to his old self—arrogant, bossy, loving—and she wouldn't change him. She looked at her phone and saw Lizzie's name appear. "What's up, Lizzie?"

"Megan, tomorrow is December 23, and I cannot believe you getting married in less than a week, so we… when I say we… your sister and I, decided that it was time that we get pampered. We rented a hotel room downtown, and we'll have a girl's night out. I've cleared it with Max, so be ready tomorrow at ten thirty. A limo will be picking us up."

Megan laughed at Lizzie's suggestion, but it was the best gift any one could give her. After the car bombing, Max getting shot, and almost getting driven off the road, they needed girl time. What better way to be with her besties? "You're on; I will be ready."

The next morning, she walked out the door with an overnight bag. Maggie and Lizzie were sipping mimosas, and both were giggling and hugging each other. "Looks like both of you started without me, and it's so not fair. I cannot drink!"

"It's okay; we will drink for you." Maggie hugged her sister as she pulled her into the limo.

As soon they pulled away, they gave Megan some sparkling water. They all looked at each other. "Cheers to a sister, a friend, and soon to be married to Mr. Alpha man himself," Lizzie said. "Salute." They all raised their glasses together, for a toast of girls day.

The ride was short this early on Saturday morning, with no traffic. The light snow was still failing as they pulled in to the Ritz-Carlton downtown Montreal. They walked into the lobby, as they stopped and admired a twenty foot Christmas tree, fully decorated. She could hear the Christmas music overhead, the cheers around her, knowing it was so close to Christmas and people walking in and out of the cold. To the left there was a stone fireplace as she watched a few people drinking their favorite drink. She knew it would be easy to lose herself in front with her favorite book.. "Wait here, I will check us in," Maggie said. She winked at Lizzie. "The place is just festive enough to have a party, don't you think?"

"Mom would have loved this place. Did you know this was her favorite time of year? Christmas, I mean. She always loved the glitter and joy." Megan looked around, and people were happy. She wanted to run up to them and hug them.

Lizzie leaned in and hugged her. "I believe your mom is with you everywhere you go, Megan."

Megan hugged her back. "I know; I just miss her."

Maggie returned. "All set. We are on the fifteen floor."

They walked into the elevator and could hear the music as soon the door opened. What Megan didn't know was that this

$$$

floor and the sixteenth floor were all reserved for the Harrison and Pierce families. This wedding was going to be a surprise, and Megan had no clue what was happening.

Megan looked at Lizzie. "Early for a party, don't you think?" She didn't care though. This was about getting away from the pressure of planning her wedding, and she couldn't wait to relax.

Maggie and Lizzie burst out laughing. "Yeah right! It's early! I think the bubbles went to my head." Lizzie started laughing again and couldn't stop. She had to stop mid-way and crossed her legs because she was going to pee herself if she didn't stop laughing.

Megan looked at them and couldn't help but laugh too. Why she didn't know. "Your nuts; you know that right?"

"Here we are. I think we are seeing double. That bubbly was more bubbles than orange juice, I think. You should open the door yourself." Maggie couldn't stop laughing and leaning against Lizzie. They turned and watched the chauffeur bringing their bags. "Hurry, Megan, I need to pee," Maggie said.

"I'm sorry, I cannot stop!" A fit of giggles consumed her. Tears were running down Lizzie's cheeks. She was bent over and laughing like a hyena.

"You girls are crazy!" Megan swiped the key and opened the door. She heard the word 'surprise!' She backed up and bounced off Maggie and Lizzie. "What's going on?" Megan looked at Maggie and heard her sister say, "Welcome to your wedding, my dear. Today is your big day." Megan looked at Maggie. "What? No…no… it's next week." She looked confused as she was pulled in by her cousin, her aunt, and people she didn't know yet. The suite was huge, and there were at least fifty people inside.

No more laughter. Maggie and Lizzie pushed her in. "Meg, you're getting married today, in about two hours," Lizzie told her.

XOXO

"You're serious, aren't you?" Megan looked at Maggie and Lizzie. "But how?"

"My dearest sister, Max had planned this about four weeks ago, so we are all here to help you get ready for the most amazing wedding. Your dream wedding." Maggie gave her sister a small glass of bubbly. "One small glass will not harm my niece and nephew."

Megan looked at her sister with wide eyes as she shoved a glass of bubbly in her hand. They pulled her aside to a private suite, where everything and everyone was ready for her. From the stylist, the makeup artist, all Lizzie's best girls were there to do everyone's hair and makeup. By the time they finished her, Megan had her wedding dress on, her tiara, and the person reflecting back at her was the most beautiful bride she had ever seen. With thousands of butterflies in the pit of her stomach, she couldn't believe Max pulled this off. She heard a knock at the door, and her sister opened it. She saw Joe and Ethan standing there in tuxedos, all handsome. Joe approached her, noticing that he had a Tiffany rectangular box in his hands. "Joe, Ethan…" A lump was building in her throat. She felt a tear building in her eyes, and she tapped it with a tissue.

"No crying, Megan. I have a gift for you from your future husband." Joe handed it to her. She opened it. Laid on blue velvet was a diamond sapphire bracelet and necklace to match. "Joe, it's beautiful!"

"Max wanted you to have this before you head downstairs," Joe replied

Maggie took the necklace and bracelet from Joe and helped to put it on her sister. She watched her sister through the mirror. It was exquisite, the jewelry complemented the dress. Max knew about everything, he thought about everything.

$$\$\$\$$$

Joe looked at his sister, knowing that his father would have loved seeing his daughter, how beautiful she was. He would have been a proud father walking her down the aisle. "Baby girl, you are exquisite! Mom and Dad would be so proud of you right now. I would be honored you asked me to walk you down the aisle," Joe said.

"Oh Joe, thank you. But you know what? Mom and Dad are with us. Maggie got Mom's wedding dress fixed up for me. I'm wearing her earrings for something borrowed. They're the ones Dad gave her. So I know they're with us right now." Megan hugged him, then hugged Ethan.

"Now, we should go before he sends an army in for you. That man is on edge right now. He hasn't seen you since yesterday, and he's ready to break down the door." Joe extended his arm and Megan took it.

Megan held onto her brother's arms in the elevator. She felt like she would pass out. She wasn't nervous to marry Max, it was just all the excitement of her perfect day. She held onto Joe's arm as they descended to the main floor. It seemed like an eternity. This is what she had waited for, to marry the man she couldn't live without him. She loved him with all her heart. She watched the floor passing. She squeezed Joe's arm again as she took a deep breath.

"Megan, if you hold any tighter, I'll lose circulation in my arm! It will be alright; it's not like you don't want this. You both do. You and Max are good for each other and what I've learned is that this man is crazy about you. I had my doubts, but he has proven himself. He loves you, Baby Girl, and this will be a piece of cake. You can do this."

"Thank you, Joe." Megan leaned up and kissed him, right before the elevator doors opened.

XOXO

## Chapter Thirty-Six

From the moment Megan walked off the elevator, everyone became silent, as whispers and looks as she walk down the hall. Then the unthinkable happened as people started to applaud, and cheer her on. Megan felt Joe hold her a little tighter as people wishing her luck and chanting how beautiful she looks. *Like I need it right, I faced death and survived not once but twice. But still, I had the eerie feeling that this was happening to me today, marrying Max Pierce my other half, my soul mate.* Joe and Megan walk further down the corridor, where two large men were guarding the two large oak doors. We stopped, and Megan looked at Joe; he took both her hands in his and smiled.

"Megan, I love you; I know that you wish Mom and Dad would be here, but they are in spirit, they are with us in our hearts. I'm so honored to walk you down the aisle. You have become a beautiful woman; sometimes I wonder where that little girl went that was always on my side. But I know that Mom and Dad would be proud of you as well. Be happy Megan, that is all I ever wish for you." Joe leaned in and kissed her cheeks and hugged her.

"Ah Joe, stop I'm going to cry."

"Now are you ready to become Mrs. Max Pierce."

XOXO

"More than you know Joe. I'm ready." Megan watched as Joe nodded his head to the guards.

The moment the doors, open Megan saw Lizzie, and Maggie waiting for her behind a white curtain, as the two doors behind her close the curtains in front of her opened up to a beautiful setting with all her closest friend and family. But that didn't describe how romantic the place looked. The white and ivory veils that surrounded the room that was hanging from the ceiling made the area more intimate. You could smell the elegant flowers that surrounded each archway as you pass through, they were handcrafted, and she knew that someone had put a lot of hours behind making them. She honestly felt like a princess on this particular day, that she never thought it would happen to her, it's was her wedding day, and the moment that she meets Max's eyes she knew it was forever.

Megan couldn't help herself. It was like everything around her disappeared. All the sound and whispering—everything vanished. All she saw was the handsome man standing there, dressed in a black tux. His emerald green eyes were sparkling his dimples were showing. She could see how happy he looked. Just one look into those emerald greens, and they were lost in each other. Megan couldn't help but smile back. The fear she once had of losing him two weeks ago was gone. Max was her universe. All she saw was him and how happy he made her feel. He made her knees weak, her heat beat faster. At that moment, there was no other place she wanted to be. Megan was mesmerized by this handsome man in front of her. What she would give right now to lose herself in his embrace, his kiss, his touch.

As the doors opened, Max was nervous. He hadn't seen her since he left the house earlier that morning. Megan was still sleeping. He refused to wake her up. He knew that today was

$$$

going to be a long day for her. When she finally came through the doors and started walking down the aisle, he was aware that he couldn't live without her. He wanted to give her everything she would ever want; he wanted to make this day the most important day of her life. When Maggie told him that she always loved their mother's wedding dress, she had convinced him to get it ready. He knew he made the right choice by listening to Maggie. She looked like a princess, his beautiful Angel. The dress did not touch the floor, but ended at her ankles. The bodice snuggled her beautiful breasts and a delicate lace sleeve covered her arms, the dress was loose from the waist down. She didn't have a veil, but she wore a tiara in her hair. Her hair was pulled up and loose in the back, which showed off her beautiful face. She held a bouquet of calla lilies. In his eyes, she was the most beautiful woman he had ever seen. He smiled at her; but the moment she smiled back at him it took his breath away. His life had no meaning before; she was his whole world. She stopped in the middle of the aisle, he started walking towards her. He didn't see anyone but her. He had waited so long for her. He stood in front of her and whispered "I Love you." Max reached up and touched her soft cheek. He felt her intake a breath. "You take my breath away." He then looked at Joe and smiled.

Joe kissed Megan's cheek and told her, "I love you, baby girl. Be happy. Max, take good care of her, or else!" He chuckled.

"I will, Joe. Thank you!"

As Joe handed over Megan's hand to Max, he said, "She's all yours!"

He leaned into Megan and whispered, "You are exquisite. You stop my heart every time I see you. I love you, Megan Harrison. There has never been anyone else but you. You are my other half.

xoxo

Are you ready to continue this journey with me? Put your faith in me." He extended his hand and kissed her cheek.

She whispered, "Show me the way, Baby. I'll follow you from here to eternity." The nervousness she felt finally subsided, and once Max had taken her hand, she felt more relaxed. She knew that she would follow him and protect him forever.

He took her hand and wrapped it around his arm, and they finished walking down the aisle to meet the reverend.

"Dearly beloved, we are gathered here today to join Megan Harrison and Maxime Pierce in holy matrimony."

They looked at each other, utterly oblivious to their surroundings. They only had eyes for each other. As the reverend recited the speech, they repeated as the vowed their love for each other, to honor, to obey, to protect and sickness and health. The next thing they knew, they were exchanging rings, and they both turned when the reverend said, "You may now kiss the bride."

"It's about time!" He took her face with both his hands and leaned in and gave her the most passionate kiss. Megan forgot where she was. She lifted her arms around Max's neck and deepened the kiss as she played with his hair. She pulled him closer to her. Her insides were now on fire, and she could not bring herself to stop. The taste of his tongue, the desire he felt for her; he was kissing her breathless.

The next thing she knew; Josh was smacking his brother on the back. "Get a room, guys! Everyone's watching!"

They broke the kiss and turned their faces, cheek to cheek, and looked at everyone. They all cheered and applauded them. Max held her tight against him. "Mrs. Pierce, are you ready to party?"

$$$

## Chapter Thirty-Seven

Megan watched the elevator move up to the last floor of Pierce Enterprises. Four months ago she became Mrs. Max Pierce and every night since then she felt like she was on her honeymoon. Today, she wanted to surprise her husband, or was it because she was tired of being home. She had to hold herself up against the wall as the elevator came to a stop. once she walked out, she held her belly, as she stops and held onto the wall, and bend over to take a deep breath. She waiting outside the elevator, leaning up against the wall now, until she knew she would be ok to walk again. She was done of being pregnant. She wanted these babies out. She had been through enough. Being shot at, being run off the road, hit on the head, then finding out she was pregnant, then Max getting shot, all within a six month period. But to her surprise, Max pulled off a wedding of her dreams, just a few days before Christmas. That day burned in her memory like it was yesterday. But now, she took a deep breath, knowing the pain would go away soon. She wanted to go to Max's office. She loved to surprise him in the middle of the day. Max had assigned a driver for her, to make it easier to get around, because staying home watching the wall was getting to her. She looked around, no one had notice her there, so she took a deep breath, stood

xoxo

straight as much as she can and wobbled done the hall rubbing her belly.

"Good afternoon, Julie," Megan said through clench teeth.

Julie ran to steady her. "Hi, Megan! You look a little flustered right now, are you okay?" Julie looked concerned as she held on to Megan.

Megan rubbed her belly to ease the pain a little. "I'm huge, and the twins are playing football in there. I'm tired from lack of sleep. I can't wait to pop these babies out! I'm done being pregnant." Megan smiled back at her.

"I can only imagine, but if you need anything, please let me know. I'm sure Max will be pleased to see you. Surprising him again today?"

"Yup, I like to see that surprised look. At first, he thinks someone is barging in, but when he sees me, he smiles." Megan opened the door without knocking as she walked in and saw Julie closing it behind her.

"This better be…" Max raised his head as he watched his wife walk through the door, looking radiant. Her hair was pulled back into a ponytail. She was wearing a beautiful dark blue tunic with matching leggings and blue and green shoes. She finished with a white scarf wrapped around her shoulders. "Beautiful. Angel, you are the most beautiful woman I have ever seen!" Max got up and walked to her as he helped her to the couch in his office.

Megan held on to Max as he slowly sat down. "Oh, please, I look like a whale! You're just saying that because it's your job to say those things!" She rubbed her belly again.

Max stuffed a pillow behind her and then sat beside her, lifting her feet onto his lap. He leaned in and kissed her senseless until she didn't remember her name. Max pulled back, breathing heavily. Her eyes fluttered open, and he caressed her cheeks.

$$\$\$\$$

"Megan, you are beautiful. I love everything about this body of yours, and you do not look like a whale. How are they doing today?" Max rubbed where she was rubbing, and with the other hand tried to relieve the tension in her neck.

Megan rested her head. She loved it when he spent this much attention to her, and she just sighed as she felt his strong hands working out the knots in her neck. "You know what I miss the most?" She inhaled his musky scent mixed with his body soap. That made her heart quicken.

"What is it you miss the most? Tell me?" He could feel the babies kicking, and he couldn't fathom what it must feel like for her from the inside. He listened to her breathing.

"I miss having a real hug from my husband! I miss the strong arms that wrapped around me, and miss seeing my feet!" She laughed. "This belly is taking so much room; I'm missing the small things. I want to see my feet; I forget what they look like." Megan looked at her feet on his lap. She watched him take off her shoes and noticed they were not the same color. "See? I cannot even see if I'm wearing the same shoes."

Max rubbed her inner foot. He heard her moan, and thought it was in pleasure, but he could see how she was biting down on her bottom lip. "Tell you what; I have just one call to make, then let me take you somewhere special for lunch."

"That sounds fantastic! Could we stop for ice cream on the way home?" Megan couldn't help herself. She had never had a craving before, but now she loved ice cream. She could never get enough of it.

Max laughed out loud. "Anything you desire, Angel. Give me a few minutes. I will make this call fast, and we can leave." Max moved and then put her feet back on the couch, leaned in, and kissed her. One thing Max loved was the feel of his wife's skin. He always wanted to touch her.

Max was listening to his manager in L.A. going over the expansion when he heard Megan screech out a cry that could break a glass. He didn't hesitate to interrupt his call and said, "I'll call you back." He hung up the phone without saying goodbye and rushed over to Megan, now sitting up, kneeling down in front of her. "Megan? What's wrong?"

Megan held onto Max's forearms as a look of terror spread across her face. She took a deep breath and she could feel that another contraction was about to begin. "Max! Oh God, Max! I'm having contractions! I thought…" she took a deep breath again. "I thought it would go away, but they are only getting worse."

"Let's go!" He helped her stand up. She grabbed hold of his arms and leaned forward as another contraction hit her, and that is when her water broke. Max looked down on the carpet, then he looked at Megan again. "Julie, get in here now!" he bellowed at the top of his lungs like a drill sergeant. A second later, Julie opened the door. "Get the car and call someone to clean this. Megan's water just broke. Call everyone. I'm taking her to the hospital." Max didn't waste any time as he escorted his wife from the building as fast as he could.

***

Josh had been pacing the waiting room for about five hours now, without a word from anyone. He watched as everyone was calm and waiting patiently. His brother Brandon was on his phone doing god knows what. Joe and Ethan were in conversation about the cabin progress, and Maggie and Lizzie were in another discussion about what they will name the babies. Why was he so nervous? It wasn't him giving birth. Knowing that Megan was in there giving birth to his nephew and niece was a lot to handle. He watched Brandon with those two giant bears, the kind that look like Ted. They were taking up space, and people were coming in looking for a place to sit, but there was none. "Man, it been five hours, if not more. What is taking so long? What the hell is going on in there? We should have received some information by now!" Josh growled.

"Josh, darling, giving birth takes time!" Helen reassured her son. "Doug, doesn't this remind you of when Max was born? It took forever, didn't it?

"Man, you need to relax! You're acting as if you're the father. If there was a complication, Max would let us know," Brandon said as he looked at his brother.

"Shit! I don't think I ever want to go through that. I don't think I'd be able to keep it under control. Megan's like my little sister now."

Brandon slapped him on the back. "Take it easy, bro. She'll be just fine. She's in good hands. I cannot wait to see these little boogers!"

"Babies are not boogers, Brandon. That is your nickname for them, Booger?" Lizzie replied.

"Hey! I'm going to be the coolest uncle. I will have them eating out of my hands." He couldn't help himself. He smiled as he sat down between the two giant bears, and smiled at everyone.

When the doors finally opened a few hours later, Max walked into the waiting room with a big smile on his face and found everyone there waiting impatiently for the news. "They are here. Both are well. Megan was a champ and did it all naturally. She's a little tired but doing great." The grin on his face was contagious. "I just need Megan to regain a little energy. They are transferring her to a private room. Once she is there, I will come back and

xoxo

get everyone. Just give us another hour or so, then I will bring everyone to meet the children." Max received a hug and kisses from his mom and a good handshake and half hug from his dad. Then Joe, Ethan, Brandon, Luc, and Maggie hugged him too. Before he headed back, he told them, "Find Josh and Lizzie and tell them the good news."

An hour later, Max and Megan watched everyone walk in one by one and couldn't help but smile at the two giant bears that Brandon was holding. Megan could see how anxious he was on seeing the twins, just by the twinkle in his eyes. "Everyone, I would like to introduce you to daddy's little princess, Emma Bianca Pierce, and this little one here is Alex Henry Joseph Maxime Pierce." Megan watch as Joe beam up with pride, the name she giving her son.

Megan watched as everyone cooed around the children and each one took a turn to hold them one by one. She knew that no matter what, this family would always be by her side. If someone would have told her that she would be this happy two years ago, she would have laughed in their face. Now she had two children and husband that loved her more than anything in the world. She looked up and sent a silent thank you to whoever was watching over her.

$$$

## Epilogue

Max kissed Megan, Alex and Emma then headed to the office as planned. Something had to give; they were both exhausted and needed help with the twins. He didn't want to force the issue on Megan, but when she decided that they did need help, he was more than happy to comply. "Good morning Julie, can you come to the office please."

"Yes, Sir." Julie was always in before him, which made his job so much easier.

Max leaned back in his chair and took a deep breath, was it selfish of him to run away when Megan needed him. Having twins is terrific, but the lack of sleep is another thing, he had a hard time managing his personal life, imagine his business, he focuses was just not into it, lately. Max needed to stay alert at all time. He knew that Josh and Brandon were dealing with more these days till he gets back into the reigns of running his empire. He loosens his tie as he looked at Julie: "We need to find a nanny to help us with the twins. Can you get a hold of a few agencies for me?"

"Yes Sir, will that be all?"

He looked at her as he pulled off his tie, and threw it on the desk. "Yes, sorry, for now, that will be all. Thank you. Let me

XOXO

know when you have a few good candidates. So Megan and I can call in a few interviews at the house." Max got up and removed his jacket and rolled up his shirt sleeves, *damn he wishes he could sleep for a week.* "Julie, please hold my calls and cancel all my appointments, and that will be all." Max looked at Julie as she smiled back at him. *Damn that woman can sometimes see right through me.*

Julie didn't question the reason why she could see it in Max's eyes how exhausted he was. The dark circle and it looks like he even forgot to shave this morning. "Ok, Sir." She left and turned and closed the door behind her.

Max was waiting till Julie closed the door and took out bottled water, as he drank the contents in one shot, then presses a button and the windows behind him darken, to block out the sunlight. He sat down on the couch in his office as he then removed his shoes and lay down. Max took a deep breath and rested his arm over his eyes as he closed them he didn't know how long it took, but all Max knew is that he finally fell asleep, in his peaceful surrounding.

Josh and Brandon walked into Max office, Julie had called canceling their appointment at one o'clock. So they decided to head down to the king's den and find out what was going on, they open the door to his office, and it was in darkness.

Josh looked at Julie; "He's still here, isn't he?" Julie nodded her head and confirmed that he had not left. But as they approach the couch in his office, he was sound asleep, they looked at each other and couldn't help but smile. "I guess having twins is exhausting." Josh whispered.

Brandon put a hand on his shoulder to shake him awake; "Hey Bro! Wake up! "

"Max? Wake up! Josh also said.

$$$

Max bolted up from the couch on full alert thinking that Megan needed him that Alex or Emma was crying; he looks around: "Holy fucking shit! I must have dozed off! What time is it?" he rubbed his faces with his hands and then ran his fingers through his hair...

"It's two o'clock, why?" Brandon looked at him. "You look like shit Max! The twins are keeping you up." He smiled at him.

Max leaned forward and put his shoes on; "I was only supposed to here for a couple of hours. Megan must be flipping out by now." He looked at his brothers "We are both sleep deprived."

"Bro! You look exhausted!" Josh replied.

"Well, I am. Does it show that much; I know I haven't been myself lately because we have been spending most of our time with Alex and Emma, catering to their needs." Max stood once he had his shoes on and reach for his cell phone to make sure that he didn't miss a call from Megan.

"Aww! Is my beautiful niece keeping you up at night?" Brandon said.

"Totally! I miss my wife if Megan and I don't do something soon... Let's just say, I need time with her alone, without the children."

Brandon looked at Josh. "Hey man, if you need help just let us know."

"Yeah, I'm sure if I call Lizzie she will give a helping hand for one night," Josh said.

"I just may take you both up on that, but first we have a nanny to find." Max interrupted and page Julie, he didn't even have to tell her what he needed she said it was on his desk; "Thanks." he told her.

"Nanny huh, I thought Megan was against it," Josh asked.

xoxo

"Hell, say the word, and we are there if you need help," Brandon said.

"You know what; Megan and I just need a full night's sleep. We need to recharge our batteries. We haven't had a moment to ourselves since the twins were born." Max press the button to remove the darkness and let the sun fill his office.

"Saturday is free for me I have nothing planned? What about you Brandon you free Saturday night."Josh ask

"Sure I'm in let me know," Brandon said.

"Thanks, guys! I'm sure Megan will appreciate it. Having twins can put a damper on a couple's love life. We both need to have some time to ourselves. We haven't had sex in six weeks; we're just too tired even to try."

"Ouch! No sex in six weeks? Damn man? Why didn't you say anything?" Brandon replied.

"The Doctor just gave the ok to Megan. We had to make sure she healed properly first, but honestly, we were just too tired even to do anything." Max said to his brother, if there was one thing he knew about his brother is how discreet they can be. "Thanks, guys I appreciate this I will run this by Megan and let you know ok." Max ran out of the office, and Brandon and Josh followed, he stopped at Julie desk.

"Brandon, Josh, thanks again, let's reschedule the meeting. Was there anything I need to know." Max looked at his brothers, knowing that the company was in good hands.

"Nope, go home to your wife," Josh said, and they both left his side.

Julie handed Max two more applicants that she received from the agency. "What would I do without you, Julie? Thank you. I'll be at home if you need me tomorrow. Sorry, I fell asleep in there. I was not very productive today."

$$$

"Not a problem that is what you pay me for, I have sent a few files for your review just have the looked at and signed over. You did look tired." She handed him the files and also told him what she considers her choice that looked good.

"Go home, Julie. If I need anything, I'll call you ok? Goodnight. Max left the office and headed home. When he arrived he saw an unknown car in the driveway, he looked inside the car, had suitcases and clothes and other things. "Baby, I'm so sorry I'm late. I didn't think it would have taken me this long." He walked into the kitchen and noticed a woman holding Alex. She was all smiles and whispering to Megan. *Who is this woman?*

"It's ok Max- I like you to meet Carla Roy. Carla this is my husband Max Pierce, don't let his gruffness scare you he's big teddy bear."

"She looked at Max and smile.

"It's nice to meet you, Carla. May I?" Max took Alex away from her. Was it possessiveness not knowing someone a stranger holding their child? He didn't care it was his son, and he wanted him in his arms.

"Max, Carla and I used to go to school together. I went to the park to take a walk with the twins, today, and I ran into her. The most amazing thing happens today, our luck is going to change, Carla is going to be our new Nanny. I was so excited when she accepted our luck was on our side." Megan said.

"What?" Alex started to cry when Max tensed up.

"Carla, do you mind taking Emma, I need to talk to Max for a few minutes." She handed Emma to Carla and took Alex so he would stop crying, "Max, can I talk to you in private, please? Excuse us, Carla, we'll be right back." Megan wanted Carla, and she didn't want a stranger in her home, where her children were, she wanted someone Megan could trust, and she wanted Carla.

XOXO

They went into Max's office and closed the door. "Over my dead body!" Max never yelled at Megan before, but she knew better, he didn't trust anyone especially some stranger. Max walked over to his cabinet he didn't like to argue with Megan. Max poured himself a glass of bourbon, as he shot back and felt the burning all the way to his stomach. He took a deep breath then turn toward her; he could sense that the fire in her was building and he was ready for a fight, hell she wasn't going to win this one. "Megan you know my rules we need a background check, and I do not trust strangers in our home. Need I remind you what happened to us; Max handed a list of applicants; "here there are a few good qualified Nannies that we can choose."

Megan was holding Alex in one arm and place the applicants on his desk; she knew she had to diffuse the situation. She didn't want these strangers; "Max, honey, she's perfect! Don't you trust me? Don't you trust my judgment?" She needs a place to live, and she can start right away. She needs our help Max, and I already told her that she could have the job. Carla is amazing;" yeah she may have come from a bad home, things that just needed to stay between her and Carla. "She's perfect Max."

"Does she have any experience with newborn babies?"

"Max Pierce? Hear me out please, we can go through the protocol of a nanny, have some stranger in our home that we do not know. I trust Carla, she is perfect for us, she's calm, and she has been around more kids than you and I ever been. She's sweet and loving she loves kids. She needs a fresh start, Max, she just left her boyfriend that didn't care about her, and she quit her job today. Please, Max, give her a try, trust my judgment on this one, I believe that she is the best person for this job, even if it's only temporary till she can get back on her feet. Give me this Max." Megan looked at him hoping that he trusts her enough with this.

$$$

"Megan, you know I don't trust many people. We need to do a background check on her."

"No Max, you don't! Do you trust me or not?"

"But Baby?"

"Max, we need help, and I gave her the job. She will get full salary, and I'm also giving her benefits."

"But Baby?"

"Max, it's only for a short period. Just until she can get back on her feet, Ok? I promise she will stay in the suite at the end of the hall. Baby, this will work out, I promise." She reached up and kissed him on the lips. "I love you Max and trust me; this will work out." Megan walked out of the office not waiting for him to second guess her decision as she walked to Carla; "Carla, it's all settled. Come; let me show you where you'll be staying."

"Megan? Are you sure? Your husband didn't look very pleased. I don't want to cause any problems."

"Everything's fine! I'd rather have someone I know taking care of our babies than to have a perfect stranger in my house. So here's the deal, will you be ok working from eight to five? You'll have your evenings unless we have an engagement to go too. The weekends are yours to do as you wish. I don't expect you to be around twenty-four-seven; you still have a life to live. You are helping us out especially me; this will give me time to re-energize myself. You are my friend and a life saver."

"Megan, you don't know how much this means to me. I'm here to help in any way possible. Even during the night. I know both of you work hard and I don't mind. Maybe I can help during the evening until the twins start sleeping their full night."

"Don't be silly. I need someone during the day. Max will not always be around, and that is when I'll need you the most."

XOXO

"Meg, for what it's worth, thanks," Carla said, twelve hours ago she was homeless no job, and she didn't know where she was going to stay, now she has a job and a roof over her head what more can she say.

"Don't thank me yet; these two beautiful children can we a hand full. It will give us time to get reacquainted with each other. Wait until Lizzie finds out!" They walked up the stairs to the second floor; "this bedroom will be yours, I'm sure it will have everything you need. We haven't done much with this room, we used it as a guest room, but this will be yours. You can do as you wish in here."

The bed was the center of the bedroom, a massive four post king size bed, with matching night tables and dresser. "I hope this will be ok, to the right you have your private bathroom with tub and shower, and you will find linen in there. If you need anything, Carla, please let me know, we want your stay to be comfortable. I will have Max bring your things up."

She held Emma in her arms, and she couldn't ask for anything more when she thought she had nothing left in her life but her beat up old car and the contents in it. She had little money to her name and this being here with Megan Harrison Pierce. After high school they lost track of each other, she was always so kind to her and always welcoming her with open arms into her family, why she hadn't stayed in touch over the years was a shame, but yet her focus there was her ex… damn him for making her lose all of her friends.

"Megan thank you this is wonderful, and I cannot believe you and Lizzie are still friends. How is she doing?

I will have to get her over here soon. I'm sure we have lots of catching up to do.

$$$

***

Max watched his wife leave his office, and he couldn't believe that he didn't win this battle. Didn't she understand that she's a Pierce now and that there are things that just needed to follow? All background checks required, anyone coming close to his family, after that brutal attack at the cabin, he didn't trust anyone and for a good reason. Megan said to trust her, to trust her judgment, but something inside him didn't feel right. It's who he is; he needed to know who this girl was, she refused to get a background check done. Max just leaned on his desk, as he finished his bourbon, he felt that burning sensation as he looked down at his empty glass. What the hell just happened? We were supposed to hire someone together! He thought to himself; but he trusted her, and if hiring this woman makes her happy, that's all that mattered to him right or so he thought. "Luc, it's Max, I need a favor." Yeah, he trusted his wife, but he didn't trust people he didn't know. Max wanted this information; it is paranoia. He was a wealthy man, and with wealth, there are a lot of people out there that would do anything to get close to him.

"How are you doing? How are the twins?" Luc asked.

"Growing faster and bigger every day. Listen, Luc, I need your services, and I want this to be confidential. Megan can't find out about this." Max said.

"What is it?" Luc ask.

"I need a background check done on a Carla Roy. My wife had this crazy idea of hiring her to be our Nanny and didn't run it by me first. You know how I am. After what happened to us, I don't want to take any chances. My family means a lot to me, Luc. I want to know everything there is to know about this woman. Family, ex's everything that I need to know, I want to find out who is staying under our roof." Max said, like any

XOXO

employee, he has always done a background check, and if she will be on the payroll this needed to be done.

"You know what Max, that name sounds familiar."

"Apparently, they went to school together."

"Thanks right, that is why I recognized her name, sweet kid, she was a few years younger, but quiet, curly blond hair, right? With brown eyes almost milk chocolate color." Luc said.

"Yeah! That's her." Max said.

"Ok, I'm on it, but Max, I can tell you this right now; the report will come back clean. She's a quiet girl; was never in trouble. She and Megan used to be friends in high school; she use to talk about her all the time, she never mingled much with other, other kids use to make fun of her." Luc said.

"Well, that's reassuring."

"Most likely, Lizzie knows her too. She was a good kid back then Max. But I will get you what you need. She was very shy, and stayed mostly to herself unless she was with Megan or Lizzie." Luc said.

"Thanks, Luc, I appreciate this. I should be in the office tomorrow."

"I should have all the information for you by then. Bye Max."

"Thanks, Luc I appreciate this, see you tomorrow."

Next morning, Luc was waiting at Max's office as he handed him the file on Carla Roy; Max looked at it, there was not much in it; graduation picture, a picture of her Father and Mother. For what it was worth he needed this. Max needed to make sure that the Carla Roy who was living under his roof is who she said she was.

Luc looked at Max knowing that the girl he once knew was harmless, she was shy, an only child, quiet that is how he remembered Carla Roy. "As I said, there wasn't much to find. She's clean

$$\$\$\$$$

except for a file that was sealed; I couldn't get to it. In most cases these files don't mean anything; it was probably something that happened when she was a juvenile. Her father is deceased; her mother kicked her out when she was eighteen, and until recently, she was living with Bruce Sumner. As I said, she's a private person, just like she was in high school, there is no threat there. She doesn't have any friends. I'm surprised that she never stayed in contact with Megan." Luc lean back in the chair facing Max, as he watched him go through the file.

Max looked through it, and there wasn't much, money little, no saving, no investment, she had nothing to her name, deed of the house belongs to her ex-boyfriend, she had nothing to her name. Was she a con artist trying to get money, he didn't know, he didn't trust anyone, but he had to believe his wife. "It's just that; I want to know about the people who are near my family. I appreciate this Luc. This research is between us; Megan should not know about this. You should come over soon; I'm sure you'd like to see Emma and Alex." Max said as he leaned back in his chair but kept his hand resting on the folder.

"I'll check the schedule, but I think I could make it over on Friday? Luc said.

"That'd be great! I'll let Megan know." Max stood up and shook Luc's hand. "Once again I appreciated this, I know if Megan finds out about this I will never hear the end of it, at least this way, my conscience is clear. You've become a good friend Luc. I can see why Megan is close to you."

"Megan has always been like a little sister to me, but now I have to go, have a potential client looking for some exclusive security," Luc said.

"Good luck with that man. So business is good." Max said.

xoxo

"Why do we wish him luck? Megan said walking into the office. "Luc! It's great to see you." She watched her husband as he smiled back at her, and Luc leaned in and kissed her cheek.

"Hi, Beautiful! What? No children?" Luc then hugged her.

"No, they're home with our new Nanny. You remember Carla Roy? Well, that's who I hired as our Nanny, for now anyway. She's still that sweet girl that I've known all my life, but she has turned into a beautiful woman now." Megan was no fool she knew her husband went behind her back and got a background check done, it was written all over his face. Luc could hide stuff from her, but her husband he had that guilty look on he couldn't hide anything from her, and he knew it also.

"Yeah, I remember her. Isn't she the one with the blond curly hair? She was the quiet one, shy didn't say much if I remember, but I didn't know her that well the age difference."

"Yep, that's the one! She's amazing. Did you know that Max and I just had our first full night of sleep in a week? Luc, you cannot imagine how that felt." she leaned into her husband and hugged him.

"Hi Baby, I wasn't expecting you in here today." Max held his wife in his arms and kissed her.

"I wanted to surprise you and to go to lunch with you. Carla is watching the kids. Luc, would you like to join us?"

"Rain check, O'Neil and I have tons of work that I need to finish up and to meet with a new client." Luc extended his hand: "Max a pleasure as always." then he leaned in once more and kissed Megan on the cheek. "Bye."

"Bye Luc, we'll see you on Friday," Max said. "So Baby, it's too early for lunch. What's the real reason?"

$$$

"I just wanted to see my husband. You left so fast this morning that I didn't have a chance to do this." She stood up on her toes and kissed him.

"Mmm... I like this! I missed you, Angel. You, Mrs. Pierce, have a date Saturday night? Brandon and Josh said that they're coming over to babysit. I can't wait for us to be alone together. I missed you so much, my love." Max move a stray hair behind her ear and touch her cheek; he likes how she blush to the slightest touch.

"Mmm... Well, you know the Doctor gave me the ok right? After a few more nights like last night, I should be back to my old self. Max, about Carla, thank you, for trusting my judgment with her. It means a lot to me." Megan still had her arms around his waist, loving the feeling that she can feel him without the inconvenience of the belly.

"Baby, I just want you to be happy." Max wouldn't tell her that he did do a background check on her, or should he. He knows he shouldn't keep secrets but telling her. If he mentioned to Megan what he did, that would mean he didn't trust her. He did believe her; it's who he was everyone that comes in contact with Pierce Enterprises it's mandatory.

"In that case, I can't wait for Saturday; I'll show you exactly how happy I am!" Megan looked into those emerald green and knew what he was thinking. She could also feel his excitement against her belly.

Now I'm the one who can't wait! Just let me finish my work here can I meet you let's say around one o'clock." Max said.

"Sure I just have a few errands to run; I will meet you at our usual place for one. Ok Baby, I'll see you later."

"Hey wait! I think you forgot about something?

XOXO

"What?" Megan looked at herself; she had her keys, her purse, her phone. She looked up questioned him.

Max walked up to her. "I think you did." He looked at her and smiled. "I think your lips missed mine! Right here!" He leaned in and kissed her. Megan hummed as he kissed her. Max kissed her hard, as he held the back of her head in place he demanded, he wanted to make her breathless and ensure that her only thoughts were of him. He kissed her with a hunger that he couldn't get enough, as he lowered his hands and cupped her ass in his hands. Max pulled away and looked down at her; she was breathless as he.

Megan had lost all thoughts when Max kissed her breathless; one thing she could count on, her husband knew how to kiss and make her crazy with need; "Oh, I do miss this! I'm so looking forward to Saturday! See you later Honey!" Megan walked into the elevator giving her hips a little extra swing.

A few days later, on Friday night… Max walked into Brandon's office: "Hey Bro? Are we still on for tomorrow evening?"

"Sure! You look like you're in a good mood! What happened?" Brandon ask

"We got a Nanny! That's what happened. Both Megan and I have finally been able to sleep at night. It's wonderful! I finally have my mojo back and can't wait for tomorrow evening." Max sat down in Brandon office as he crossed his leg over the other and smiled.

"Is she cute?" Brandon asked.

"Is who cute?" Max said

"The Nanny man! Is she cute?" Brandon asked

"I don't know! I haven't paid any attention to her; I only have eyes for my wife." He looked at his iPhone and text message that was coming in.

$$$

"Wow! She must be ugly if you didn't notice her." Brandon asked

"Who's ugly?" Josh asked as he walked in and sat down in the chair next to Max.

"Max here has got himself a Nanny, and I was asking him if she was cute? But our brother didn't notice." Brandon said.

"Well? Is she cute Max?" Josh asked.

"I don't know! I guess! I haven't been paying attention, to be honest! Unless you like the girl next girl, kind of girl." Max told them.

"What the hell Max? What does that mean?" Brandon replied.

"Come on guys! You know I only have eyes for Megan. All I know is that she's single. I guess she's cute; I haven't paid that much attention to her. So you guys are still coming right tomorrow?" he needed to get out of here to beat the traffic to get home.

"Yes, I'm in. Will the Nanny be there?" Brandon asked.

"She lives in the suite; of course she'll be there. Megan and Lizzie went to school together. Anyway, I'll see both of you tomorrow around one. I need to go; See you tomorrow afternoon. Have a good night." Just like that Max walked out of the office ending the story about the nanny. He walked out of the office, signing a tune he loves so much, and hoping he can whisk Megan away. He was finally going to get his wife for himself for one night, and he had booked a suite downtown, with champagne and the works, he was going to lock them in the suite from the time he arrived till they had to check out. This weekend was about one thing only pleasuring his wife. With no crying kids or diapers or feeding, all the nutrition he was going to do was of Megan and just that alone made him hard thinking about it.

### The End!

XOXO

# Dedication

I Hope you enjoyed Max and Megan journey. This book took me years to finish. I guess in a way I wanted it to be special being the first one. There are so many characters in this book for a reason, because I have more stories to tell. I want to thank everyone for your support from when the first book came out in 2016 Billionaire's Love. So to all my support team, family, friend, and fans thank you without you I couldn't do it.

To Derek, I know you feel I'm always on my computer, and I sometimes forget this but thank you for your support knowing that you are there when I need clarification on something. I love you.

To my niece Gabrielle Pearson thank you for helping me with Social Media, you are beautiful and loving, and you have an amazing heart. I love you so much.

To my Aunt Marjorie, thank you for proofreading my work, and encouraging me, when I didn't know where to go with the story, especially when I had to cut stuff out that had no meaning. Your guidance, made me see my story much clearly. You will always be a treasure in my heart.

To my Mom, thank you for your support and helping me spread the words about my book. Billionaire's Love. Love you.

XOXO

To my BFF – Lizette, words cannot express how much I love you, you are my sisters, a connection that could never be broken, near or far you are with me.

I cannot express how grateful I am to have a family that stand behind me, I love you all dearly.

I hope you enjoyed Billionaire's Forgiveness, because you will fall in love with Brandon Pierce in Billionaire's Rescue. So here is an Excerpt on more to come from the Pierce Brothers. Also coming soon Billionaire's Mistake, Josh Pierce story watch for it on my website.

*Brenda*

I can be followed on the following website
www.bpearsonbooks.com
www.twitter.com/mbrendapearson
www.facebook.com/bpearsonbooks

$$$

EXCERPT

# Billionaire's Rescue

BRANDON PIERCE

Brandon Pierce never went home early, but lately, he felt something was missing from his life. After a good night's sleep, well deserved; what better than an early morning run. He needed to get his shit together. Today he would be spending time with his niece and nephew, and he couldn't wait until they were old enough to do things with him. He plugged in his iPhone, turned on his music, stretched, and took off, starting slow. Running made him feel better. It cleared his mind and made is blood flow. He always pushed himself. He made it to the park, pacing himself in a full run. As he rounded the corner after the bushes, he jumped trying to miss running into a woman bent over, and went flying over the bench, and face-planting to the ground. *Fucken hell!*

"Hey are you okay? Sorry about that!" Carla didn't know what to say. She almost tripped when her lace came undone and she bent over to tie it back up.

XOXO

Sitting on the grass, he looked up. "What the hell were you doing there? You shouldn't be stretching where people cannot see you."

"I'm sorry. I wasn't thinking."

"Typical. Watch it next time!"

"Hey, you don't have to be rude. I said I was sorry."

"I don't care for your apologies. Just don't do it again." He was pissed. He didn't like to be humiliated, and he shooed her away.

"Fuck, you're an asshole. I said I was sorry. Take it or leave it." She left. *Man what a prick, if he wasn't so cute… What are you thinking, Carla? The guy's an asshole.*

Brandon watched her leave, as he got up and decided that he was heading back home, he couldn't help but watch her run in the other direction. *What the hell is wrong with people? She said she was sorry asshole, should he run after her and apologies, hell no he did nothing wrong.* When he got back home, he had time to take a shower and pack an overnight bag. *Today I'm spending time with Emma and Alex, my niece and nephew.*

Carla arrived back from her run and entered the kitchen. She was pissed. "What the hell is wrong with people?" She mumbled to herself, as she drank glass a water before heading to her room to change.

"Carla, are you okay? You seem upset." Megan looked at her, knowing that Carla was the sweetest person she had ever met, she never got anger.

"Some jerk was running in the park and I was tying my shoelace. I know I should have moved over, but he was coming too fast and didn't see me and he jump over me and then went flying over the bench to the ground. Anyway, I said I was sorry, but he had an attitude about it. What is wrong with people? I said I was

$$$

sorry. I swear, Megan, I'm not going to let guys walk all over me anymore. Anyway, I told him he was an asshole and left."

"Good for you" Megan smiled at her; Carla, I meant to ask you, are you okay with this today? I know I told you that the weekend was yours to do as you wish."

"Megan, it's my pleasure. I should be fine with the twins."

"Brandon and Josh will be here to help and Lizzie should be here around five. I will leave our cell phone numbers in case anything goes wrong."

"It's fine, trust me. I will take good care of Emma and Alex. You don't need to worry. Now let me go take a shower and change and I will help you burp them after the feeding."

"You are a godsend. Thank you, but Max should be out of the office with Emma soon. We will take care of the eleven a.m. feeding before we leave."

Carla looked at herself. Would she feel uncomfortable around two men she had never met before? She was no supermodel, only five foot three, blond curly hair, shoulder length, fair skin, and God gave her curves. Living with Bruce for ten years, she lost who she was, and also added extra pound that she now wanted to drop. That was why she started jogging again. She needed to shed those extra pounds. For some reason, it always went to her breasts and hips. Taking one last look at herself in the mirror, she left the bathroom. It was hot outside for June and her body was warm still from the run, so wearing a summer dress, just felt right. She heard the doorbell, then voices downstairs telling her that Max's brothers had arrived. This is going to be awkward, being with strangers for a few hours. She was glad that Megan had decided to stay a while before leaving her with them. This was about Emma and Alex. She fell in love with those beautiful kids. For once in her life she had a purpose, and she was

XOXO

happy living here. Megan was so kind to her, but she was always that way even in high school. She opened her door and headed downstairs. She heard voices in the kitchen and headed in.

Megan came from behind her. "Carla, let me introduce you to Max's brothers.

Josh, this is Carla Roy, my friend, and our new nanny. She is helping for a few weeks.

Carla, this is Josh Pierce, Max's brother."

Josh came up to her and extended his hand. "Nice to meet you, Carla. I hope this lovely girl here hasn't been giving you too much trouble."

Carla couldn't help but stare at him. She thought Max was intimating, but he was gorgeous. Josh had the dark hair, but where Max had green eyes, Josh's were blue. "Nice to meet you too, and no, she is a sweetheart. They are just adorable."

"Hope you don't mind us crashing here for the night." Josh always had a way to ease the tension. She looked shy, and he just wanted to make sure she felt at ease. He knew how to read people. That innocence was there, and she blushed a little.

"Not at all I'm happy for the help." She liked Josh. He was easy going and she heard that he was dating Lizzie.

"Carla, this is Max's other brother Brandon, the younger of the two." Megan saw Brandon come out of the office with Alex in his arms.

Brandon was cooing to Alex as he approached. "And the better looking one of the three." he replied as he turned the corner.

"You!" Carla raised her voice a little too high.

Brandon looked perplexed. "Have we met?" His smile was gone as he looked her over.

"Megan, that is the guy I told you about from this morning." Carla turned to Megan, not wanting to be there.

$$$

They all turned to Megan, confused. She laughed and looked at Carla. "Oh, the asshole. Right!"

Brandon's grin disappeared. "I am sorry, have I met you before?"

Carla looked at him. "This morning when you tripped over me, you were insulting and arrogant and rude. I tried to apologize."

Josh looked at Max. "Bro, this will be an interesting afternoon. Are you sure you don't want to stay?" He laughed.

Brandon looked at Carla. "That was you?" His grin started to return. *Dang, she's cute.*

"Megan, I am sorry, but I cannot stay. I will go somewhere else for the weekend. Please accept my apologies." She turned and left the kitchen. *She was not going to stay in a place with an arrogant asshole, that he thinks he's god gift to women.*

Megan went up to Brandon. "Give me my son. Brandon Pierce, you are going to apologize to that girl right this instant! I cannot afford to lose her." She looked at Max. "If he doesn't apologize, we are not leaving this house!" She walked away.

Max was confused. "Brandon, can you explain to me what she is talking about?"

Brandon took his hand and swiped it through his hair. "Well, I was kind of rude with her this morning. I was jogging and turned the corner and she was right there, and I went flying over her, then hit bench and face-planted onto the grass. So I told her off, in a not so friendly manner."

Max walked up to his brother, face to face. "What the hell, Brandon? Fix this now or I swear it will not be nice. My wife is not happy right now and that makes me unhappy."

Josh leaned in. "Glad I am not in your shoes, man." He slapped him on the back.

"Shut up, Josh! I swear I didn't know she was your nanny Max."

XOXO

"Then fix it. NOW!"

"Okay!" Brandon left the kitchen, and waited at the bottom of the stairs for Carla to come back down. He heard the door open, and she slowly came down the stairs with a bag and her purse. He looked up. "Carla, can I talk to you, please?"

"I do not think we have anything to say to each other. You made it clear this morning."

"Carla, I am sorry. I can be a real dick head sometimes and most of the time I do not hear what people tell me in the moment of anger. My mouth gets in the way of speaking without thinking. Please accept my apologies for this morning." He looked at her. She was pretty with those curls and dark eyes. Something inside him stirred, a pull he wanted to get closer to her. He looked her over from her lips to her curves, and her legs, but his eyes lingered on her breasts. He was a breast man, and he loved what he was seeing.

Carla was facing him from one step higher. She looked at him and saw that he was sincere—or was he looking her over? A shiver went through her.

"Can we start over, please?" Brandon extended his hand and waited for her response. He could still see that she was angry at him, but not as much as before.

"Hi, my name is Brandon. Nice to meet you, Carla." He turned on the charm and gave her his million-dollar smile. He knew she would forgive him just by the way she was standing, he could read people in the business he's in.

She put her bag down, extended her hand, and said, "Nice to meet you, Brandon." That is when it hit her like a lightning bolt. It went through her whole body. She looked at him and then pulled her hand away in shock. Her heart skipped a beat, and

$$$

she just stood there looking at him. He smiled back at her. *What the hell just happened?*

"So you will stay then?" Brandon looked at her. He wasn't sure what had just happened. She looked stunned. He wanted to wrap his arm around her and kiss her, and then he wondered how it would feel to have his hands in those curls. Shaking off that thought, he said, "Carla, will you stay and babysit my niece and nephew with Josh and me, please?"

"Okay, let me put my stuff back in my room, and I'll come right down."

"Here, let me help you bring your bag back upstairs." He was reaching for her bag, but she pulled away.

"No, I'm fine. I will just be a minute." Carla gave him a small smile.

"Okay. Let's order in tonight, my treat. Carla, I'm truly sorry for the asshole I was today."

"You're not going to hear a complaint from me for a free meal." Carla walked back up the stairs to her room.

He laughed. "I like a woman that will not argue."

Carla turned and him a smile. "But wait, you have the first diaper duty as punishment for being a jerk." Carla couldn't believe that she was flirting with him. Where was this coming from she never flirted?

He laughed even harder. "Oh, but I have ways to convince you otherwise."

Brandon returned to the kitchen. They all looked at him like they were going to jump him. He raised his hands in defeat. "Okay, sorry. I was wrong, but it's okay now. She is staying, and I apologized. I'll be paying for dinner."

"Now Brandon, was that so hard? She's a nice girl, and I don't want you to go all macho man on her. I need her, so hands off,

xoxo

you got me? She's my friend, so if you hurt her, you will have me to deal with, got it?" Megan knew that Brandon was a big teddy bear.

"Trust me, Megan, I do not want you to be angry at me. You are one scary woman when you're mad." Brandon walked over and kissed her on the cheek.

"Wait until Lizzie find out you are paying for dinner. I hope you have lots of cash on you, bro." Josh smiled at him.

Carla was looking at herself in the mirror and put a hand to her heated face. *What the hell just happened? God, that guy is gorgeous. Holy shit, when he smiles it's like Mount Saint Helen erupted. Those dimples and those ocean blue eyes… but more like a violet color. Get a grip, Carla! Guys that look like that do not date average girls; they date supermodels. Okay, he apologized, so suck it up and go downstairs.* Carla looked herself over again and splashed a little water on her face to cool down her heated body.

"Hi Carla, welcome back to the party," Josh said. "Don't worry about my brother here. If he gets out of hand, I will beat the crap out of him. Alex and I will beat him up. Isn't that right, little guy?" Alex gave one of those gaga faces as he cooed to him and smiled back at Josh.

Carla couldn't help but laugh. "I am sure that Alex can take him."

"Hey, I resent that. He's my nephew. He wouldn't beat up his Uncle Brandon, right big guy?" Brandon took Alex little hand and high-five him.

"Okay guys, Megan and I will be back tomorrow around one o'clock, so play nice." Max leaned in and kissed Alex, and held his little princess for belly kisses. A little laughter came out of her.

"Here, I take her." Carla held out of her arm.

$$$

"Thanks. Carla, you have my number, so if these guys get out of hand, call me," Max said as he looked at his brothers.

Megan kissed her daughter. "We'll miss you, princess." She turned to Josh. "Where is my little man?" Megan kissed her son. He held on to her hair and she tickled him. He let out a little laughter. Megan looked at Josh and Brandon. "Be nice. I'm warning you both."

"Yes mommy, pinky swears." They laughed. "Now go so we can tell Carla all the dirt on you both," Josh said.

"Thank you, Carla, for staying. I trust that they will behave, and Lizzie will be here around four." She hugged her friend.

"No problem, Megan. I am sorry about before."

"You have nothing to be sorry about, these guys can be intimidating when you do not know them, but they are just big teddy bears inside. They are good guys and I trust them with my life."

"Angel, please, we will miss our reservation. It's time to go." Max couldn't believe he was going to have a weekend without diapers, puke, and babies crying. The only crying he wanted was from Megan, screaming out his name.

"Yes, Honey, I am coming." She closed the door behind her.

XOXO

CPSIA information can be obtained
at www.ICGtesting.com
Printed in the USA
LVHW02s1111120518
576973LV00001B/1/P